"Are you avoiding people?"

Sutter narrowed his eyes as he looked across the field and didn't answer.

"Is that what your success has gotten you?" Megan asked. "The feeling of having to hide from people? What, are you afraid we're all going to ask you for money or something?"

He brought his gaze around to her sharply. "Do I insult you every time we meet?"

She paused. "Not every time." Her dark eyes met his.

He'd never insulted her, he was sure of it. He wanted to challenge her to tell him when he had, but he couldn't take his eyes from her wet lips, naturally pink and plump and parted just enough . . .

By Elaine Fox

Elaine Fox

GUYS & DOGS

AVON BOOKS
An Imprint of HarperCollinsPublishers

This is a work of fiction. Names, characters, places, and incidents are products of the author's imagination or are used fictitiously and are not to be construed as real. Any resemblance to actual events, locales, organizations, or persons, living or dead, is entirely coincidental.

AVON BOOKS
An Imprint of HarperCollins*Publishers*
10 East 53rd Street
New York, New York 10022-5299

For my great pal, Sarah Ferrell.
Nobody knows dogs better or loves them more.

And in memory of my dear friend Greg Cunliffe,
who I'm sure would smile from the heavens
if Ashley Judd were to star in a movie version of this book.

Acknowledgments

The author wishes to thank, for their invaluable help, Dr. Terri Horton, DVM, for her extensive experience, wonderful imagination, and her generosity in sharing both; and Maureen Redmond, for her help with the language of an expat Brit, as well as her knowledge of Great Danes.

Any mistakes in this book are entirely mine.

One

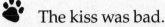 The kiss was bad.

His tongue was everywhere—across her lips, on her chin, her cheeks . . . but he looked something like Brad Pitt so she went with it.

It didn't improve.

Plus, he smelled bad. She turned her head away and noticed a crick in her neck. Then she realized she was not on a Caribbean island but in her own bed, in Fredericksburg, Virginia. Finally, she opened her eyes.

Jerking awake, she gasped into the hot breath of a hairy, grinning face.

Megan was on her feet in the center of her bed before she realized that she'd moved.

Beside the bed, with its dirty front paws on her pillow, stood a young golden retriever, wagging a long feathered tail and grinning with the friendly

2 ❀ 🐾 Elaine Fox

self-confidence only a golden retriever could ex-
ude while being gaped at in shock.

Trouble was, Megan didn't own a golden retriever.

Nor had she ever seen this dog before. Which
might have been unusual considering she was the
vet who ran the local animal hospital, but she was
new to the job. And the town.

As her heart rate slowly edged back toward
normal, Megan knelt down on the bed and
reached out a hand to the dog, who licked it
twice, then recommenced smiling and wagging
at her.

Megan wasn't fooled. This dog had broken into
her house. It was not bent on pleasing people for
anything other than its own purposes. She raised
a skeptical brow at it.

"Well, hello, uh . . ." She leaned on one elbow
and craned her neck to look under the dog's hind
end. "Hello, girl. Where'd you come from?"

Edging to the side of the bed, she scratched the
dog behind an ear and did a cursory examination,
mostly out of habit. The dog—a mere adolescent,
six or seven months by the look and build of her—
stretched luxuriantly under her touch. Since it put
up with that so magnanimously, Megan went for
the collar.

True to form—and in the spirit of most dogs' favorite game, "catch me if you can"—the pup
twisted sharply the moment it realized what she

was up to and writhed expertly out of her grasp, taking off down the stairs.

Megan sighed. *Teenagers.*

Getting out of bed and pulling on some sweatpants under her tee shirt, she listened for any sounds of destruction. From what she heard downstairs, she surmised the puppy had found her own dog, Peyton—a big, tricolored bear of a Bernese mountain dog—in her crate next to the stairs. The sounds of toenails on hardwood mixed with frantic tail thumps on the side of the crate and throaty whines of longing were clear giveaways.

How the pup had missed Peyton on the way up was a mystery, but after a bit of scratching and whining the interloper resorted to a short, high bark. Then another. By the time Megan reached the stairs the golden was down on its elbows, butt in the air—play bowing—as if Peyton weren't actually closed up in the crate but for some reason just playing hard to get.

"Come here, puppydog," she called, walking past the golden on the way to the kitchen, thereby short-circuiting the dog's play instinct to run away. A Milk Bone would convince it that having its collar and tags examined was not tantamount to torture. "Come on! Come let me find out who you belong to."

She entered the kitchen and found her father, hair mashed and spiky from sleep, threadbare bathrobe hanging from hunched shoulders, seated at the table, nursing a cup of coffee.

"Oh. Hey, Dad," she said, looking for signs of vitality in his sagging face. He hadn't been home when she'd gone to bed last night, and she was fairly certain he was the reason she'd woken up at three this morning. He never seemed to learn that those late, hard-drinking nights resulted in these less-than-idyllic mornings. Either that or there was so much brain damage from years of this that he forgot by the time night fell again that it was a bad idea.

He looked at her with watery eyes. "Hey, doll."

Despite the fact that Megan had grown up thinking it was just his nickname for her, she'd come to learn that her father called all women "doll." The mistake was understandable—she'd only spoken to him about once a year after the age of nine, when her parents had split up—but she still felt a pinprick of disappointment whenever he called her that now.

A few months ago, in a fit of missing her mother, who'd died of cancer several years before, Megan had decided to leave the animal hospital in Connecticut where she'd worked since graduating from vet school and move to Virginia to get to know her father better. In the week since she'd moved into his home here to take over his veterinary practice, she'd not only learned that women were "dolls" but that men were "sports." Unless they were "assholes." And the later in the evening it was, which meant the more he drank, the more dolls and assholes there seemed to be.

Now he mustered a wry smile and said, "What's with all the barking? I thought that dog of yours was supposed to be quiet."

"She is." Megan looked at the back door, noted that the dog hatch was not locked as it should be, and concluded that this was how the extra dog had made it onto her bed. "Didn't you notice someone strange coming through the dog door just now?"

He straightened. "Huh?"

Grabbing the box of dog bones and shaking it, she whistled sharply. The apparently delicious sound of meat treats in cardboard had the desired effect on both dogs. The puppy came running, while Peyton whined pitifully in her crate.

"Who the hell is that?" her father queried.

She held a bone out and the puppy nabbed it like a Zen master capturing a fly. She inhaled it just as fast and looked expectantly back up at Megan.

"An unexpected visitor," Megan said. "She just woke me up. And on a Sunday, the *one day* I can sleep in. Bad dog."

Her father chuckled.

Megan held a bone up out of reach and said, "Sit!"

The dog continued wagging its tail and gazed at her in gleeful ignorance.

Her father harrumphed. "Probably not house-broken either."

Megan folded her arms across her chest and sustained eye contact with the puppy, whose optimism that another bone was in the offing was undiminished by her stern look. "I don't know. It recognized the dog door. And it's wearing a collar. Somebody obviously owns this dog."

She dropped her arms, lowered the treat to knee level and said, "Come!"

The puppy bounded toward her and snapped up the bone.

"Good dog!" Megan grabbed the collar and before the dog could resist offered another treat. Distracted, the puppy stood chewing while Megan examined the tag.

" 'Baywatch,' " she read, then laughed and looked at her father. "This dog's name is Baywatch, can you believe that?"

He stirred his coffee. "That's a weird name. Think it came from somewhere near the river?"

"No, it's an old TV show." The dog was starting to resist, twisting in her grasp but she had the collar tightly this time. She reached behind her for the box and produced another bone. "Big-breasted girls running on the beach, that kind of thing. I think they're supposed to be lifeguards or something."

Her father's brows rose with interest. "I haven't seen that one."

"Come on, Baywatch, settle down. *Baywatch, no!*" The dog showed no response to the name, or the command. Megan sighed. "Oh brother."

She finally got the puppy in a leg-lock and looked at the tag again. "BAYWATCH, 17 Washington Ave., Fredericksburg," she read. "No owner's name. No phone number. That's strange. You'd think someone on Washington Avenue, of all places, could afford a phone."

She let the puppy go and walked across the kitchen to lock the dog door. She didn't want Baywatch to run out and risk getting hit by a car. Since she couldn't call, she'd just have to take the pup to the address once she got dressed.

"Seventeen Washington Avenue?" Her father rose out of his chair and shuffled across the kitchen toward the coffee maker. "Did you say 17 Washington Avenue?"

"That's right," Megan said, going to the hall to release her dog. Peyton bounded out of the crate and bee-lined for Baywatch. She and the pup sniffed each other a few moments with guarded exuberance before playfully lunging and nipping at each other.

Megan went back to the kitchen, both dogs following and knocking into each other's shoulders in the dog version of "me first."

Her father regarded the puppy with renewed interest. "I think that's Sutter Foley's address."

"Sutter Foley?" Megan repeated, surprised.

Sutter Foley was Fredericksburg's resident celebrity. He was the founder of SFSolutions, Inc.—a company second only to Microsoft in the computer software industry—and architect of the worldwide software revolution called FoleyWare. He was, at the very least, a multimillionaire, and quite possibly a billionaire. And he lived in Fredericksburg, behind a wrought-iron fence posted with security signs, in order to keep in touch with his regular-guy roots, or to stay away from the public eye of a big city, or to make it harder for the media to stalk him—strangers being more noticeable in a small town—or some other such similar tale that varied according to whom you talked to.

"Are you sure?" she asked her father. If it was true, the last thing she wanted to do was go traipsing up to his door uninvited. He was, after all, famous. Not to mention famous for guarding his privacy. But then there being no phone number didn't leave her much choice in the matter. Something told her he wouldn't be listed in the phone book. Thinking about it, this was probably why there was no phone number on the tag, either.

That was taking a risk, she thought irritably. How many people would make the effort to go to someone's house to return a dog? It seemed irresponsible to her. If you were going to own a dog, you owed it to the dog to be reachable if said dog got loose. That was just common sense. And surely Sutter Foley, of *all* people, had enough money to get a phone line that didn't have to be unlisted. Heck, he could afford to have a phone line dedicated to the dog tag alone.

She shook her head, wondering how much of her annoyance was due to the inherent shallowness of naming a dog Baywatch.

"Hell yes, I'm sure," her father said, scratching the side of his shaggy head. "I've lived in this town twenty-seven years and if there's one thing I know it's where Sutter Foley lives. Time was, this place was known for its history—George Washington, James Monroe, hell, the Civil War! That's a big thing, isn't it? But no. Now we're known for Sutter Foley. Seems an awful come-down to me."

Megan suppressed a smile. "Sounds like sour grapes. He stealing your women?"

Her father scoffed. "We don't exactly travel in the same circles."

Megan tilted her head. "I don't know."

He had a dog named Baywatch, that sounded like the same circles to her.

Megan put one of Peyton's leashes on the puppy and opened the back door. Her father had gone upstairs to bed. Apparently the morning coffee had been a kind of midnight snack for him. Since his retirement he'd kept the hours of a college student—up 'til 3 a.m., sleep 'til 3 p.m. and start the whole cycle over again.

The early June day was beautiful. Warm and sunny, with a caressing breeze that promised summer was here to stay. The trees sighed and birds darted as the world slowly opened its eyes. Baywatch pulled her along with all the gusto of an Iditarod contender.

It was 9 A.M. on a Sunday. Early to be knocking on someone's door, but Megan knew if it were her she'd be frantic about the whereabouts of her dog. Besides, much as she loved dogs, if the puppy wasn't housebroken she didn't need to add cleaning up dog poop at home to cleaning the entire animal hospital during her working days. Mr. Millionaire could take care of his own problems.

Washington Avenue was just a dozen blocks away and while that was close, it was a crucial dozen blocks, as far as property values went. Her father's house was large and charming, a southern Victorian with a wide porch and welcoming façade, but it was nothing compared to the places on Washington Avenue. For one thing, George Washington's sister's estate was there, and the houses around it—while not of the same time period—reflected the same affluence.

She had to admit, she was a bit nervous. She'd never met a true celebrity before, and certainly never because she'd shown up at one's door. She was counting on Baywatch to keep her from looking like some kind of computer geek in search of an idol.

She enjoyed walking down the broad, stately street, reveling in the sunshine and admiring the houses. Dividing the east- and westbound lanes was a large public green lined with trees and hosting a statue of Hugh Mercer, local eighteenth-century physician and Revolutionary War hero, in the center. It was the perfect spot for games of Frisbee or impromptu picnics or just lying on the grass with a good book. She halfheartedly looked around for someone who might be Sutter Foley amidst the few out walking this morning, but based on what she knew about his aloofness she was pretty sure he didn't show his face in public without an express purpose.

She'd seen a picture of him once, so she had a vague idea of what he looked like. Handsome, in a groomed corporate way, with that killer look in the eyes that many CEOs tried to adopt when photographed but few could pull off. Most of them ended up looking like soft-palmed, doughy-faced, privileged white guys.

Not so Sutter Foley. He'd been on the cover of *Forbes* or *Fortune*, one of those magazines she only saw in doctors' offices, and she'd paused over it because he looked so intense. She had the feeling he always walked around with that expression, rather than having donned it to look intimidating in the photo.

She hoped he didn't answer the door with it.

Of course, *he* wasn't going to answer the door. No doubt he had lackeys for that. No, he was probably in some bunker in the basement, far from prying eyes, alone with his computers and peripherals and surge protectors and God knew what else.

In no time she reached number seventeen. The house was imposing, tall and wide, brick, solid-looking in that way that historic homes had.

She paused outside the wrought-iron gate and looked for a buzzer or an intercom or something with which to ask for admittance. But there was nothing.

Great, she thought, strong-arming Baywatch to a sloppy sit next to her ankle and examining the brick pillars into which the wrought iron was cemented. What was she supposed to do now? Scale the fence? She reached out and experimented with the latch and was shocked to find it unlocked. This was hardly consistent with Foley's reputed obsession with privacy. The gate swung open on well-oiled hinges.

Baywatch took this as permission to shoot up from the ground like a firework and yank Megan's arm from its socket. Dog and walker landed on the front walk—dog swimming upstream like a spawning salmon as walker stumbled behind until she was able to control the animal by assuming the position of a water-skier.

No doubt about it, the pup recognized this as

home. When they got to the front stoop, however, Baywatch veered right, into the bushes, and began peeing.

Megan waited, quickly looking self-consciously around, then, realizing the puppy had stopped peeing and started sniffing the bushes, all without changing position, she gave the leash a quick jerk and walked up the steps. This was silly. The man may be a celebrity, but she was only returning his dog.

She rang the bell and waited what felt like an eternity. The door was huge, one of those oversized ones that some of the grander older homes had. She wondered if it was supposed to be a subliminal kind of thing, that she was supposed to think whoever lived here was not only richer, but actually larger in some superhuman way than herself.

In the corner of the entryway, trained on the porch, was what looked like a surveillance camera. She looked around and spotted two more. She had no doubt the house was covered with them.

She rang the bell again, sure that he wasn't home. After all, if he were looking through that camera he'd see that she had his dog.

She was surprised, however, that there was no hireling to answer the door. She rang the bell again, for the heck of it, wondering how long she was going to be stuck with this puppy, who was now winding itself in an intricate pattern around a topiary tree in a large pot next to the front door. Just as she noticed the dog had actually threaded itself through the railing too, the front door opened to reveal *the man* himself.

In an instant Megan noticed three things: first, he was taller than she'd expected; second, he was much better looking than his picture; and third, his expression was every bit as intimidating as *Forbes*, or *Fortune*, had portrayed.

Baywatch let out a yelp and lunged for the door, only able to move about two inches, which was enough to shake the topiary tree in a way that startled all three of them.

Megan and Sutter Foley backed away. Baywatch cowered backward and cried, thereby setting up a continuous loop of cowering—shaking the tree—cowering, etc.

"May I help you?" His words were polite but his tone was sharp and his expression grew, if possible, darker.

Good lord, he was British, she thought. Did she know that? And had his eyes been so green on that cover? Maybe it was the casual clothes, the width of his shoulders in the untucked white shirt and the way he filled out his worn jeans, but she felt shocked at his youth and vigor.

He wasn't the colorless corporate giant he'd appeared on the magazine cover.

Megan jolted herself into action. "I'm sorry she

got so tangled up. I wasn't paying attention and as you probably know she's awfully fast." She leaned down to unhook Baywatch's leash so she could pull it free without having to drag the dog back through the motions.

"Why on earth would I know that?" he asked, sounding impatient.

She looked up at him from the corner of her eye as she yanked on the leash, sending some kind of evergreen needles from the topiary into her face and hair.

Not only was the arrogant jerk not helping her, he seemed annoyed that she was even here.

Giving up on the leash, she pulled Baywatch out by the collar and sat her forcibly in front of the man.

"Because she's your dog," she answered, pulling an evergreen needle from her hair. "I'm sorry if I interrupted something. I just wanted to return her. So you didn't worry," she added archly. With that she gave the pup a little push and sent her careening into the house.

"What the—" Sutter Foley jumped away from the animal as if she'd just loosed a gator in his direction and glared from her to the cavernous interior of the house into which Baywatch had disappeared. He turned back to her. "What in God's name do you think you're doing?"

"Returning your dog," she insisted again, but

something began niggling at her brain. He did not look like a man overjoyed to see his pet. Indeed, his expression bore absolutely no recognition for the animal.

He took two steps back into the hall, gazed into some adjoining room, then faced the door again.

"*I don't own a dog,*" he said through what seemed like clenched teeth. "I don't know what the devil you're about, but get that animal out of here before I summon the police."

Trepidation curled her stomach but she stood her ground. "The tag had this address. And no phone number. Which made sense what with you being such a . . . ." She lifted a hand up and down in his direction.

"Such a what? Dog lover?" He was utterly condescending. "Tell me, do you see any evidence of my owning a dog? Muddy ruts in the garden? Messes in the grass? Cheesy little plastic toys lying about?"

Megan put her hands on her hips and answered with equal impatience. "Forgive me. I didn't stop to examine the yard. The address on the tag was enough evidence for me."

Foley ran a hand through his hair and looked from her back into the house.

"Look," he said finally. "I don't know what you're up to, but if you've come for—"

The sound of breaking glass reached both of them at the same time.

Foley's face froze and he looked at her as if she'd just discharged a shotgun into the front hall.

"Well? Aren't you going to *do* something?"

"Are you saying," Megan asked dumbly, becoming aware of the enormity of her mistake and wondering if she had possibly misread the tag, "that's *not* your dog?"

"No, it's not my bloody dog," he roared as another crash sounded.

Megan raced past him into the house, following the noise, vaguely registering the luxury of the appointments, until she found the puppy. She was tangled in some curtains by a rear French door, hurling herself at the windows in an apparent attempt to vanquish a squirrel. The crashing they'd heard came from an ornately carved breakfront filled with crystal, between the French door and which Baywatch was bouncing. The breakfront was filled with wine glasses of all shapes and sizes, many now in much smaller sizes as they lay shattered on the shelves.

She grabbed the puppy by the collar and dragged her from the door, noticing as she did that she was now in a cozy dining room, complete with fireplace and velvet flocked wallpaper in deep green and gold. It was opulent and old world and utterly charming.

Foley was right behind her. "I don't know what your angle is but you've seen the house, now I'll thank you to leave. And if any photos or descriptions of the place turn up in the tabloids I shall know whom to have arrested for trespassing."

"Wait just a second," she snapped. "I was *trying* to do you a favor. I *thought* this was your dog."

"Well it's *not* my bloody dog."

"Okay, we've established that." She shook her head and sat down on one of the dining room chairs. "Does this room have a light, by any chance?" It was a sad fact of her character that Megan usually countered condescension with impertinence.

He looked at her as if no one had ever said 'boo' to him before.

"I want to check her tag again," Megan explained.

With a long-suffering sigh, he turned on a light, adjusting the dimmer to its brightest.

Megan took the quick opportunity to look at the rest of the room. One corner held a rack filled with wines, and a selection of serving platters stood on a sideboard. The carpet was a rich dark green that was springy under her feet and revealed their footprints in its just-vacuumed pile.

Foley stood in front of her with his arms crossed over his chest.

Refocusing on the task at hand, she turned Baywatch's collar around as the puppy sank to the ground, exhausted by her early morning adventures. *17 Washington Ave., Fredericksburg.*

She looked up at Foley. "Take a look."

He leaned down and glanced at the tag, giving her the chance to smell shampoo, laundry soap, man. He straightened abruptly, looking disturbed.

"That's not my dog," he said again, with much less force this time. "Surely it's not difficult to get a false . . ." He trailed off.

Megan had to concede this. "That's true. Anybody can go to PetsMart and get a tag for five bucks, but I assure you *I* didn't. And I don't know who did. I just live a few blocks away and this dog found its way into my bedroom this morning. I was only trying to return her to her owner."

She glanced around the room again and into the living room through which she'd run to find the dog. It too was lushly furnished and immaculately clean, quiet, and dark. Almost as if no one lived here.

"Are you all alone?" she asked. Then, realizing how provocative that sounded, added quickly, "I mean, I just thought you'd have like a butler or housekeeper or something. You know, a whole staff of people."

He was studying her with a curiosity that made his expression much less forbidding.

She smiled and shrugged, her fingers idly petting Baywatch as the dog drifted off to sleep. "Just curious."

"I don't like having a large staff," he said, the

words emerging almost reluctantly. "I dislike people wandering about when I'm trying to concentrate. Quiet is very important to me."

"So . . . I can imagine Baywatch and I have been a pretty unwelcome distraction." She laughed lightly, watching him.

His eyes flitted over the tangled curtains, the jostled breakfront with its broken glasses, back to her. "A distraction indeed," he murmured.

"I'm sorry. I had no way of knowing the tags were faked." She stood and found herself closer to him than she'd anticipated, looking up into his handsome face, those green eyes steady and unnerving.

To her amazement, he lifted one hand gently toward her face. Was he going to *kiss* her? Touch her cheek? What? Instinctively, she jerked her head back, then could have kicked herself. If a good-looking, fabulously wealthy, famous man gets an urge to touch you, *give him the benefit of the doubt*.

Even more unbelievably, his cheeks colored. "I was just—there's a spider, there, in your hair. Must have come from the plant outside. I was going to remove it."

It took Megan a minute to absorb his words, then her hand flew to her head and her fingers felt the insect. "Oh my God." Suppressing a squeal, she flung it away and rubbed her hands over her hair to be sure there were no others.

He gazed impassively in the direction she'd hurled the bug.

"Sorry," she said.

"Listen," he said finally, "I think I might know what happened. I just had to let my groundskeeper go. He was living in the carriage house and to the best of my knowledge he did not have a telephone. A down-on-his-luck sort. I was hoping to . . . well, in any case, the dog might well have been his. Indeed upon further notice it does look a bit . . . familiar."

He frowned in the direction of Baywatch, who had made herself completely at home and was stretched out sideways on the plush carpet.

Megan exhaled, relieved, and gave him a smile. "Oh, thank goodness. I was afraid you didn't believe me. I'm not a fame whore, I swear."

He looked startled. "A what?"

"You know, one of those people who wants to get close to the rich and famous no matter what the means." She paused, then extended her hand. "I'm Megan Rose. I'm the new veterinarian at Rose's Animal Hospital."

He took her hand in his. This was no milquetoast handshake, no wimpy clasping of her fingers, this was a warm, palm-to-palm embrace. Megan's heartbeat involuntarily accelerated, even faster than when she'd felt the spider. Or when Baywatch had woken her up this morning. Come to think of it, she wasn't sure her heart could take much more adrenaline this morning.

"Sutter Foley," he said quietly, his eyes on hers. After a second, he gave a ghost of a smile. "But you knew that."

She laughed. "I knew that. Yes."

The moment drew long, until Megan realized she was holding her breath. With an unladylike exhale she dropped his hand and looked away. "Okay, well, I'll just get going. You, uh, you can have the leash on the front porch, I've got a million of them. So, um, sorry to disturb you."

She stepped over the sleeping dog and headed for the door.

"Just a moment," he said after she'd gone several paces.

She turned, the absurd hope that he might ask her to dinner springing like a cartoon light bulb into her head.

"You're not *leaving* it here, are you?" The imperious tone was back. "The dog?"

"You said you knew whose it was."

"Yes, but he's gone. I don't know where." He looked at her expectantly.

She raised her brows. "Can't you *find* him? Don't you have references or an application or something?"

"No, I—well, he . . ." He stopped, frustrated, then said, "I don't have a way to trace him. He left . . . rather abruptly."

"Well, *I* can't find him. I don't even know what he looks like."

"He's quite distinctive, actually. Short, with some tattoos on his arms, rather a shifty expression—"

Megan laughed. "You've got to be kidding. Maybe he'll come back for the dog."

Foley seemed to be remembering something, perhaps an ugly scene upon firing the man. "I sincerely doubt it."

"I'm sorry, but the dog obviously feels that this is home." She indicated the place where Baywatch lay.

"That dog has never been in this house," he said firmly.

"That you know of." She paused a significant moment, as the plausibility of her words sank in, then turned to the door.

"You can't just leave it here," he insisted, stopping her again. "It's not my . . ." he started. Then, realizing that tack had already taken him nowhere several times, he reached into his back pocket and extracted a wallet. "Here, listen. I'm sorry to further impose, but why don't you just take the dog down to the pound. Here's some money, enough for a donation and . . . and something for your time." He extended a wad of bills toward her.

Megan hesitated. She could take the dog to the shelter. It wasn't far out of her way. But something about Sutter Foley made her think he needed this dog. Not to mention that the dog needed him. Maybe it was the fact that he was all alone, maybe it was the sterile silence of the house, maybe it was the arresting depth she saw in his eyes . . . In any case, she figured she had nothing to lose. "You're used to that, I suppose. Solving problems with money and never having to leave your . . ." She opened her arms and gazed around the room. "Sphere."

His arm sank. "I beg your pardon?"

She shook her head. "I'm sorry. I don't mean to be insulting. But maybe you should take this as a sign. The universe might be telling you you're spending too much time alone or something." She shrugged, smiling.

He gave her a look dripping with disdain. "Am I to believe you're here to speak for the universe?"

She felt her resolve harden. "What I'm trying to say is, why don't *you* keep the dog? It could be good for you. Humanizing."

For a moment he looked shocked, then he laughed. It was short—incredulous more than amused—but his face was so transformed she found herself smiling automatically in response. He looked completely different than Mr. *Forbes*, or *Fortune*, whichever.

"You must be joking," he said. "I don't want a dog." He said it as if the idea were preposterous.

She frowned. "Why not? You've got a yard. You've got this enormous place." She spread her arms again, thinking of the cramped cage the puppy would likely be put in to await an adoption that might never materialize. "Why put another dog on death row when you've got what must be unlimited resources to look after it? Think about it. What possible reason can you give for not sharing some of your abundance with that poor little creature?" She gestured toward Baywatch, still sleeping sweetly upon the deep green carpet, looking like a prop for a *Town & Country* photo shoot.

Foley seemed momentarily struck by the picture as well. But he turned back to her and said coolly, "The reason is, I do not want a dog. I've never wanted a dog. I don't even like dogs."

Megan could not have been more disappointed in him if he'd ripped off his own handsome face to reveal Darth Vader underneath. "You don't want a dog," she said finally, choosing the least offensive statement.

"That's right." He reextended the money. "Now please. You needn't look at me as if I've just confessed to kicking small children. I really haven't time to deal with a dog. Especially one as . . . as unwieldy as that one. Please, just take it to the pound."

She took a deep breath. "Look, if you don't want her that's one thing. Though I don't know how on earth you live in this big empty place all by yourself. But I'm not going to do your dirty work for you. You're going to have to take her to the shelter yourself. I've got to go."

She turned on her heel and headed for the door. Once there, she turned back to see Sutter Foley, corporate cover boy, staring morosely down at the sleeping puppy.

"I'm leaving the leash," she called, and as she opened the door she saw Baywatch's head rise.

She slipped out the door before the puppy—or the man—could ask her for more.

Two

Times like this, Sutter Foley wished he did have an entire staff milling about waiting to do his bidding. After sacking Charlie, however, all he had left was Martina, his housekeeper, who had Sundays off, and Berkley, his chef, who did not live in. He eyed the sleeping dog distrustfully, remembering how quickly it had darted into the house and created mayhem.

That vet was right about one thing. The dog certainly seemed at home here. In addition to Charlie's other infractions, he'd obviously had the mutt in the house, probably when Sutter was away on one of his many business trips.

He ran a hand through his hair. He hadn't slept well in a week and it was starting to show. He was irritable and exhausted, and his workload—

usually so energizing—felt overwhelming. The last thing he needed to deal with was this damn dog.

He looked malevolently at the sleeping pup, thought about opening the door and letting it go, then pictured it getting hit by a car and shook his head. Sod it all, he thought, he was going to have to do something with it. Leave his "sphere," as the cheeky vet had said.

He smiled grimly to himself. She'd actually been right about that. He'd been cooped up in his home office all weekend. Though he didn't employ much household help, he had enough that he never had to leave the house if he didn't want to, not even to retrieve the mail.

Maybe that was what was the matter with him, he thought. His internal clock was off. He hadn't seen sunlight in days so his body didn't know when it was supposed to sleep.

Sounded like something the vet would conclude, he thought. Maybe the universe *was* trying to tell him something.

It was telling him to leave the house before the bloody dog woke up.

Sutter was sitting on the front stoop, absorbing as much sunlight as he could before the ceaseless thoughts of work drove him back to his computer, when a black Jaguar, much like his own, pulled up in front of his house.

Kristen Montgomery, his assistant VP who preferred to be called by her last name alone, would get out and he had no doubt she would be trussed up neatly in a suit, either beige or gray. Occasionally it was blue, but that seemed to be for important meetings and such. He used to think she'd surprise him one weekend—for she showed up every weekend with some work-related issue—and have a special pink or purple suit to denote the off-hours, but she never had.

She did not disappoint today. Gray.

Sutter watched her close her car door, hit the remote locks, and clip-clop in her low heels up the front walk. She was so absorbed in getting her suit straight and her briefcase situated that she didn't notice him until she was practically on top of him. She gave a short squeal and stopped abruptly.

Perversely, her surprise pleased him. She was so tightly wound that any break in the businesslike façade was a welcome change. Even her hair never moved, cut into a short severe style that could not be reshaped if she'd wanted to do it. She was somewhere in her thirties, he happened to know, but by her looks could easily have been a well-preserved fifty or an overdressed minor.

"Hello, Montgomery," he said, leaning back against a porch column and looking up at her with eyes that felt puffy with fatigue.

"Sutter," she said, "what are you doing out here?"

She was used to seeing him in *his* weekend attire

of jeans and natty shirt. Why did she never take the hint?

"Readjusting my circadian rhythms." He tilted his face toward the sun.

"I see." She stood stiffly before him. "I needed to talk to you about the accounting system package. Myers has totally screwed up the product overview and I wanted your input so I can set him straight first thing tomorrow morning."

"You have a meeting with him first thing tomorrow?" Sutter asked, mentally comparing Montgomery's tight form and stern demeanor with the jean-clad softness of his earlier visitor. The vet's face was pretty, yes, and her worn jeans had fit her with admirable precision, but there was something else, a glow of some sort that made her seem ready to smile at any instant. It had been . . . nice.

"A breakfast meeting, before work. Don't worry, it won't cut into regular time." She nodded once, curtly. She'd have saluted, he was sure, if it had been remotely appropriate.

Sutter blinked slowly, feeling fatigue wash over him. Maybe he should have Montgomery call him every night before bedtime; something about her seemed to wear him out.

"You do know he has a newborn, don't you? I imagine it's something of a hardship for him to schedule an early meeting."

"On the contrary." She shifted, her shoes obviously uncomfortable the longer she stood. "He said he never sleeps anymore, so being up early should be quite easy for him."

This reasoning struck him as so funny he laughed, causing a look of consternation to cross her face. "Is something wrong?" she asked.

"I laughed, Montgomery. There's nothing wrong." Had he done this? Had he created this rigid imperative around himself? He feared he had. He motioned toward the stoop next to him. "Have a seat."

She looked toward the step as reluctantly as if he'd asked her to lie in the bushes. But after a minute, when he did not elaborate, she clopped forward, turned, and folded herself down next to him.

"It's quite a nice day, isn't it?" he said, attempting a pleasantry to offset his irritation. A low breeze kicked up and rustled the leaves in the trees, carrying away an overhead cloud. Sutter looked up into the clear blue sky. The air felt good, the sun warm on his cheeks. Why did he never do anything outside anymore? How long had it been since he'd noticed the sky?

"Still not sleeping?" Montgomery's voice exuded disapproval.

He sighed. "Not with my eyes closed."

"You should call a doctor. They have drugs that can help you sleep."

"I don't need a doctor. All they'll do is give me some narcotic I can certainly do without."

"Yes, you're obviously handling this quite well yourself."

He shifted his eyes sideways and looked at her, surprised at the remark. She was positioned just as she'd been when she was standing, back straight, briefcase under one arm, head erect, except her legs were bent demurely together as she sat.

"Have you got a boyfriend, Montgomery?" he asked.

Her dark eyes, lined with an obvious but professional level of makeup, darted toward him. "No, sir, I don't. What's gotten into you? You haven't gotten another email from your ex-wife, have you?"

Sutter straightened involuntarily. "No. Why do you ask?"

"Because you always get sleepless and preoccupied with odd things when you have."

"Do I?" He thought back, but could find no reason for this conjecture.

"Listen, sir, I've got something else to talk to you about too. And you're not going to like it." She paused, looking at him with obvious misgiving.

He raised his brows. "All right, then. Spill it."

"Not here." She looked around them as if the very bushes might be inhabited by spies, here to hear what she had to say.

Sutter looked around too. Nobody was near. Hell, apart from a sunbathing college student a block down on the green there was nobody out.

"The trees aren't bugged, Montgomery, tell me what you've got."

She sighed. "Can't we just go inside?"

"I'm afraid we can't. There's a savage beast in there that I am not sufficiently rested to deal with."

She looked at him, blandly unamused.

"Charlie's dog. It's a bloody terror," he elaborated.

"Where's Charlie?" she asked.

"Gone. Sacked. Shown the door. Escorted from the premises."

She began to nod, an oddly smug smile tugging at her lips. "So you know."

"About the interview? Yes. I saw it."

She shook her head. "Such disloyalty, it's disgusting. That's what I wanted to tell you. I'm glad you already knew. I hated to be the one to break it to you."

She may have hated to but she looked strangely disappointed not to have been able to. "Berkley 'broke it' to me last night and I was furious. Didn't handle the firing too well either, I'm afraid. Maybe that's why he left the dog, as payback."

"What's wrong with it?" she asked. "Is it vicious?"

"If you're a squirrel." He laughed dryly. "No, it's just a puppy. An untrained one."

"What on earth are you going to *do* with it?" She looked horrified at the prospect of having to deal with such a thing.

Sutter thought about the vet—what was her name? Rose . . . ? How disappointed she'd looked when she'd told him to take it to the pound himself.

Then she'd made that ridiculous conjecture that the universe was trying to tell him something. He chuckled.

Montgomery looked at him sharply. "What is it?"

"Nothing, I just . . . thought for a moment about keeping the damn thing."

She looked scandalized. "The *dog?*"

He lifted one shoulder and let it drop. "Silly idea."

"Have you any idea what your life would be like with a dog? You have to walk it and feed it and make sure it goes outside. They need to go outside all the time."

"Yes, I understand it's not a piece of furniture," he said.

"And the vet bills! You have no idea how much that could cost."

He slid her a look. "Money's not exactly an issue, Montgomery."

"Yes, but the *time*." She exhaled the word *time* as if the very thought of it was exhausting. "You'd probably have to hire someone to take care of it. You can't be taking time off work just to walk the dog or take it to the vet. And some of them you have to take to the vet *all the time*, Sutter."

"Really?" He thought about that, about having

to go see the veterinarian who'd been on his porch this morning *all the time*. She was so . . . refreshing.

"God, yes. My mother has a cat with diabetes and that thing is always having to go in for check-ups and blood work and insulin shots. It's a nightmare. She says she spends more time with Dr. Prichard than she does with my father."

Sutter looked at her, a half smile on his face. "Does she?" he asked, picturing it for himself. "How intriguing."

After a second, Sutter stretched his legs and looked out over the grass. The urge to lie down in it was powerful. Clearly he was going to have to get some kind of sleep aid, but he was damn sure not going to any doctor. If he did, the next thing he knew it would be splashed all over the tabloids that he had the clap or something. For some reason, ever since his divorce a few years ago he'd become fodder for every gossip sheet around.

No, maybe after Montgomery left he'd go to the pharmacy himself and get something. Venture even farther outside of his sphere.

Monday morning Megan got dressed for the day in her "uniform" of khaki chinos and pink polo shirt with the words "Rose's Animal Hospital" embroidered where the breast pocket might have been. She'd ordered shirts for all the staff in an effort to counteract any impression her father's wrinkled, ill-fitting shirts and shapeless pants might have left on clients before he retired, but she hadn't counted on the pink (a color she'd imagined as being closer to *rose*) being quite so electric.

Still, the fact that they were all wearing the same thing created a feeling of organization, she thought, and organization made people look competent. Not that her father hadn't been a competent vet. He had been. It was just that as he got older—and his evenings got later and his beer steins got deeper—his actual ability to deal with reality got weaker and he was as likely to ask a client for a loan as what the problem was with his pet.

This had driven most of the better-heeled clients away. At least, those who weren't already offended by his indiscriminate flirting and afternoon beer breath. The ones who were left were usually too poor to pay for their visits—or claimed to be—causing her father, who was actually quite soft-hearted when it came to animals, to neglect to charge them.

Megan had been aware that the books were a mess and the hospital a failing enterprise, financially, but she hadn't quite realized why. She'd thought maybe they were charging too little, spending too much, or running inefficiently. But in the short week since she'd been a full-time resident of Fredericksburg, her father's social reputation had revealed itself to be behind many of the animal hospital's problems. In short, he was a tiresome philandering drunk around whom people did not generally want to be.

It shouldn't have been a surprise. After all, that's the reason her mother had left him—or he'd left her, it was never entirely clear—all those many years ago. In fact, Megan had grown up associating the smell of stale beer and cheap perfume with her father, whom she'd barely seen after the age of nine when she and her mother had moved to Connecticut.

Now, she had chosen to revisit that part of her past and here she was. A vet, just like dear old dad, taking over the business he had begun twenty-odd years ago.

For his part, her father seemed glad to have her here, cleaning up the house and taking over the animal hospital. But whether that was solely because he was now getting dinner every night and somebody else was worrying about the hospital's accounts payable Megan wasn't sure. It didn't matter, really. The fact that she was here was her decision, not his. She was just glad he hadn't told her he wasn't interested in her taking over when he retired.

Still, it had been a bit of a surprise to find her father was so little respected in this town where he'd lived for so long. She'd even heard the receptionists joking about him one day, about how the bruises on their asses were nearly gone without "old Doc" there to pinch them and how they kind of missed discovering all the places a bumper of beer could be hidden—in the cooler with the blood samples, under a blanket in an unused cat crate, inside a carton of heartworm medicine in the storeroom. They even lamented the fact that their boyfriends now had to content themselves with being jealous of whistling construction workers and the like.

She just shook her head. It had nothing to do with her. She was completely independent from her father, so much so she felt as if she were living with a stranger. Watching a movie about a character the director had not quite made her care about yet.

Well, she cared, she thought. She just didn't feel connected.

Megan slipped her watch on, checked that she'd tucked her shirt in smoothly in the full-length mirror behind her bedroom door and headed back toward the stairs, her footsteps hollow on the uncarpeted hallway of the old Victorian's second floor. As she passed her father's bedroom door she paused, just until she heard him snoring, then descended the steps, grabbed her purse from the hall table and Peyton's leash from the new hook on the wall.

"Come on, Peyton, we're going to the dog park. You remember the dog park, don't you?"

Peyton scrambled up from the spot she'd been lying in, then sat, as she'd been trained to do, in front of Megan while she snapped on her leash. As usual, the dog's eyes beamed up at Megan in apparent comprehension of everything she said, her tail sweeping slowly in good-natured response.

The dog park was about four city blocks away, on the corner of Kenmore and William streets, and Megan had vowed to go every work day, if only to advertise the hospital and the fact that there was new management and a new vet. That it was exercise for Peyton and a joy for Megan to watch the antics of the other dogs was an added benefit.

She arrived today to find the place teeming with dogs and their humans. The perfect June weather had brought them all out and Megan breathed deeply of the warm, grass-scented air. There was something about the Virginia soil that smelled dense and fertile when the sun shone after a rain, making her think of secret garden paths and honeysuckled trellises, illicit assignations under a moonlit sky. She pictured Sutter Foley for a second, but quickly banished the thought, as she did all thoughts of him since yesterday, as the ridiculous ramblings of a sex-starved mind.

She unsnapped Peyton's leash and watched her lope across the grass toward a pack of dogs alternately sniffing each other and examining a Frisbee that seemed to be stuck in the mud.

A light breeze rustled the greening leaves in the trees and caressed her bare arms with its round balmy touch. Megan inhaled again, tilting her face to the sun.

"Excuse me," a voice to her left said, in a southern accent so strong it sounded like "ex-key-use may."

Megan turned to see a woman of indeterminate age (thirty-five? forty-five? it was hard to tell) approaching, wearing a white sweater appliquéd with dog heads. Her fluffy blond hair blew in the breeze, revealing a perfectly made-up face and large, startlingly direct blue eyes. Megan wasn't sure, but she might have been wearing false eyelashes.

"Is that a Bernese mountain dog?" the woman asked, gesturing toward Peyton.

Megan smiled. She, like every dog owner, loved talking about her dog. "That's right. You're one of the few people who recognize the breed. Most people think she's a Saint Bernard and rottweiler mix. Or border collie and something."

"Oh, I recognize the breed all right. Dogs are my life," she said without the trace of a smile. She held her hand out to shake. "My name's Georgia Darling. That's my Great Dane over there, Sage."

Megan shook her hand and glanced over toward the fence, where a giant steel-blue Great Dane was standing like a muscular sentry carved out of marble.

"Oh my," she said, taken aback by the dog's size and beauty. He was one of the largest and most perfectly formed Great Danes she'd ever seen, and she'd seen her share. They—along with all the giant breeds—were not the healthiest dogs on the planet.

"Isn't he magnificent?" Georgia looked appreciatively at him herself. "A champion, of course. One of the most sought-after studs on the East Coast."

"Just the East Coast?" Megan angled her head for a better look and frowned. "But . . ."

Georgia chuckled. "That's right. He's neutered. Just too damn big to let testosterone run free, but I've got his sperm on ice at the bank, and believe me, honey, it's in demand." *De-may-and*, it sounded like.

Megan smiled. She loved a strong accent, particularly southern, though the British accent she'd heard yesterday had been every bit as enticing as scones and clotted cream.

Megan tore her gaze from the dog—and her mind from the man—and turned back to Georgia. "I'm sorry, I never introduced myself. I'm Megan Rose. I'm the new vet at Rose's Animal Hospital."

"Nice to meet you, Megan." Georgia's eyes flicked from her face to the embroidery on her shirt and back. "Rose, huh? Any relation?" She started to laugh.

Megan smiled back, unsure what the joke was and afraid it was her father. "Actually, yes. I'm Dr. Rose's daughter."

Georgia's smile faded. "Oh." Her perfectly plucked brows rose. "Well, bless your heart. I wasn't aware Doc Rose even had a daughter."

"My parents split when I was nine. I grew up in Connecticut, where I've been living until I moved here a week ago." Megan's eyes moved toward the group Peyton was in, which was now chasing a small beagle in ever-widening circles. A boy of about twelve stood in the middle watching them go round and round. His sneakers created a twist of grass and mud beneath his feet as he turned.

"Well, welcome to town. Funny, I can't recall Doc even mentioning an ex-wife," Georgia said, then shrugged. "Isn't that just like a man."

"I suppose so. Are there always this many people here so early in the morning?" Megan asked. She didn't want to start dissecting her father with everyone she met.

"No, I think it's the warm weather. We've had a pretty cold, wet spring," Georgia said. Megan could feel the other woman's eyes still on her. "Anybody ever tell you you look like Ashley Judd?"

This startled a smile out of her. "Ashley Judd!"

"You know, the actress, real cute—"

"No, I know who she is. It's just . . . well, thanks." Megan laughed and put a hand to her shoulder-length dark hair. "Same color hair, maybe."

"Same smile, I think. Are you married?"

"No, divorced." Were all southerners this direct? She liked it, tried it on for size. "You?"

Georgia nodded and looked toward her dog. "Divorced. Thank the good lord."

At that moment another woman approached the gate, slid the heavy iron barrier back a few inches, and sidled in with her dog, a black Labrador retriever. She entered quickly, before any of the dogs in the park could spot the opening gate and try to bolt. She was a pretty woman of about thirty with long, extremely shiny dark hair. Once she'd unhooked her lab from the leash, her eyes sought out Georgia and she waved.

"Here comes Penelope," Georgia said to Megan. "She owns a shop downtown, Pen Perfect. Have you seen it?"

"I've seen the sign." Megan watched the woman approach. This was great. This was exactly what she'd hoped would happen by visiting the dog park. She would meet some people, advertise the animal hospital, maybe even make a friend or two.

"Hey," Penelope said briefly when she joined them, bumping Georgia playfully with her elbow and looking curiously at Megan. "Big day here, it seems. I haven't seen this many people out at this hour in a long time."

"We were just talkin' about that," Georgia said.

Penelope's eyes took in the shirt Megan wore as Megan took in Penelope's dancer's posture and porcelain complexion. Pen *was* perfect, Megan thought, mentally clinging to Georgia's Ashley Judd compliment.

"So, you work at Rose's? Doc Rose pinched your ass yet?" Penelope laughed, her brow furrowing slightly as she glanced at Georgia's unsmiling face. "Did you already ask her that?" she asked Georgia.

Megan felt her cheeks go scarlet. Whether it was embarrassment for herself, for her father or for the awkwardness Penelope would feel when she found out, Megan wasn't sure.

"Megan here is Doc Rose's *daughter*," Georgia said. "And I'm afraid you've just insulted her."

"No, no," Megan began.

"His daughter! Oh I'm so sorry! I mean, about what I said, not that you're his daughter." Penelope's face went prettily pink.

"Please don't worry about it." Megan waved a hand. It was easy to feel separate from her father when she heard tales about him from a distance. Now that she was here, however, it seemed it might feel different to be openly associated with him.

"Oh I just feel awful." Penelope turned a tragic face toward Georgia.

"Please don't," Megan said firmly. "I know he's got a . . . well, some kind of reputation. I'm just here trying to drum up business for the animal hospital. I'm the new vet there. My father has retired."

Peyton galloped over toward her, the fur around her neck damp from being playfully chewed by the others, and stopped, leaning against Megan's leg and sitting squarely on her feet.

Unsure what else to say, Megan pulled one foot out from under Peyton and looked at her watch. Good lord, she was late. Had Peyton's inner clock known that before she did? The dog was always saving her from time-lapse problems, though it was usually just when she was late to provide dinner.

She extracted the leash from her pocket.

"Oh no, don't go," Penelope said, "I was just making a stupid joke."

Megan laughed, but for some reason it came out stilted. This was more awkward than she knew how to fix. "Please don't worry. That's not why I'm leaving, really. I'm just late."

"I can't believe I said that. Usually Georgia says the rude things." Penelope laughed too quickly. "Really, I'm such a jerk. Normally I don't even listen to gossip. Not that there *is* any gossip, I just meant—"

"Oh *stop*, Penelope," Georgia said, laughing. "You're just makin' it worse. Megan knows you didn't mean anything by it."

"Of course I do. No, I just have to go, is all," Megan said, realizing that she herself was making it worse by leaving so quickly, but it was too late now. It was nearly eight-thirty and the hospital opened at nine.

"Hey, we meet here most Tuesday and Friday mornings," Penelope said. "Georgia and me and our friend Lillian, but she's in Boston for the summer. We'd love it if you'd join us."

"Thanks," Megan said. "I was planning to come every morning anyway. Hopefully I'll see you. Nice to meet you both." She gave a short wave and turned away.

Megan didn't know why she was so bothered by Penelope's comment, but she was. Maybe it was having it said to her face, having to endure another person's pity for being related to Doc Rose. *Old Ramblin' Rose*, as one of the receptionists had dubbed him. Or maybe it was the uncomfortable novelty of having herself compared to him, even obliquely.

Megan shook herself as she strode vigorously up William Street toward the animal hospital. This was stupid. *She* was the one thinking bad thoughts about her father, fearing they'd see him in her. She tried to imagine someone feeling ashamed to be related to her and it made her so sad she felt a lump of pity grow in her throat.

Quit feeling so goddamn sorry for everyone. It's insulting. Her ex-husband used to say that to her all the time and he was right. She should save her pity for the animals, about whom she was also frequently choked up. But they, at least, deserved it. This preoccupation with her father was nothing more than glorified self-pity and she was the last person in the world she should feel sorry for.

Her life was going great, and was only going to get better.

Three

Sutter Foley was sitting in his car at the light at William and Kenmore streets when he noticed the new veterinarian talking with his ex-wife's friends in the dog park.

He should bring that damn dog here, he thought, instead of waiting until it needed some kind of medical attention. He'd locked it up in the laundry room that morning, thinking the worst-case scenario would be that the destructive beast chewed its way into the dryer or something, in which case he could take it to the vet and tell her it wasn't working out. A kind of lose-win situation.

On the other hand, if he brought the dog here, it might look like he'd made some sort of commitment to keeping it. Which he most certainly hadn't. He'd spent less than an hour on the front stoop yesterday only to discover upon reentering the house that the animal had mutilated the corner of an oriental rug, distributed the stuffing from an armchair around the room, inspected the contents of the kitchen garbage, and relieved itself on the dining room carpet.

The car behind him lay on its horn.

He glanced into the rearview mirror. The driver of a rusted white van exaggeratedly motioned him forward. He accelerated slowly.

He told himself he was not anxious to get to the office and that's why he was driving slowly enough to get a good look at Megan Rose. He'd remembered her name last night, as he was striving to fall asleep.

She was pretty, yes, but not dramatically so. There was something else about her. Something that drew his eye like an optical illusion that needed to be figured out.

He accelerated more, before his creeping pace became stalkerlike, and sighed, turning his thoughts to the office. He didn't think he could handle Arnetta today. Previously, going to work was the thing that made getting up in the mornings worthwhile, the office was a place he could relax in, a place where the rest of the world fell away.

For the last couple weeks, however, it had become something else. It had become the place where he dealt with Arnetta.

Arnetta Suggs. His new assistant. Hired at the behest of Sutter's sister, Liz, the only one of his siblings who lived in the states (in nearby Charlottesville) and the only one he enjoyed keeping in touch with. Liz, with her soft heart and do-good drive, didn't understand that Arnetta's experience as an academic secretary in no way prepared her for the job of assistant to an executive like Sutter. That and her seemingly limited mental capacity made for a daily challenge. For both of them, he supposed.

He parked behind the old brick building, circa 1824, in downtown Fredericksburg, and locked his Jaguar with the remote. Arnetta's car, a faded blue Ford hatchback, was already there. That was one thing he'd say for Arnetta. She was *always there*.

He sighed again.

"Good morning, Mr. Foley," Arnetta said, jumping up from her chair as Sutter came through the door. No small feat as she was very tall, at least six feet, and rail thin. She was also all elbows and knees, making unfolding that lanky frame seem like a project that could not be completed without knocking something over on her desk and ramming the chair back into the filing cabinet behind it.

"Good morning, Arnetta," he said. "Please sit down. I've told you, you don't have to get up every time I enter the room."

She smiled as if proud of doing something she didn't strictly have to do. "I know, sir, but I wanted to give you your calendar for the day. Franklin Ward says it's important to have a roadmap for the working week."

Franklin Ward, Sutter had learned on Arnetta's first day, and every day thereafter, was an efficiency guru whose entire oeuvre of tapes, texts, and workbooks Arnetta studied with feverish intensity.

She handed him a neatly written sheet of appointments that he glanced at as he entered his office. A moment later, after setting his briefcase on the desk, he turned around and headed back into the reception area.

"Ah, Arnetta?"

She sprang to her feet, knocking over the pencil holder on her desk. Sutter closed his eyes as the metal wheels of her chair clanged into the file cabinet at approximately fifteen miles per hour.

"Yes, sir?" Her bony fingers twisted together.

He took a deep breath. "You've got 'two-thirty' written here . . ."

She hurried to his side and bent her head over the sheet. Sutter was given the opportunity to contemplate the back of her curly gray-brown hair.

"Yes, two-thirty," she confirmed, nodding and looking back at him with a smile.

He hesitated, then, "Well, you see the problem, yes?"

She looked again at the sheet and the moment stretched long.

"There's nothing written next to it, Arnetta," he said finally. "So something is to happen at two-thirty, and I don't know what it is."

"Oh!" She took the sheet from him, frowning at it as if the answer might be discernible if only she could achieve total concentration.

"Could it be a conference call?" he prompted. "An appointment?"

"Um . . ." Arnetta said.

He waited.

"Someone's not likely to show up here, are they?" he asked, barely containing exasperation.

She looked up at him, stricken. "Oh. Oh, that would be bad, wouldn't it? Without knowing what they want or anything?"

"It would not be good." After a moment he took pity on her. "Though it's not likely. Remember, this is just my satellite office. Mostly what we get here are conference calls and external appointments." He paused. When she said nothing he asked, "You haven't scheduled any external appointments for me?"

"Oh no, I don't think so," she said, grimacing as if that would be a terrific breach of etiquette on her part.

"Fine, then, we'll just see what happens at two-thirty." He turned briskly back to his office.

"Mr. Foley!" She took several strides after him, reminding him, as she always did, of a baby giraffe. "You forgot your schedule."

He took the paper from her and thanked her, wondering what on earth good it was now that they'd so conspicuously established its unreliability.

When Megan arrived at the animal hospital she set right to work. There may not be many appointments yet, but there was plenty of work to be done. Even though cleaning was a daily affair, it was obvious much had been overlooked for a long time, judging by the filthy floors and disorganized back rooms. There was also updating the records and putting everything on the new computer, which she had the receptionists doing while she and the vet techs moved furniture and equipment to clean and rearrange.

She could do this, she thought. She could turn this place around just as she could rise above the stuff associated with "Doc Rose." Before long, she told herself, people would barely remember her father's transgressions and "Dr. Rose" would come to symbolize safety and healing.

"Dr. Rose?" Allison, the afternoon receptionist, poked her head into the back room with a tentative smile, where Megan was scrubbing out a cat crate. At least Megan thought it was Allison. She and Bethany looked an awful lot alike. Her father tended to hire receptionists who were petite, blond and exceptionally smiley. Megan had inherited three of them. Two of whom, if things didn't improve soon, would have to be let go. "Someone's here to see you."

Megan's heart rose. A client? Excellent.

She looked at her watch—one-thirty, no wonder her stomach was growling—then down at her white lab jacket to be sure the morning's cleaning hadn't made her look like a chimney sweep. "I thought we didn't have any afternoon appointments. Is it a walk-in?"

Allison's blond curls bounced as she shook her head. "No. This is a visitor, for you."

For no reason at all, Megan thought of Sutter Foley. What if he'd come to apologize for his curtness yesterday? What if he wanted to make it up to her with a fabulously expensive dinner somewhere with mind-blowing sex afterward? What if he was the leader of a spaceship teeming with aliens?

They were all equally plausible.

She glanced quickly at the glass-fronted cabinet next to her and nearly burst out laughing. Even her reflection looked like it had been cleaning decades of animal hair from corners not seen since the Carter administration.

She'd better hope it was the aliens.

She had just enough time to tuck an errant wave of hair back into her ponytail when Penelope— perfect Penelope—came through the swinging door from the reception area. She was dressed differently than she'd been that morning, when she'd been in jeans. Now she wore clothes that had an elegant, yet artsy look about them. A trim skirt that accentuated her slimness and a deep emerald shirt that had to be silk, nothing else could get color that rich. In her hand she held a small white paper bag with handles.

Megan couldn't hide her surprise. "Hi."

Penelope smiled. "Hi. I'm sorry to barge in like this. Are you busy?"

Megan laughed. "Hardly. We've just been cleaning the place. We don't have all that many clients yet." She glanced at her fingernails, saw they were nearly black, and put her hands in her pockets. "What can I do for you?"

"I just brought you a little something. To apologize for this morning."

"There's no need—"

"Yes there is." She waved off Megan's words. "Now, you've probably already had lunch, so this is dessert." She smiled conspiratorially and handed her the bag.

"Actually I haven't had lunch." Megan took it and looked inside. The divine smell of chocolate wafted out. "Oh my God. Truffles?"

"Just a few. I have a friend with a chocolate shop. But if you haven't had lunch, do you want to go grab a bite? I'm starving."

Megan knew this was a sympathy visit but she didn't care. She had a lunch date! Just a week in town and she might actually be making a friend.

"I'd love to go," she said.

They decided on a restaurant called Sammy T's, a Fredericksburg institution with many vegetarian entrees since Penelope didn't eat meat. They sat in one of the high-backed wooden booths and both ordered salads.

They started off with polite conversation, moving effortlessly from "Where are you from?" to "Where did you go to school?" to "What are your hobbies?" Penelope was apparently an avid tennis player, playing whenever she got the chance, but Megan had to disappoint her when she asked if Megan played.

Then Penelope got to what Megan suspected might have been the point of her visit. Or at least a secondary point, after the unnecessary apology.

"I wondered if you might like to join the board of the local SPCA," Penelope said, leaning a little bit forward and putting her forearms on the table.

Megan paused. "I'd be delighted," she said truthfully, "but I'm not sure I have the time. I'm the only one manning the fort right now, until I can get enough clients to hire another veterinarian. So I won't have much discretionary time."

Penelope was shaking her head. "That's all right. It's really kind of honorary, since we have volunteers who do most of the work and organizing. But it's great to have vets on the board even in just an advisory capacity. One meeting a month, tops. Maybe even every other month. What do you think?"

"Well . . ." Megan picked up her napkin and placed it in her lap. "It sounds like I could do it. If you're sure nobody would mind me playing such a small part."

"Mind?" Penelope beamed. "They'll be thrilled just to have you there when you can make it. And if it turns out to be too much for your schedule, you can always quit."

Megan smiled. "All right then. Thank you for thinking of me."

"No, thank you! This'll be great!"

A short silence prevailed, then, "Georgia tells me you're divorced," Penelope said. "I am too. So's Georgia, and so's our friend Lillian, whom you haven't met because she's away for the summer, but who's usually at the dog park, too. Isn't that funny?"

"I guess it's true what they say. Divorce is epidemic." Megan shook her head. "Stinks to be such a common statistic, doesn't it?"

"I'm pretty new to it, myself." Penelope looked down at her hands, making Megan wonder if the divorce might not have been her idea. "It still feels funny to say it. I'm always saying 'my husband' and then having to insert the 'ex' afterward. I guess I should just stop talking about him at all."

Megan sighed. "It is tough to get used to. It took

me a couple of years to be able to say I was divorced without automatically adding in all the reasons why." They both laughed. "Took me a while to figure out nobody cared. In any case, it's four years now and not that many people even ask anymore."

Penelope rolled her eyes. "You're lucky. People are always asking me about Glenn. And they're not single men looking for dates, either. Just busybodies wanting to hear all the gory details. Either that or be the first to tell me the latest gossip about him."

"I know what you mean. That used to happen to me and I'm so glad to be away from it," Megan said. "I left it all behind in Connecticut. Ex, in-laws, and meddling gossips. And boy, does it feel good to finally move on."

Penelope's lips pressed together. "Move on. That's what everyone says to me. 'You have to move on.' Like I don't already *know* that. They just never say *how*." She gave Megan a wry look. "I hate to be the one to break it to you but you haven't exactly landed in a hotbed of eligible bachelors."

Megan shrugged. "Fortunately, I'm not looking for another relationship. Certainly not marriage. Not again. An affair might be nice," she smiled slyly, "but right now I have too much on my plate even for that. And it seems an awful lot of work at this point."

"I know, sometimes I feel tired just thinking about it. But when I think about the future . . ." She made a rueful face, then continued briskly, "Around here it's mostly families with young children, or older types who've been here a long time. Most of the women I know who date are seeing men who live in Richmond or Washington." She shook her head. "Either way it's a long haul for a date. A lot of work, as you said."

"Especially for those of us who work Saturdays too," she said, guessing that Penelope, with her shop, was also a slave to the six-day week. "In any case I'm going to have my hands full for a while getting the hospital back on its feet."

Unbidden, Sutter Foley sprang to mind once again. She'd assumed he was single, based on the emptiness of his house, but he could well be married despite the lack of a ring. A lot of men didn't like jewelry. And she couldn't recall what she might have read about him in that department. She'd like to find someone to go out with, just to have the occasional fun, but Megan didn't fool around with married men. Not that Sutter Foley would ever be interested in *her*.

"I did meet an interesting man yesterday," she said, then sipped her water.

Penelope gave her a significant look of interest just as the waitress arrived with their food. Conversation paused.

Once their salads had been deposited, silverware arranged and their beverages checked, Penelope immediately asked, "Did you meet him at the dog park? I keep thinking that would be a perfect place to meet someone, but I never do."

"No." Megan started to chuckle. "It's a funny story, actually. His dog woke me up yesterday morning."

Penelope picked up her fork and pushed the top of her salad around as if looking for something better underneath. "Oh I *hate* it when the neighbors leave their dogs out to bark. It's not the poor animal's fault, it's just bored. But to leave a dog out in the yard all day? It's irresponsible and you should call animal control."

"No, no." Megan laughed. "The dog actually got into my bedroom." Megan wrestled an oversized piece of lettuce from her Caesar into her mouth.

"Your bedroom!" Penelope's eyes widened.

"It got in the dog door and came right on up." Megan chewed while shaking her head at the memory. "Scared me half to death. When I finally got a chance to look at the tag, you'll never guess who she belonged to."

"Wait, maybe I can. What kind of dog was it?"

"Golden retriever mix. Very young, six or seven months, maybe."

Penelope paused, her glass of iced tea suspended between the table and her mouth. "Hm, a mixed golden . . . we had a puppy like that about a month ago at the shelter, but it was adopted. Oh and you know who—" She stopped.

Megan looked at her, grinning. "You know who it was, don't you?"

Penelope's eyes were wide. "Was it Sutter Foley's groundskeeper?"

Megan laughed and wiped a tiny bit of dressing from her cheek. "The man himself, actually."

Penelope, who'd been about to sip her tea, put the glass back down and leaned forward. "It was *his* dog? That's so strange—wait, you didn't go to his house, did you?"

Megan raised her brows. "Didn't I?"

Penelope leaned back in the booth. "But the dog wasn't his! Not really, was it? What did he say?"

Megan laughed. "That's pretty much what he said. Repeatedly."

"It was some guy he'd hired who lived in his carriage house that adopted the dog. And the only reason I know this is because everyone at the shelter was thrilled that one of our dogs was going to live with a multimillionaire."

"A *multimillionaire*," Megan repeated. "It's hard to even imagine that kind of money. And the house was nice but with millions . . . it's not like he had a helicopter pad on the roof or anything. Not that I saw anyway."

Penelope gaped at her. "You were *in* his house? What was it like?"

Megan thought. "Nice. Plush. Filled with obviously expensive furniture and china and all that." She thought of the shattered wine glasses and wondered if they were Waterford or anything. "But it wasn't overblown. Nothing . . . ostentatious about it."

Penelope stabbed the salad with her fork. "You know, I was friends with his ex-wife but was never invited to the house. I always got the impression she wouldn't do it because he wouldn't like it. Apparently he's *obsessed* with privacy."

"I would be too, if I were him. The weird thing was he was alone in the house. No one to even open the door. I thought he'd have servants or a butler or something. A housekeeper at least. Someone to deal with the riff-raff who might knock on his door."

"That's the weird thing about Sutter," Penelope said, shaking her head as if mystified. "Even though he's rich as Croesus, and he does apparently love his luxuries, for the most part he supposedly tries to live like an everyday guy. That's why he stayed in this town when he struck it big. A lot of people who know him now, knew him when he first moved to this country fifteen years ago with Bitsy, so we're not overawed by his wealth. At least, we say we're not." She grinned. "But for the most part the town tries to protect him a little bit."

"Protect him? From what? Sounds to me like he could afford to build a fortress with a moat and hire enough assistants to never have to leave the house."

"That's what I'd do," Penelope admitted. "You'd be surprised how often the press comes looking for him. And the wackos looking for money—they're endless! And when someone asks where he lives, you know, 'just out of curiosity,'" Penelope brought her fingers up and mimicked quote marks, "you never know if it isn't a thief or something. He's even got some kind of geek fan club following. One time, this guy set up a giant wooden computer on the green across from Sutter's house with 'God Bless SFSolutions, Who Delivered Us From Microsoft' painted all over it. And then there're the *women*. Oh my God."

Penelope took a bite of her salad and chewed thoughtfully.

"The women?" Megan asked.

Penelope nodded and swallowed. "Whenever there's an article or anything that includes a picture of him, women begin turning up in town posing as his sister, or his cousin, or his girlfriend, or whatever, looking for his house. One of them claimed he'd asked her to marry him over the Internet." Penelope chuckled. "Sheriff Hill likes those trespassers the best."

"He *is* awfully good looking." Megan speared a cucumber and put it into her mouth. So much for meeting an eligible man in Fredericksburg. She finds one and the whole world is after him. *Not*, she told herself again, that she'd ever thought he might be interested in her.

Penelope nodded. "He is."

"Do you know him? I mean, personally?"

"A little. I met him once or twice with Bitsy, his ex-wife, when they'd come to a function in town. But they've been divorced a while now, so I don't see him very much. Or when I do, he doesn't condescend to talk to me."

"So he's a terrible snob, huh?"

Penelope shrugged, as if his snobbishness would be kind of inevitable, what with him being able to buy small countries and all.

Despite herself, Megan asked, "*Ex*-wife? So he's single?"

Penelope gave her a cagey smile. "Interested?"

Megan laughed. "I'm really not. Believe me, I know myself too well to believe I could live the life of a multimillionaire's girlfriend. If nothing else, my wardrobe isn't up to the challenge."

"Oh come on, nobody would turn down a multimillionaire out of wardrobe concerns."

"The wardrobe's just the tip of the iceberg." She thought about her father asking clients for money, buying drinks for preposterously young women, coming home drunk and brimming with tales of barroom "networking."

Penelope's smile turned benign. "Well, I wouldn't blame you for being interested. Who wouldn't be? He's a great-looking, extremely wealthy, available man. But trust me, you don't want to get mixed up with him."

"Why not?" This time Megan leaned forward. Did Penelope know some sort of scandalous secret about Sutter Foley? How close *was* she to the ex-wife?

"He's dating someone, for one thing," Penelope said.

"Well, of course he is." She laughed. "Though if he knew there was an average-looking, single, impoverished veterinarian in his midst I'm sure he would dump her in an instant. Who is she? Does she live in Fredericksburg?"

"She didn't, but I heard she just rented a house a couple blocks away from his. The rumor is she's an ex-model from New York, but she's not. She's a Massachusetts blueblood who's pretty enough that millions of dollars can make her *look* like a model."

"They never mention that in *Glamour*," Megan mused. "How millions of dollars is really the ultimate fashion accessory."

"That's for sure," Penelope agreed. "Look at Paris Hilton."

"Who?"

Penelope looked up. "You're kidding. Don't you watch TV?"

"I don't *own* a TV," Megan confessed. "I don't have time to watch."

Penelope shook her head, smiling. "Good for you. I, on the other hand, am an "Entertainment Tonight" groupie. Anything you want to know about the rich and famous, just ask me."

"All right," Megan said, "what's the other reason I wouldn't want to get involved with Sutter

Foley? You said he was dating someone, *for one thing*. What's another?"

Penelope paused, then sighed. "All right, but you have to *promise me* you're not going to go straight to the *National Tattler* or anything."

Megan grinned. "Sure, I promise. I might be a reporter who moved to town and impersonates a struggling veterinarian to get near him, but I promise. Feel better?"

Penelope chuckled but eyed her a tad warily. "All right. But only because I know Doc Rose is your father."

"That's the first time *that's* ever given me an advantage," Megan cracked.

"Sutter Foley," Penelope said in a low voice, leaning forward, "is an emotional cripple."

A brief silence passed.

"An emotional cripple?" Megan finally asked. This was a far cry from the gossip she'd hoped for—like a criminal record, a penchant for dressing in women's clothing, or a mad wife in the attic.

"Yes," Penelope said, her expression intent, "you know, the kind of man who doesn't have any."

Megan frowned. She was always leery of psychobabble and "emotional cripple" smacked of just the kind of thing women make up to tell each other to soften the blow of being dumped. "How do you, uh, know this?"

"Because," Penelope said, nodding sagely, "he hates dogs."

Four

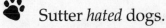

Sutter *hated* dogs.

He looked from the hall to the living room to what he could see of the dining room and as far as the eye could see was toilet paper. A long unbroken string of it stretched from the half-bath under the stairs to the front room, and beyond that were chewed bits and small wads and little gobby things that looked like gum. Interspersed with the toilet paper was a generous sprinkling of garbage, some carpet fringe and a bit more of the stuffing from the armchair.

The bloody beast had gotten out.

How? How on earth had the thing gotten free of the laundry room? The door had been closed and, to the best of his knowledge, dogs were not adept at doorknobs.

He thought of Briana and the horror she would

feel at this desecration of his "charming parlor," as she'd called it. He imagined one of her expensively clad feet stepping into a pile of this beast's making and gritted his teeth.

Briana would abhor whatever it was that had made him relent in the face of the veterinarian's logic that morning. She would consider it weakness, not kindness or anything that could be considered laudable, to have kept the dog even overnight. He would think so too if it had not been himself arguing with the implacable Dr. Rose.

And he would have been right. Look at how his charity had been paid back. No, some people were pet people and he was not one of them.

He took a deep breath and set his briefcase on the floor.

Where was it, he thought, setting a pile of mail on the hall table. Where was the sodding dog?

He gave a whistle, sharp in the quiet of the house. A scurrying of toenails on the wood floor overhead responded. Sutter looked up. *It had gone upstairs.* Sutter's blood threatened to boil. A moment later the pup hurled itself down the steps, its back legs almost going faster than the front ones. It hit the front foyer, u-turned and threw itself at Sutter as if expecting to be caught in his arms.

Part of the dog—snout? leg? he couldn't be sure—caught him all too close to the groin and he doubled over, pushing the dog's next attack away.

Finally, when the puppy rebounded one more time, he grabbed its collar and dragged it to the door.

"That's enough from you," Sutter growled. "I can't be dealing with this blasted nonsense. Coming home from work," he muttered, "long day, bleeding bastard at VamTech, pain in the ass Lizzy wanting favors, damn senseless memo, *Arnetta*, for Christ's sake. It's too much, I tell you. *Too bloody much.*"

The dog's tail wagged furiously, whacking him in the legs, as he opened the door and dragged it out to the car. He opened the back door, grabbed the hairy thing, and tossed it unceremoniously onto the petal-soft, dove-gray leather of the Jaguar's back seat.

He straightened and looked at the pup panting up at him, happy as a halfwit, dripping saliva onto the seat.

God, he was knackered. He'd slept all of two hours last night and all he'd wanted to do when he arrived home was eat and go to bed. It had seemed he might be tired enough at last to sleep.

Not now, however. Now he was wound up. Now he was going to see that veterinarian and get rid of this whole sodding problem.

Then he was going to get some sleeping pills.

Where in the hell had Martina been, anyway? Dropping her sister off at the airport, he remembered. The house had been empty for only an hour, but apparently that was enough time for pandemonium to break loose.

He opened the front seat and got in, slamming the door behind him. A long wet tongue found his ear.

Sutter shot forward, throwing one arm back into the dog. His other hit the car horn, startling them both.

"No!" he barked, glaring at the dog. What was its name? Didn't matter. He was getting rid of it.

He drove swiftly down Washington Avenue to Lewis, turned and gunned it toward Princess Anne Street. He wasn't exactly sure where Rose's Animal Hospital was, but he was pretty sure he'd seen a veterinarian's office down on Sophia Street. Waste of prime property, he'd thought at the time, as it was sitting on the riverfront and not taking advantage of the view. Not that a bunch of animals would care, which made it another crime.

He pulled up in front of the two-story clapboard structure and threw the car into park, congratulating himself on being right. *Rose's Animal Hospital* was painted in chipped letters across the front of the building above the front door and below the second-story windows.

He got out of the car and looked in the back seat. The good news was the puppy had laid down and was no longer drooling. The bad news was it had thrown up. From what he could tell, most of it was toilet paper. Whatever Martina, his housekeeper, had fed the dog for dinner had already been processed and was probably sitting at home somewhere on one of his carpets.

He looked dolefully at the dog and took a deep breath, expelling it slowly. He hadn't brought the leash, he realized.

He opened the back seat and the dog sprang to life. He grabbed its collar and pulled it off the seat, avoiding the mess, and up to the front door of the hospital. Unfortunately the door was locked, and there in front of him were the hours. Open at ten, closed at six. He looked at his watch. Six-thirty.

Blast.

Through the glass door he could see a light glowing from a back room. He rapped on the glass. A moment later a shadow crossed the doorway and to his immense relief Megan Rose herself came out and headed toward him.

She had a smile on her face until she spotted the puppy. Then she frowned, and shook her head ruefully as she unlocked the door.

Sutter loosed the dog and the animal took off, slipping and sliding on the linoleum into the back room. Sutter stepped into the waiting room. Megan pushed the door closed behind him and locked it.

"Well, hello," she said, sounding as if she were not at all surprised to see him. "Let me guess. You don't want a dog."

It wasn't until this moment that he realized he should have taken the dog to the pound, not back here to Megan Rose. She was going to make him feel guilty about this. She was going to try to talk him into keeping it again. She was not going to take this lying down.

He thought of her lying down. Then shook his head.

"You," he said, sounding accusatory even to his own ears, "wouldn't believe the shambles I found when I returned home this evening. This dog is a menace. Beyond a menace, this dog is—is—the dog is a threat to itself." *Yes! Brilliant.* "With all the toilet paper this mongrel consumed, much of which it just vomited up on my back seat on the way over here, it's a wonder the thing hasn't already expired. I tell you it does not belong with me. It doubtless does not belong with anyone who values the state of their home. Nor should it be anywhere it is likely to injure itself by consuming things it oughtn't. Like heirloom furniture, for example."

Megan Rose listened in silence, her arms crossed over her chest, her expression benign, if not sympathetic. She didn't attempt to interrupt, nor did she laugh at him or roll her eyes or otherwise editorialize while he spoke. No, she just let him waffle on until he had no choice but to stop and await her response.

Effective technique, he thought. She'd be good in the corporate world.

"You know, dogs can be trained," she offered finally.

He shook his head. "I haven't the time, nor the inclination. Neither do I wish to invite yet another person into my home to do it. I prefer to be alone and I require quiet, Dr. Rose. Absolute, uninterrupted silence."

After a moment she sighed. "I'm wondering," she said slowly, "what it's like to live your life."

He raised his brows. "I beg your pardon?"

She uncrossed her arms and regarded him thoughtfully. "I'm serious. I'm really curious. You come home to an empty, *silent* house each evening and you seem to want it that way. You could have *anything*, and you choose nothing."

Sutter hesitated. Was that what she saw? Is that how he appeared to others? *Did* he choose nothing? Why *was* he so upset about that chair? It wasn't, as he'd characterized it, an heirloom. If it were it would have been a piece of MFI junk purchased third-hand at a car boot sale. His parents had been far from wealthy.

Perhaps it was because Briana had called his room "charming" that he'd been so upset at its disruption.

That was ridiculous. He didn't care a whit what anyone thought of his decorating style, including

Briana. He was simply angry that a nice belonging had been arbitrarily ruined, as anyone would be. His peaceful place had been thrown into chaos and that's what had rattled him. What he had was quiet, not nothing.

"Sometimes," he said, "nothing is everything."

She smiled. "Yeah, right. And solitude is not loneliness, but nature abhors a vacuum. Your isolation was bound to be interrupted one way or another, someday."

"I have the right to make my own decisions about how I live my life. And besides, Berkley is frequently there when I arrive home. As is Martina. So you see . . ." What was he doing, justifying this to her?

"And they are . . . family members?" she asked.

His cook and his housekeeper, actually, but that would just feed her argument. Regardless, he nodded his head slowly, "In some ways."

"Don't tell me they're your gardeners," she laughed. Her eyes glittered, her face so purely amused that her prettiness turned to beauty.

Of course, she was essentially right, which was annoying.

He said stiffly, "I'm under no obligation to keep this dog simply because you don't understand my choices."

She quieted and he knew he'd got her. Why he didn't turn around that instant and leave was less clear.

She tilted her head. "You were married once, right?"

"I don't know what that has to do with anything."

She lifted her hand to guide a lock of hair behind one ear. "Don't you miss the companionship? The everyday routines, the interaction? I mean, even if it wasn't very good most of the time, you still had somebody, you know, kind of in your same orbit."

"Are you suggesting I should orbit this dog?"

She laughed. "No, I actually had the dog cast in the role of satellite, but I suppose that's up to you."

"Ah. So something *is* up to me," he said. "Thank you."

She inclined her head graciously.

Something niggled at the back of his mind and he asked, "Were *you* married?"

It seemed an impertinent question, and maybe that's why he asked it—she was so frequently impertinent herself—but he was also curious. She seemed too young to have gone through both marriage and divorce. But then, perhaps she was not divorced.

"You ask that like I might have hit the nail on the head," she said evasively.

"No, I ask that like you just revealed something about yourself. Clearly you desire something instead of nothing. If indeed one's own company can be considered nothing."

"One always has one's own company," she said. "That's not a positive or a negative."

He didn't rise to the bait. "You didn't answer the question."

She flushed. He thought, *Lovely rose rising to Dr. Rose's cheeks*.

"Okay, yes," she said, "I was married. And it didn't work, in the long run. But *parts* of it did. Parts of it worked."

There was something in her eyes, he thought, something wounded. He decided, though he could have pegged her further, to let it lie. "Why are you so dead set on my keeping this dog?"

She sighed. "I don't know. You just . . . seem like you need it. And I *know* it needs you."

He felt himself weakening and did his damnedest to fight it. "Got your ear to the universe again?"

"Look," she said, "I'll make it easy for you. Come on." She turned and headed toward the back where the light was on.

Reluctantly, Sutter followed. What would make this easy for him would be to leave, and never see either her or the dog again. But something about her was compelling and he could think of no good reason not to pursue the reason why.

In the back room, which sported a number of metal cages, most of them empty, the puppy was tormenting a cat in an upper cage. The dog would leap up to look at the cat, causing it to arch its back and hiss, then she would sit down wagging her tail until the cat lay back down before jumping up again. Sutter watched this maneuver several times before Megan came back from a darkened storage area carrying a large plastic box with holes on the sides and a door on it.

"This is a crate. Every time you leave the house, or if you're home and can't keep your eye on Baywatch, you put her in this and close the door. She won't be able to chew anything and she'll learn to hold her bladder and bowels until you let her outside. Dogs are naturally averse to soiling their beds."

"You want me to put the dog in a cage?"

The vet pursed her lips, obviously displeased. "You have no trouble with the idea of taking this dog to the pound where it could well end up euthanized, and yet you can't stand the thought of putting it in a cage?"

"If you will notice," he said tightly, "I brought the dog back to you, not the pound."

She *humphed*, unimpressed. "In any case, it's not a *cage*, it's a *crate*. It's a very humane way to housetrain a dog. Think of it as a crib. Eventually she'll come to regard it as her den. And you won't lose any more heirlooms."

He shook his head, frustrated. "Surely you know someone with a farm, someplace where the dog can run around. Someplace more suitable than my house."

"You mean set it loose so that no one has to think about it again?"

"Something like that, yes."

He realized he'd said something wrong by her swiftly darkening expression. She had lightning-quick expressions, exactly mirroring, it seemed, whatever it was she was thinking. So unlike Briana with her Mona Lisa smile and unreadable porcelain perfection. If Briana was a question mark, then this girl was an exclamation point. Mystery and transparency, ever at odds.

"If I let you take this dog—"

"*Let* me?"

"—I can be sure, can't I, that you won't just open the door and let it go?"

She studied him a moment as he began chuckling. He was not so easily led down the path of reverse psychology.

"You'll never know, will you?" he said.

Her lips curved and her dark eyes narrowed. "I'll risk it. Now, you'll need to bring her back for her shots. Since we don't know what she's had already, if anything, we'll have to start from scratch . . ."

She went on in this vein, detailing all kinds of medical attention the dog would require over the next several weeks and for some reason the prospect had him feeling more generously toward the animal. It wouldn't be that difficult, he reasoned, to keep the thing in this box and let it out every now and again. If it was under control, then it would barely be noticeable and he wouldn't have to do battle with this willful woman on the issue anymore. Maybe it would be nice to come home to something, though this tornado certainly didn't seem like something he'd want to see every day.

Still, if he kept the dog, at least for a while, he could see Megan Rose again. She was, he could admit to himself, entertaining, if only because she didn't tiptoe around him as so many other people did. Virtually everyone, in fact, except for the people he'd known before SFSolutions had taken off, flattered him and served him and generally acted as if he might order them beheaded. There was something about wealth—extreme wealth, wealth beyond one's wildest dreams—that intimidated people. While he found it frequently convenient, it was also disturbing.

His ex-wife, Bitsy, was about the only other person he trusted to be completely honest with him. Probably because she had known him in the darkest depths of poverty. She'd married him when he'd had no money and divorced him just when he was becoming rich. It was the fame she couldn't stand. But she hadn't cared about his money—of course it helped that her family had plenty—and that more than anything else had endeared her to him forever.

His assistant VP, Montgomery, was pretty blunt around him but usually only on safe subjects.

Clayton Van Werner, his senior VP, could be terrifically acerbic, but only on subjects other than Sutter himself.

And Briana . . . well, Briana was something else entirely. Removed from everyday life and concerns, she was like dessert. Delicious when he was in the mood, but not necessary for survival. Not, in fact, necessary for anything but pleasure. And he could afford the most expensive pleasures now . . .

Before he knew it, Megan Rose had produced a bag of dog food and a box of dog bones to go with the cage—er, crate—and was hustling him out to the car with all of it.

"Don't forget," she said, as she propped the bag of dog food up against the crate in the boot of his Jaguar, "that she still needs a rabies shot so you'll have to bring her back. Or," she added with a sly look, "you can send one of your servants or lackeys or whatever you have."

"I haven't got any lackeys. As you recall, I have chosen to have nothing."

She smiled. "Then you'll have to come."

He looked at her, his eyes trailing from her dancing brown eyes to her curved lips. "I can't believe I'm letting you do this to me."

She paused, her lips parting. After a second of silence, he brought his gaze back to her eyes. "I'm not doing anything *to* you," she said, her eyes steady.

"Aren't you?" He lifted one brow, was tempted, without reason, to touch her cheek, to see if it was as soft as it looked. He imagined running a couple of fingers along that downy surface to just beneath her chin. He imagined tipping it up and stepping in close, touching her lips with his.

What would she do?

What would she taste like?

Almost without thinking, he took a step toward her and she looked swiftly up at him.

If he kissed her, she would want to know why. And he didn't know why. He only knew he wanted to.

"Aren't we forgetting something?" he said finally.

Her eyes were still on his face. "What?" She sounded breathless.

He gave a slight smile. "The dog. I seem to have all the accessories and no pet."

She laughed then. Relieved? And with a promise to be right back, ran back inside the building.

Megan stopped as soon as she was out of view of the front door, and leaned against the back wall. Baywatch was jumping up in front of Mrs. Houseman's overweight cat, giving it a better workout than anything Megan could prescribe, while Megan held one hand to her heart to still its frantic pace.

He'd been about to kiss her, hadn't he? His eyes were on her lips and the expression in them had been positively smoldering.

Unless she was losing her mind. It was possible. She'd gone so long without a man that she could be reading something into nothing, but she'd felt it as surely as if he'd reached out and touched her. He had thought about kissing her.

The question was, what should she do about it? Why had he stopped? Thought better of it, most likely. Or maybe he thought she wouldn't like it. It was a tough call, but this could be her last opportunity to find out. Only at the risk of looking like an utter fool, however.

But maybe she didn't care about that.

Maybe it was worth it.

She pushed herself off the wall and grabbed one of the hospital's thin slip leashes. Catching Baywatch as the dog descended from her last jump, she slipped the leash over her head and turned to the door.

"Come on, Baywatch," she said. "We don't want him cooling off too much."

She stepped back out the door into the warm summer evening. The sun had already dipped below the horizon and a slight breeze caused a rustling in the nearby trees. The light was just the way she liked it. Soft and low, the dimming of the day.

Sutter was leaning in the back seat of the Jaguar,

a nice-looking car if ever she'd seen one. The black surface was shiny as onyx, and the whole car looked like a jewel. When she emerged from the building he pushed out of the back seat, the sound of crumpling newspaper reaching her.

She liked the way he moved. He was tall but not gangly in any way. He had a kind of grace, an efficiency of movement to go with that tight British reserve. She tried to imagine him tripping or slipping or doing something uncoordinated and couldn't do it. He was too contained. He would never allow it.

"Here you go," she said, extending the leash. Baywatch tugged at her arm, pulling her toward him.

He, in turn, extended the crumpled newspaper toward her. "Have you got a trash can? That's the best I could do cleaning up the seat. Martina will have to go at it with some kind of cleanser in the morning."

He took the leash from her by grabbing it in the middle and held the wad of newspaper out toward her. She reached for it.

"Careful," he said. "You don't want to touch . . . that . . ." He manipulated the wad so she could catch hold of the clean edges.

She got it and turned toward a trash can near the front door. So much for renewing the potentially romantic moment, she thought. Maybe she was crazy. What had she planned to do, anyway?

Throw herself into his arms and kiss him? Women must throw themselves at him all the time, she thought. Why should she be just like all the rest?

Besides, that would probably be the end of Baywatch's chances.

She hurled the newspaper into the trash with a little more force than necessary and brushed her hands together as she turned back to him. "Well, that's it, then. You're all set."

He had wrestled the dog into the back seat and closed the door as she returned. "Listen, I'll do this for a while if you agree to look for a more permanent situation for the animal."

She shouldn't feel disappointed, she knew she shouldn't. Taking the puppy had seemed an indication of . . . something. But it wasn't true, and it didn't matter. She was dwelling completely in her imagination now, it seemed.

"All right. Agreed. You'll foster her. But in the meantime . . ."

"Yes, yes, in the meantime I won't set it free in a field somewhere or let it get hit by a car." He grinned, obviously proud of himself for reading her thoughts, and she was caught by how boyish he looked. Without the austere veneer he was even more handsome, which irked her. Nobody should be so favored by the fates.

"You laugh but it happens all the time." She

frowned, hunching her shoulders and pushing her hands into her pockets.

He opened the driver's door but didn't get in, merely leaned an elbow on top of the window frame and looked at her, his lips quirked. "*Now* what have I done?"

"What do you mean?"

"I mean a moment ago you were happy I was taking the dog. One joke later you've lost that triumphant glow." He cocked an eyebrow. "And it was very becoming."

She smiled reluctantly. "Gloating becomes me?"

"Indeed it does."

She chuckled. Handsome, rich, *and* funny and perceptive. The man was like a cosmic joke to single women everywhere. She wondered about the blue-blooded beauty he was dating.

"I'm just . . ." She contemplated telling him the truth. While she had no pretension to feminine wiles, she didn't think he deserved her every thought. "You're just a lucky man, is all."

At that his eyes seemed to shutter and he lost *his* glow. "So they say." He got in the vehicle and closed the door, starting the engine, then rolling down the window. "Thank you, Dr. Rose. Ought I to make an appointment for the next shot or is it the kind of thing I can simply show up for?"

She moved closer to the car door. "Make an appointment," she said, deciding she'd need some warning when this guy was coming back. Unexpected beauty in the workplace could really throw one off one's stride.

"Have you got a card or something with your number on it?"

She patted her front and back pockets, told him to wait a minute and ran inside for a card. Back outside, she handed it to him and their fingers brushed, causing her to wonder what it would be like for this man to touch her in a nonbusinesslike way. How would it feel for those hands to grip her with desire, to touch her face with tenderness?

If he'd still been standing outside the car she would have kissed him. She would have, she insisted to herself. Just to see what he would do.

"Thanks." He looked down at the card. Long, elegant fingers held it in the dashboard light.

"Sutter?" she said. The name felt strange on her lips, incomplete, almost rude. As if she'd just met Michelangelo and called him Mickey.

He looked up, brows raised inquiringly. His eyes looked very green in the twilight glow.

"Thanks for taking Baywatch," she finished lamely.

"Who? Oh." His eyes shot toward the back seat, though not enough to really look at the dog. "Sure."

She suffered a slight misgiving. He *would* treat the pup well, wouldn't he?

"That reminds me," he said, putting the Jag in

gear. "Can I change the name? I don't believe I can bring myself to use the one it's got and I've got to call it something, haven't I? I mean, I can't just let it wander about without identity."

Megan's smile blossomed. If he was worried about the pup needing a name, then of course he was going to take care of it. Worrying about a dog's identity was a great sign. She congratulated herself on being right the first time. He *needed* this dog.

"Of course you can change the name," she said. "Anything you want."

He smiled, perhaps the first truly unfettered smile she'd seen from him and it made her positively weak in the knees.

"There it is," he said gently.

"There what is?" she breathed.

"That triumphant glow. I knew it wouldn't be gone for long." With that and a wink she might have imagined, he backed out of the parking space and drove off.

Megan watched until his taillights disappeared around the corner. Only then did her heart climb back from her throat.

Five

🐾 "Will that be all?" the clerk at the pharmacy chirped.

"That will be all." He pushed the bottle of sleeping pills closer to her and fingered through the bills in his wallet.

She picked it up and scanned it with her hand-held gun. "This stuff is great. My boyfriend Dwayne used it. Well, he's really my *ex*-boyfriend." She leaned down for a plastic bag. "You know, we went out for a long time but it just wasn't working, so I pulled the plug. He was real into, like, sitting on my couch watching sports? Like he never took me out or anything? So a girl's gotta do what a girl's gotta do, you know? I mean, these are supposed to be the best years of my life. I can't be waiting on a guy who can't even commit to a whole night's sleep, you know what I'm saying?"

"I thought you said it worked for him," Sutter said, immediately sorry he'd encouraged the conversation. He'd been holding out a twenty to her for the last three minutes but she hadn't noticed. He remembered now, vividly, why he usually delegated these tasks.

"No, I said he *used* it. And it might've worked for him, really, if he didn't find out he liked to take 'em with beer. Get kind of a high, you know? Dwayne's an idiot." She handed him the bag.

"I see." The idea would appeal to him too, in the sick part of his brain that longed to be unconscious, except for the risk of permanent insensibility. "Uh, how much?"

"Oh, sorry!" She giggled. "Seven ninety-seven. It's like, twisted, you know? Everyone says alcohol's bad for sleep, so to take a sleeping pill with a beer, well it's just stupid. I told him he could wake up dead some morning. He just said at least he'd of fallen asleep." She shook her head. "Twisted."

Sutter rued the fact that he understood this side of the couch-dwelling Dwayne.

He held the twenty out farther. She took it and made change, counting it out into his palm. He wondered if the woman in line behind him was ready to spit nails yet. Or maybe people who shopped all the time were used to this kind of thing. All Sutter knew was it would drive him batty, and he vowed to let Martina do all the shopping from now on, no matter what it was he wanted her to purchase.

"Good luck. You let me know if that works, now," the clerk said, smiling at him. "If not you just bring it on back and we'll see what we can try next. There's lots of stuff, you know? I know 'cuz of my boyfriend. But maybe this'll work on you."

"We'll see," he said, turning away from the counter. "Thank you."

"My name's Trudy!" she called after him. "Just ask for me, I'll help you. I've helped plenty of people who couldn't sleep. Between 'em they've tried everything there is out there."

Sutter kept walking until he was out of earshot. He'd just bet they tried everything. A little oblivion around talkative Trudy would be a blessed relief.

He arrived at the office fifteen minutes later only to be greeted by Arnetta and her theme song: the spilling of the pencils and the ramming of the file cabinet. In her fist she held a wad of pink "while-you-were-out" slips.

"Mr. Foley," she said, giving him her most ingratiating smile, the one that made him feel simultaneously sorry for and fatigued by her. "I've got your messages."

"Wonderful, Arnetta," he said without missing a step as he headed for his office. "You can bring them in here and put them on my desk."

"Yes, sir, although Franklin Ward says it's better

if I read them aloud to you. Would you like me to read them aloud?"

He didn't look back to see if she'd followed; she always did. "No, thank you, Arnetta. I prefer to get to them in my own time."

"All right," she said in a tone that made clear she thought it was not all right.

He laid his briefcase on the desk and removed the file he was working on.

Arnetta sidled out of the room. "I'll just be out here if you need anything."

"I know." Once she'd closed the door, he sat in the chair and picked up the messages.

The first one had two phone numbers, the "please call back" box checked and written on the bottom the note, "says you can reach him at first number until noon, second number until five," but there was no indication of any sort whose numbers they might be.

He looked at the second one. A name, "John," and no accompanying message or phone number, just the "please call back" box checked. He knew at least three Johns and could think of no reason for any of them to call.

The third had a long message about copier needs with no name or number or box checked. He wadded this one up and threw it in the trash. The fourth had no name either, but an 800 number with the message, "Urgent," underlined three times.

He leaned back in his chair and closed his eyes. The first thing he wondered was if Arnetta would have noticed her mistakes had he let her read the messages out loud. The second thing was how much longer he'd have to endure this before he could honestly tell his sister he'd given the woman every opportunity. He knew, however, that the first thing Lizzy would ask him would be what Arnetta's mistakes had cost him and the truth was nothing, except for a lot of hair-graying aggravation.

He thought about calling Arnetta in to point out the mistakes, but honestly he was getting tired of correcting her all the time. It was like chastising a toddler for not knowing algebra. Neither the chastising nor the algebra was going to do the child any good, and either would only make the child cry. He was tired of making the child cry.

He thought about the vet last night, how her face had glowed at him just before he'd driven off with the mutt. He'd made her happy just by keeping the damn dog, and it had made him feel good. How long had it been since he'd made a woman happy like that? All pleased and glowy and surprised at him.

And it had been easy. The more he thought about it, the easier it seemed it would be to keep the pup. Martina would deal with it during the day, and hell, maybe he'd take it for a walk at night. Do him good to get a little outdoor exercise. Despite working out in his home gym, he needed some activity in the fresh air. Might make him sleep better too, to do something cardiovascular.

His intercom buzzed. "Yes?" he answered.

"Miss Montgomery is here," Arnetta said.

He told Arnetta to send her in.

"Sutter," Montgomery greeted him with a brisk nod. "I'm sorry I'm late."

"Are you late?" he asked, looking at his watch, then searching for the daily schedule Arnetta had given him last night. He looked at it for the first time and saw nine-thirty with the word "meeting" next to it. No wonder he never paid these schedules any attention.

Montgomery gave him an arch look that accused him of forgetting her.

"I just arrived myself," he said. "Martina was late so I had to take the dog out."

"You've still got that dog?" She gaped at him. "I thought you were getting rid of it."

"As did I." He cleared his throat, pulled the file onto his lap and opened it. "The vet talked me out of it."

"The *vet* talked you out of it?" she repeated. "I thought old Doc Rose's powers of persuasion only worked on drunk females."

For a moment he was taken aback. Drunk *females*? Was Dr. Rose . . . ? No . . . she couldn't be. There'd been a . . . a *vibe* between them last night, hadn't there? A little flirtation? He pictured her dazzling smile, the curve of her cheek, that blush.

"What do you mean?" he asked.

Montgomery chuckled. "Oh, only that the good doctor is kind of known around town as, well, a ladies' man. To be generous about it."

"A ladies' man? Dr. Rose is a *woman*."

"A woman? Oh, I thought you went to that place on Sophia Street, the animal hospital."

"That's the one."

Montgomery sat back. "Huh. That was Doc Rose's place. Older guy, close to sixty, I'd say. Drinker. He's got a real shabby reputation around town."

"Does he then?" Sutter looked at her with interest. "Could be her father, maybe. Uncle. Some sort of relation."

Montgomery shrugged, indifferent. "Could be, I guess. I didn't know he had a daughter but that doesn't mean anything. My mother, like I told you, takes all her pets to Dr. Prichard."

Sutter nodded thoughtfully. Could Megan Rose have a father who drinks and picks up women? Why not? She just seemed so . . . confident. That didn't quite go with a father who had a "shabby reputation."

"I'm certain she said her name was Rose. I remember because . . . well, no matter." He picked up the file in front of him again and tried to focus on it. He'd remembered because when she blushed the color was a definite rose, but he wasn't about to tell Montgomery that.

After a moment, Montgomery said, "So she talked you into keeping the—what did you call it the other day? The bloody raging beast?"

He looked up to see Montgomery regarding him with uncharacteristic intensity.

"She must have had a pretty good argument," she added, for all the world like she was miffed about the whole thing. "You're not one to do something you don't want to do. Generally speaking."

He eyed her steadily. "I hope that I am not above doing something altruistic every now and again."

"Altruistic?"

"Yes. I'm fostering the pup. When Dr. Rose finds an appropriate home for it the dog will go. Now, shall we concentrate on VamTech or would you like to examine this further?"

Ordinarily that would have been enough to put Montgomery squarely back in her place.

Not this time.

"What does Briana think of the dog?" she asked.

The question hit its mark and Montgomery knew it. He could see the sharp look in her eyes, the look a woman gets when she knows she's cornered a man.

"Briana is not yet aware of the dog. I'm sure she'll love it." He couldn't help frowning even as he said the words. "It's been my experience that women have a soft spot for puppies."

He could actually think of none of his acquaintance other than Dr. Rose who might appreciate the animal. And Lizzy, but then she had a soft spot for everything helpless.

His assistant VP snorted in a most unladylike way, not that he'd ever accuse of her being ladylike, and put a hand to her mouth.

"I gather you don't agree," he said stiffly.

"I'd rather not speculate, sir." She hauled her briefcase onto her lap and opened it.

Then why the devil did you bring it up? he wanted to ask. But it was his own fault for even engaging in the conversation. With effort, he turned his attention back to work.

"You won't believe what I just found out," Georgia said, stalking over to Megan and Penelope, who had just found each other at the dog park.

The day was overcast, the clouds heavy with unshed rain, and a low breeze moved the humidity around them like a veil. Even the dogs seemed affected by the weather, moving about with obvious fatigue, as affected as the humans by the meteorological malaise.

It was Saturday, early afternoon, and the park was nearly empty, no doubt due to the foul weather. Megan rather liked it, however, this thick calm before the impending storm.

"What did you find out?" Penelope asked, petting Sage's giant head as he lumbered by, intent on Penelope's dog, Wimbledon.

"That bastard Clifford and his new wife are having a litter, due any day." Georgia nearly spit the words and raked a hand through her blond curls, something she rarely did as it dislodged the carefully tousled and heavily sprayed look she favored.

"Who's Clifford?" Megan asked quietly, looking at Penelope.

"He's my asshole ex-husband," Georgia supplied, "who slept with our show handler and then had the bad taste to marry her when our divorce came through. Cheap little bit of Christmas trash that she is. And her dog too." She shook her head, her mouth compressed into a mean red line.

"That harlequin Dane she's got?" Penelope asked.

"The one with the short snout and bad front end? Yep. Why anyone would breed that animal is God's best guess." Georgia put her hands on her hips. "And I know I left Gretyl behind when I moved out but if I'd known Clifford would cheapen her stock by breedin' her with that Wal-Mart Dane I'd have taken her with me too."

"Oh Georgia," Penelope said, sympathy in her voice. "But you've still got Sage, and his frozen sperm. You can have a litter any time you want. Find the right bitch and have a *perfect* litter. Just forget about Clifford."

"Does he still show the bitch?" Megan asked.

"*She* does, the twit. Gretyl is past her prime. She's only hurtin' her reputation by trottin' her out as a has-been. And that harlequin—Danny, of all the stupid, stupid names for a dog—is just second rate all around. Oh it's just so infuriatin'." She ran both hands into her hair and made fists, as if she were going to pull it out.

"Sweetie, it's not your problem anymore," Penelope said gently. "Clifford can screw up his reputation in the ring all he wants. It'll only be good for you, in fact. You should be glad Monique—"

"And don't call her Monique! Her name is *Mona*, she changed it to Monique herself. Backstabbin' French-wannabe harlot."

Penelope looked at Megan and they raised their eyebrows at one another as Georgia let fly another string of curses, her eyes following her beloved Sage.

Silence reigned as the three watched the dogs. Two older men with corgis were sitting on the picnic table on the other side of the park. Their dogs scouted the fence near a neighboring house. The men looked up at the sky, speculating.

After an interval, Georgia said, "I'm sorry, Pen. I didn't mean to snap at you. They just make me so angry, Clifford and that slut of his. They're so ignorant and they think they're so goddamn smart."

"I know, Georgia. Please don't worry about it." Penelope ran a hand up and down her friend's arm reassuringly. "You know, it's funny," she said after a while, "most women are upset to learn their husband's new wife is going have a baby, not a litter of puppies."

Megan and Penelope looked at each other and chuckled.

"They don't have their priorities straight," Georgia said, causing Megan and Penelope's laughter to increase.

"Hear, hear," Megan said.

"As a matter of fact, I wish she *were* goin' to have a baby. Serve Clifford right," Georgia said, her face still dark with anger. Then she laughed. "You know, it really *wouldn't* bother me a bit if *she* turned out to be pregnant. Even though she has more shortcomin's than her dog."

They all laughed.

After a minute, Penelope sighed. "It would kill me, though," she said, thoughtfully, "if Glenn were to have a child with some other woman. Especially before I even found a man. I just don't know what I'd do."

Georgia scoffed, still caught up in her own drama. "Clifford is welcome to whatever brat she can produce. And you can be sure that offspring won't have a short snout! That woman's got a schnozz on her looks like someone erected a flight of stairs between her mouth and her eyes." She laughed uproariously at her own joke.

"I mean it," Penelope said, looking more horrified by the minute. "All I ever wanted from my marriage was a child and it was the one thing he wouldn't give me. It was what split us up." She turned to Megan, her broken heart in her eyes. "If he were to turn around with some new woman . . ."

"He didn't want children?" Megan asked.

"No." She shook her head, incredulous. "But he didn't know it, apparently, until ten years into our marriage. When I think about all the wasted time . . ." She looked as if she were going to be sick.

"Honey, you're getting upset over a disaster of your own makin' now," Georgia said. "It hasn't even happened yet."

"*Yet?*" Penelope practically wailed.

Megan wished she knew her better, knew what to say or do to comfort her. "I can't have children," she blurted in desperation.

All eyes turned to her and she blushed.

"I mean, not to diminish what you're saying in any way, Penelope," she hastened to add, "but you're still young. You could meet someone else and have a child. Someone who not only wants one but wants *yours*."

Penelope's eyes were the soul of kindness. "You can't have children? Oh that just breaks my heart, Megan. Are you okay?" She reached out and touched Megan's arm, as she had Georgia's, only in a more tentative way.

"I'm fine." Megan waved the concern away like a fly. "It was tough to take at first, of course. Million to one shot, is what the doctor said, and of course it was a problem with me and not my ex-husband, who wouldn't have given a damn one way or the other. But still, in a strange way it made me look at the world in a whole different light."

"How so?" Georgia asked.

"Well, it was little things at first, or subtle things, I should say, because they grew to feel huge. I found that my sense of what was important was different. Like, I don't save things the way I used to. For posterity, you know. Nobody's going to care about my old love letters after I die, for example. My old yearbooks and photographs . . . I just started looking at things like that as a waste of time and space. I stopped looking back so much, I guess is what I'm saying. And I approach things more for the moment."

"You didn't throw any of that stuff away, did you?" Penelope asked, scandalized.

Megan smiled ruefully. "Some of it. Not all. I'm still getting used to the idea, I guess. I haven't added to the collection, though."

"That's just sensible," Georgia said. "Even if you had kids, who'd want to wade through all that mess when you die? It's just plain arrogant to think you're goin' to be that fascinatin' to your kids."

"I've saved it all," Penelope said archly. "My love letters, my old yearbooks, corsages from just about every dance I went to, old school papers, tests. It's a record. It's who I am."

"It's not who you are, Pen," Georgia scoffed. "I know who you are and I've never seen any of that stuff."

"Maybe I'm not who you think I am." Penelope gazed enigmatically across the park.

Georgia shook her head, chuckling. "I know you're full of horse manure, Porter. Have you ever looked through your mother's old junk?"

"As a matter of fact, I have," she said, not looking back. "Unfortunately a lot of it burned in a fire when she was in college."

"Yeah, right." Georgia laughed. "She threw it out in a fit of sanitation insanity. Penelope's mother is about the cleanest person you'll ever want to meet," she added to Megan. "She dusts the *pantry*, for pity's sake. Now who in the world does that?"

"I do," Penelope said. "Don't you?" She passed her gaze from Georgia to Megan.

"This is a discussion I'd better not participate in," Megan said, holding up her hands. "You might never come to my house otherwise."

"I'll come," Georgia said, "because I'll know you're a woman with better things to do than dust jars of applesauce."

Drops of rain started to fall and Megan saw the men at the other end of the park get out their leashes and call their dogs.

"Darn," Penelope said. "I bet this rains out my afternoon match."

"Well, that's that," Georgia said, pulling a clear

plastic rain bonnet out of her pocket, the kind that looked like they were made out of kitchen wrap. "Sage and I melt in the rain. Any minute now he'll have his head in a bush like it's gonna keep his whole body dry. Besides, Sage's got his acupuncture appointment this afternoon up in Springfield."

"What's he getting acupuncture for?" Megan asked, sorry they were leaving so soon.

"Arthritis. I swear it's helped him tremendously. He moves like a puppy again after a session."

The drops got more frequent and Penelope made a hassled noise as she pulled Wimbledon's leash from her pocket.

Disappointed, Megan watched the two women gear up for going home. She'd wanted to tell them about Sutter Foley, about how he'd come by the hospital and been so charming. She wanted to ask them about this woman he was supposedly dating. But she couldn't bring it up now, the skies were clearly about to open up completely.

"Aren't you coming?" Penelope asked, noting that Megan had not gotten out Peyton's leash or called her.

"No, I'm going to let Peyton run a while longer. She's been cooped up a lot lately," she said. "And I don't mind getting soaked every once in a while. It seems . . . healthy in some way."

Georgia laughed. "Whatever."

"Are you sure, Megan? I can give you a ride

home if you walked." Penelope was backing toward the gate, Wimbledon secured on his leash.

"I'm sure. You guys go on. I'll see you next
week."

"Oh, don't forget about the SPCA meeting on
Monday!" Penelope called. "I'll pick you up at the
animal hospital. Six-thirty."

"Okay!" Megan waved.

Peyton did a dog's version of a canter toward
the gate, tongue lolling, mouth grinning. She
wasn't intent on escaping, she was too much of a
momma's girl for that, it seemed more that she
wanted to usher them out. She was probably eager
to see them leave so she could re-pee on every uri-
nary message the other dogs had left, Megan
thought.

The rain started to come down harder and
Megan turned her face to the sky. As people ran to
their cars, ducking their heads as if able to dodge
the drops, she let the rain pelt her from the air. The
water was warm, the sensation soothing. There
was something about resigning yourself to getting
wet that made you let go of everything you were
hanging on to, she thought. For the first time in
weeks, she was completely in the moment.

While she stood, listening to the frying-pan
sound of the downpour on the street and the gentle trickle of water from the leaves on the trees, she
thought about where she was now. A new town. A
new job. A new direction. As the rain dropped

onto her head and sluiced through her hair like fingers, she realized that she was a new person. She was whoever she wanted to be, here in this town. She had a clean slate.

She raised her arms out beside her and felt the water on her skin, God tapping her on the shoulder.

She smiled. How Sutter Foley would laugh to hear *that*, she thought. And yet, there was something about him that made her want to say those things to him. It was as if he was so caught up in being him, that he forgot to see what else was around him.

She laughed at herself. What egotism to think she knew him at all after a couple of chance meetings. And yet there was something about him that cried out to her. Something that wanted to be set free.

She thought about that picture on the magazine cover. That stiff, stern visage that was so at odds with the charmer who had winked at her as he'd driven off last night. Or maybe he hadn't winked. It had been pretty dark. And she was more than capable of seeing things in a man that weren't there. Just look at what she'd done to Ray. She'd imagined him a dedicated husband, a man who'd be true to her forever. Instead he'd been true only to himself and cheated on her effortlessly, and repeatedly. No wonder he'd seemed so happy.

Well, that's what one got for expecting monogamy, she told herself. It was an unnatural state, she knew that.

She wandered across the park toward the picnic table and noted another figure with a dog coming down the sidewalk toward the gate. She'd have thought he was another rain lover but he wore a hooded sweatshirt and hunched down into it against the weather, hands jammed into his jeans pockets. Someone who'd obviously started walking to the dog park and gotten caught in the downpour.

She sat on the picnic table and looked to make sure Peyton wouldn't head for the gate as it opened. A moment later she leaned forward and studied the hooded figure more intently. He walked a small dog that strained at the leash. A dog that looked a lot like . . .

Megan's breath stopped and she froze, watching man and dog enter through the gate.

Sutter Foley leaned down and let his dog run.

Six

The puppy immediately took off.

Sutter stood and gazed in the direction the dog ran, then froze.

He knew the figure on the picnic table instantly. What were the odds, he asked himself. He'd come to the park in the rain specifically to avoid people, but now that he was here, he realized she'd been the one person he wouldn't have minded finding.

He started across the field toward her, his eyes taking in the effortless yet affectionate way she deflected the spastic puppy. She looked incredible, her lithe body perfect in her drenched, form-fitting tee shirt and rain-darkened jeans.

Soaking wet, her hair curled to her shoulders and dripped down her cheeks, tendrils clinging to her neck. As he got close, he noted the long dampened eyelashes over her rich dark eyes. Her lips were parted, half smiling.

She said, "Fancy meeting you here," in a voice that made desire crawl straight up his back.

He almost didn't know what to say. Despite, or perhaps because of, having thought of her the entire way to the park, he was shocked to find her right here, right now, on the one day he'd thought to come. Of course, for all he knew she was here all the time. Or only came when it rained. But to him it was a kind of miracle.

If, that was, miracles were sent to plague a man.

She looked even better than she had in his memory, but that was not going to matter to him. She was simply not the kind of woman with whom he should get involved. All of the warning signs were there. He needed to stick to his own kind. Or rather, the kind he had become.

Fame was a tricky thing, he'd discovered. Some people could take it and some couldn't. The ones who couldn't, it seemed to him, tended to be the most candid and open-hearted. The type who said what they meant and did what they wanted, only to have it all wind up in a tabloid, twisted beyond recognition.

His ex-wife Bitsy had been that way. "Flaky," they'd called her, though he'd always considered her free-spirited. Happy, disingenuous, a little offbeat.

Like Megan Rose, with her talking universe and orbiting dogs.

"As you can see," he said as mildly as possible, "I have not killed your dog yet."

She smiled and he felt as if the sun had come out. "Oh, Baywatch isn't mine. Besides, I didn't really believe you had petricide in you."

"Petricide? That's not a word."

"I know." She grinned. "I have to admit I had my doubts about you a time or two."

"Did you?" He tilted his head and wondered if she really was the type who never told a lie or if she just *seemed like* the type. He'd been fooled before.

He turned to watch the pup chase after a large black dog—the one he'd seen with Megan before, obviously hers—who appeared more irritated than excited to have such a companion. He understood.

"My cook's been calling the dog Twister," he said, "as she seems to have the same effect as a tornado whenever I let her out of the box."

"Twister," she said, trying it out. "I love it. It suits her."

He glanced back over at Megan to see her eyeing him appreciatively. "Glad you approve," he said, and he was, though there was irony in his smile.

He turned away again and though he felt her eyes linger on him he did not look back. It was strange, even though the rain streamed down around them they stood there talking as if they were chatting on a sunny street corner. Or rather, he stood, she sat on the picnic table, leaning back on her hands, openly contemplating him.

"Do you want to sit down?" she asked.

He looked at her and she patted the picnic table next to her.

"Thank you," he said and stepped onto the bench seat, turned and sat a respectable distance away. When she didn't say anything else, he looked over at her.

She blinked against the rain, but looked at him steadily.

"What?" he asked, a bit nettled. "Have I done something else wrong? Is the dog not happy enough? Too skinny? Too fat? Should I have kept it in away from the rain?"

She started to laugh. "No, I was just thinking you look pretty good wet."

God help him, so did she. "Thank you. I think."

"And I was wondering how often you do this, walk in the rain. It shows an unexpected side to you."

He couldn't look at her, her shirt was too revealing all wet. And he was having a hard time remembering why he shouldn't reach out and trace the path of the rain down her neck to the curve of her perfectly outlined breast.

Briana, he thought, Briana Briana Briana. Who once he could have sworn had actual tears in her eyes when a frilly pair of her shoes got wet in a puddle. He could not even picture her sitting serenely on a picnic table in a downpour, ignoring streams of rain dragging her hair down her back and making her clothes cling to her skin. But she loved the limelight, and she was excellent at keeping her mouth shut about anything important. She manipulated the media on both her own and his behalf with consummate skill—something he admired more than he could say.

Briana belonged in this crazy world into which he had climbed. Not Megan Rose.

"Never," he said. "I only came out in this weather so that I wouldn't run into anyone."

He didn't even have to look at her to know her brows rose at that. "Why? Are you avoiding people?"

He narrowed his eyes as he looked across the field and didn't answer.

"Is that what your success has gotten you?" she asked. "The feeling of having to hide from people? What, are you afraid we're all going to ask you for money or something?"

He brought his gaze around to her sharply. "Do I insult you every time we meet?"

She paused. "Not every time." Her dark eyes met his.

He'd never insulted her, he was sure of it. He wanted to challenge her to tell him when he had, but he couldn't take his eyes from her wet lips, naturally pink and plump and parted just enough . . .

Without another thought, except maybe the ridiculous one of having to do this to shut her up, he leaned forward and captured her lips with his. The sensation was immediately overwhelming. Her softness yielded instantly, her body arched toward his—he could feel it though it did not touch him.

He drew back a fraction, looked into her dark unreadable eyes with his own startled glance. His breath came heavily, as if he'd just been punched, and yet he could tell that hers did too.

One long second, their look held, before she pushed up off of her hands and put her lips back on his. Her hands grabbed hold of his sweatshirt and pulled, and before he knew it his mouth was opening under hers. His hands, of their own accord, rose to either side of the long slick column of her neck, the skin there so soft and warm and wet. Their tongues found each other and danced as if they'd been waiting all their lives to meet.

Sutter lowered one hand to her back, felt the supple strength of her muscles, her hot skin through the thin wet cotton of her shirt. She curved into him, her damp hair playing against his fingers, her tongue playing mind-blowing games with his. Electricity shot along his nerves, making him wonder if they'd been struck by lightning.

And the rain poured down from the heavens. Soaking them. Dousing them. Surely sizzling against their heated bodies.

She pushed back first, breathless and flushed. Her eyes were nearly black, the pupils huge, her lips puffy and pink. He wanted to draw that lower one into his mouth once more, but he drew back.

She swallowed, but didn't say anything, just looked at him with that heat emanating from her. It was a wonder they weren't surrounded by their own steam.

Slowly, sanity returned and he turned his head away, gazing sightlessly across the field.

"I must go," he said abruptly, pushing off the picnic table to stand awkwardly next to it. "I do apologize."

He had no idea what the hell he was doing.

"Really?" she said, but her tone held no clue as to what she was thinking.

"I . . . I didn't mean to . . ." He stopped, took a deep breath and commanded himself to return to his senses. "I didn't expect to see anyone here. In the rain. I'm sorry."

Jesus, he was a moron. But what in God's name did one say when one had just accidentally kissed someone? He shouldn't be kissing her at all. He did not want her, not Megan Rose. And she didn't want him, she just didn't know it yet. She had no idea how being with him could ruin her life.

No, he was with Briana and that was for the best. For everyone. And besides, Briana was moving to Fredericksburg. And he was losing his mind.

"I must go." He turned back to her, looking at

her but not seeing her. His eyes would not clearly focus on her, as if he had to look at her obliquely to let him gaze in her direction at all. "Again, I apologize. That was . . . uncalled for."

He turned and whistled sharply for the dog. Miraculously, she came tearing over. As did the other one, which gave him enough time to capture Twister and snap the leash on.

He headed for the gate, amazed and perhaps disappointed that the normally audacious Dr. Rose had nothing to say as he did.

His only mistake was looking back, to see Megan Rose still sitting on the picnic table, looking more beautiful than she ought to, with one hand touching her lips.

From: "Elizabeth Powell" Bitsy@ worldnet.net
To: <SF@SFSolutions.com>
Date: Mon, 25 Jun 19:09:30-0800
Subject: Re: Sleeping

Sutter, darling, I'm astonished that you who've always prided yourself on self-reliance have turned to sleeping pills. What paltry aides to your own immaculate self-control! I don't understand your resistance to seeing my hypnotherapist. Yes, yes, the bloody tabloids, but, Sutter, they're as likely to say things about you if you don't do them as if you do. And a hypnotist's methods only enhance your own abilities to control your life. Darling, if you look beyond your preconceptions it is right up your alley.

Don't misunderstand, my dear, I'm glad to see you have lost none of your stubborn streak, it only confirms how right I have always been about you. But you must do something or you will go as mad as your Aunt Edna. And the elegant Miss Briana Ellis wouldn't like that at all. Yes, I heard about her. But lord, Sutter, isn't she a little high maintenance for you? And is it true she's moving to tiny Fredericksburg for you?

Got to run. Have a massage at 2 followed by a seaweed wrap and pedicure. Love to Berkley.

—Bitsy

The mere mention of Aunt Edna was enough to infuse him with guilt. He hadn't been to see her in two weeks, and while she seemed to have a great deal of trouble keeping things straight sometimes—like who his sister was, that Sutter was himself and not his father, that she, Edna, was not sixteen anymore—she always seemed to know exactly how long it had been since Sutter had come to call.

He met his sister Lizzy in the foyer as he entered Sunrise Hills—a name that always made him wonder if they'd considered *Sunset* Hills first before realizing that was a bit bleak.

She rolled her eyes as she approached. "I

wouldn't even think about it today, Sutter, unless you've got several hours to listen to all of Mum and Da's failings. I spent the better part of this morning trying to convince her I wasn't actually Mum only to be told that I'd always been a spineless pillock and not to get shirty with her."

Sutter chuckled. "Ah, the fiesty mood."

Lizzy sighed and ran her hands over her pulled-back hair. She always wore her dark blond, shoulder-length hair pulled back into a black barrette, perhaps so that the large, unusual earrings she wore would show to best advantage. She was a jewelry designer who taught art at the University of Virginia, and was always wearing something she or one of her students had made.

"The *exhausting* mood," she said. "Oh, and by the way, Mrs. Markham wants to speak with you about the fees. Apparently they're going up again."

Sutter removed his suitcoat and draped it over his arm. The day had gotten hot, and the air conditioner could not keep up with the sun in the atrium foyer. "That's not a problem."

"I know it's not." She gave him a warm smile. "And I think you're an absolute prince never to complain about footing the whole bill here. Mrs. Markham did say there was an opening for a semiprivate room if we wanted to move her, but I told her you probably wouldn't hear of it."

"Absolutely not. Can you imagine Aunt Edna with a roommate? She already steals the attendants' keys at every opportunity. Imagine what she'd knock off from a roommate."

Lizzy shook her head. "She likes the sound of them. You'd think they'd let us give her a set of her own, if it would make her happy. I think it makes her feel as if she might just be able to hop out into the car at any moment."

"Yes, and the next thing you know she'd be doing just that."

Lizzy sighed again. "I know. And starkers at that, no doubt. Yes, I'm sure this is the best place for her . . . It's just, well it's the principle of the thing. I mean, really, for this price we could all be living in Trump Tower with a private nurse for her."

He smiled at her gently. "Now Lizzy, we've talked about this. When she was with me she nearly burned the house down in the middle of the day, with the nurse in the next room. She needs to be here, as you well know. And you need your privacy. How is Noel?"

"He's fine. He's in Atlanta this week for a show."

"Good on him," Sutter said. "His paintings have gotten a lot of exposure lately."

"That they have. Oh, by the way, do you think you could help me out sometime with a project I've got up your way?" she asked.

"Certainly, what is it?"

She glanced at her watch. "Bugger, no time now. I've got to fly. I'll ring you!"

She gave him a quick kiss and was gone.

Sutter made his way down the hallway to Aunt Edna's room. Before he even got in the door he could hear her waffling on about something over the voices of other people.

He knocked once and entered.

"You bloody wanker," Aunt Edna pronounced, pointing a gnarled finger at the television screen. "You came home arse over elbow last night and got all rumpy pumpy with Brittany, now, didn't you?"

"Language, Auntie," Sutter said, suppressing a smile. Aunt Edna had always taken her soap operas seriously, but on the "bad days" she seemed to believe the characters were actually in the room with her.

Aunt Edna glanced up at him and narrowed her eyes. Her steel-gray hair was wild, with several locks wound haphazardly around pink plastic curlers and the rest standing up straight all over her head. Her lined face was devoid of makeup.

"Well, stone the crows," she said, glaring at him. "It's my no good brother, Edgar, after two long weeks. Been too busy abusing your timid little wife to come visit? She was just here, you know, telling me all about your nasty ways. He's about as classy as you are, Lance," she added, addressing the television. "Always was, too. Even back as a little boy when he killed my kitten, Tuffy."

Sutter sighed. Not the Tuffy story again. Lizzy had been right, it was going to be a long visit.

* * *

Megan stood by the ice cream section in the grocery store, transfixed by a pint of Ben & Jerry's
called "Chubby Hubby." She used to buy that for
Ray, pleased that it was one of his favorite flavors.
And yet she'd hated being married. Hated being a
"wife," or maybe it was just being called a "wife."
It was almost embarrassing. As if she'd signed up
to become a cliché and was supposed to be proud
of it.

Since her divorce, however, she wondered if
she'd just minded being *Ray's wife*. Maybe the
cliché was having a husband who ate too much
and drank too much and eventually cheated on
her. She'd come to the conclusion that monogamy
wasn't natural, but maybe it was just marriage.
The sense of overwhelming responsibility to the
titles and obligations, to the expectations of every
other person in the world who had engaged in
that institution.

What had bothered her most about Ray's infi-
delity had been not so much the sex, but the lying.
The fact that he'd created such an elaborate façade
to hide the affair had been the most hurtful thing
of all. He'd made up an entire second job, complete with a wretched boss and unsafe working
conditions. One night he'd come home with
scratch marks on his back and had invented a
"sorting machine" that had gone berserk when his
back was turned. She'd thought it sounded odd,

had advised him to look into OSHA requirements. Ray, of course, had never followed up.

The reasons why became obvious soon after, but until then she'd been too engrossed in her job to really care. When the truth came out she remembered being aghast at the web of lies he'd constructed. Not to mention the utter oblivion on her part that had made it all work.

Divorcing him had been easy after that. She'd even marveled at the fact that she felt no jealousy, not one whit. It was all indignation.

She thought about Sutter Foley, about that unholy kiss in the park on Saturday. That had nothing to do with marriage or commitment, or even understanding. It was only about the heat in her blood and the hunger in her hands for him.

That was the way it should be, she thought. She wanted him, plain and simple. What's more, she was pretty sure he wanted her, even though he resisted it, there at the end.

She opened the freezer door and plucked out a pint of Ben & Jerry's Phish Food. She didn't need a Chubby Hubby. She needed some kind of chocolate decadence. She needed her appetite sated, her craving satisfied, her needs provided for.

She pushed her cart up to the checkout counter where there were three checkers open, each with only a couple of people in line. It was nice that she could shop during the off hours like this, even though it was because she had no clients or appointments, had no money coming in and was on the brink of total financial devastation. Still, she could look on the bright side of the situation; she could avoid weekend crowds at the store.

Unloading her groceries onto the conveyor belt her eye was caught by one of the tabloid papers on display. "Sutter's Sumptuous Digs" was the headline, with the tagline "Is the handsome Brit hooking up with American royalty?" Beneath these was a picture of Sutter Foley and a woman named Briana Ellis, who was, it had to be admitted, stunning. Maybe not beautiful in the modern sense, but classically gorgeous, with dark hair pulled demurely back from a strong-featured face with dark eyes and sparkling diamond earrings that looked huge and expensive even reproduced in black and white on cheap tabloid newsprint.

No chirpy-looking Ashley Judd wannabe for Sutter Foley, she thought. He went straight for old-world beauty.

"Ma'am?"

Megan looked up.

"Paper or plastic?" the checkout woman asked.

"Oh, paper, please." She plucked the tabloid out of the rack and opened it to the article on Sutter. True to form, the actual prose was short and sensationalistic, speculating that Sutter, in an effort to fit in with American "high society"—whatever that might be—was most likely going to marry Briana Ellis, of the Boston Ellises, who was reputed to be worth several hundred million dollars. That, in addition to Sutter's *billions*—the *National Tattler* actually speculated he had *billions*, she noted—would create such enormous wealth that they and any children they had would become the next American dynasty, á la the Kennedys.

Then, as if this wasn't speculation enough, it went on to say with galling authority that Briana Ellis, beautiful and wealthy as she was, was *not* the love of Sutter Foley's life. She was only a runner-up to his first wife, Elizabeth Powell, from whom he was divorced and with whom he was still in love. They were also in very close touch, according to their unimpeachable "source."

In addition to two full pages of surprisingly low-quality pictures of the house, they detailed the interior as having an indoor pool, racquetball court, and movie theater. They said that despite its modest exterior it also housed seventeen bedrooms, ten bathrooms, two kitchens, a swimming pool, gymnasium, and four hot tubs.

Megan could not be sure, of course, but if that house had all of those things, ninety percent of it had to be underground. It simply wasn't big enough, and while the inside seemed wonderful to her, it still felt like a charming historic house, not one that had been refurbished so beyond its modest beginnings that it had its own movie theater.

She skimmed the article for the "source" and found one line that began with "according to Foley's gardener," and it all clicked into place. The groundskeeper had adopted the dog; the dog was left behind by an employee who'd been fired; the firing had been so sudden and adamant that Sutter was fairly certain the employee would not return for the dog.

Obviously the caretaker had supplied the photos and story to the *Tattler* and had been fired for it.

Sutter Foley did take his privacy seriously. Not that anyone wouldn't be upset to have this sort of thing made up and aired without his knowledge.

That is, she *assumed* it had been made up. As far as she knew, every word of it was true. And the fact that he'd kissed her, Megan Rose, small-town veterinarian, in the park on Saturday would not even rate a footnote to a story like this.

"Ma'am?"

She looked back up at the checker, who'd finished scanning her items.

"Are you buying the magazine?"

"Oh. Uh, yes." She handed her the tabloid and the woman glanced at it as she swiped it across the reader.

"Reading about Sutter Foley?" the checker guessed, with a knowing smile.

"Yes, actually. Interesting guy." She pulled her check card out of her purse. "Do you really think he's got *billions*? I mean, no offense to Fredericksburg or anything, but billions . . . you'd think he'd be living in Paris or something."

The checker shook her head and handed the magazine back to her. "I'd be living in California myself. Where it's sunny all the time without all this humidity. My hair looks like steel wool in this weather."

"Hm." Megan flipped through the pages of the tabloid again.

"Tell you one thing, though," the checker added, "I'd like to see inside that house he's got, I would. I always knew he lived nearby but I never knew it was right there on Washington Avenue. That's one of the houses right across the street from Kenmore, ain't it?"

Megan hesitated. "Is it?"

"I think it is. I saw him once, you know." She put the last bag in Megan's cart and totaled the order. "Forty-seven, seventeen."

Megan swiped the card and wrote the total in the check register.

"He was better looking than that picture even," the checker said. "Younger than you'd think, too. But you're right. He seemed like the kinda guy who'd want to live in New York City or LA, some-place like that."

"Maybe he wants to stay anonymous."

The checker snorted. "More chance a that in a big place. No, I think it's more likely he wants to be a big fish in a small pond."

Megan punched her PIN into the machine, glancing at the woman's name tag. "*Billions*, Hazel, it says in here he has billions. Any pond would be small for him."

"Might be you're right." She handed Megan her receipt. "All I know is whenever I tell someone I live in Fredericksburg, all I get is, 'Where Sutter Foley lives?'"

Megan laughed.

"I mean it. And this where George Washington grew up and all." She shook her head. "Imagine being more famous than George Washington."

"I can't. It sure wouldn't be what I'd want," she said, "but to each his own, I guess."

"I'd take the money," the checker said, nodding as if at least that decision was easy. "The devil can take the fame."

Megan agreed, thanked her, and left, thinking as she walked to the car about George Washington and Sutter Foley, and wondering if Sutter Foley could say he never told a lie either . . .

"What is this here?" Sutter asked Arnetta, pointing to the 7:00 P.M. timeslot on the daily schedule, which was followed by the letters "SPCA."

"Oh, that's your meeting with the SPCA board." She smiled brightly at him, obviously pleased to have remembered this one.

"But I'm not *on* the SPCA board," he said, wishing he could crumple up this damn schedule and throw it into the trash without causing this giant giraffelike human being to cry. She even had oddly huge, long-lashed eyes like a giraffe.

"Yes you are!" She spoke excitedly. "Lizzy signed you up. She said you'd be excited. Or, wait a minute, she said you'd be 'chuffed to bits.'" Arnetta laughed, coloring. "I had to ask what it meant. I'm not very good at English accents."

"On the contrary," he said between clenched teeth, "the impression was uncanny." He turned back to his office. He was going to kill Lizzy. String her up and throttle her. "Get Lizzy on the phone for me, would you?" he called back to Arnetta, slamming the door behind him.

A moment later the intercom buzzed. "Lizzy on line one," Arnetta chirped.

He grabbed the receiver. "What the devil is this SPCA thing? And is *this* the reason you bullied me into hiring that incompetent out there, so you could trick me into participating in your bleeding heart causes?"

"Lovely to hear from you, Sutter," Lizzy replied, unperturbed as she always was by Sutter's temper. "I'm fine, thank you."

"I'm serious, Lizzy. I'm going to sack her if this is how it's going to be." He picked up a pen and tapped it irritably against the edge of the desk.

"Relax," she said, drawing the word out. "I asked Arnetta to put it on your schedule because I can't be there tonight. You're just filling in for me. And I *did* ask, if you'll recall. I asked if you could help me out once in a while with a project I had up there."

"Yes, but you didn't mention the project." He closed his eyes. "Or what kind of help you required or when. I would rather you inform me instead of ambushing me with it through Arnetta."

"Fine. I'll note that for the future." She sighed. "It's just a planning meeting, Sutter, and I thought you'd be a big help. They're trying to find ways to cut costs and increase donations. It's just the kind of thing you'd be good at."

"Bollocks, Lizzy, you know I don't even like animals. What on earth makes you think I'd be good at it?"

She clearly tried to repress a laugh, but did not succeed. "Well, you do have a dog now, Sutter. Surely that indicates some kind of change of heart."

Sutter leaned forward and put his head in one hand, elbow on the desk. "That's it. I'm sacking Arnetta. I'm doing it tonight and I'm telling her it's your fault. Not only have you made her an instrument with which to control me, you've gotten yourself a spy. I only wish the woman would get my own business as straight."

"This *is* your business. Come on, Sutter, admit it," his sister said, laughing outwardly now. "You and I are not so different. I may be the bleeding heart of the family but you've got your own soft side. Why else would you take in strays like Arnetta and that poor little pooch?"

"Because of *you*," he said to the sister who drove him crazy with arguments just such as this. Then he thought of Megan and made a disturbing connection. "And women just like you, dammit."

Seven

Megan opened the door to Penelope's Mercedes sedan and slid onto the leather seat. Economics in the writing implement business must be much better than those in the veterinarian business, she thought, hearing the quality *whump* of the car door as she closed it.

"Okay! Where is this shindig?" she asked, gazing up through the sunroof at the summer's early evening sky.

The day had been warm and humid but that made the evening perfect. She wore a sundress and sandals, hoping to make a nice impression on the board. Though she hated having to consider it, and barely even admitted it to herself, she didn't want anyone thinking she was too much like her father.

"It's at the library. There's a room in the basement they let us use for meetings." Penelope shook her hair back from her face as they gained speed and a warm breeze billowed through the sunroof. She looked at Megan. "Don't you look nice."

"So do you." Megan noted another casual but gorgeous outfit on her new friend. "Where do you shop? You've always got the prettiest things."

"I'll show you sometime." She smiled enigmatically. "So, you'll get to meet the sister of a friend of yours tonight."

"A friend of mine?" Megan asked. As far as she knew, Penelope and Georgia were the only friends she had in town.

Penelope shot her a sideways look. "Sutter Foley's sister is on the board."

"His sister?" she repeated, then laughed. "I didn't know he had a sister. And I'm not sure I'd call Sutter Foley a *friend*, exactly."

She wondered if she should tell Penelope what had happened between her and Sutter at the park, then thought better of it. She liked the other woman a lot, but didn't know her well enough to trust her with confidences. Not yet, anyway. One thing she was certain of: the last thing she wanted was gossip about that kiss floating around town.

They arrived at the library and clomped down the stairs to the basement behind two other people where a round table had been set up and several people sat chatting. They took their seats and almost immediately the meeting was called to order by a large woman with gray hair and kindly eyes. This must be Wilma Jones, Megan thought, the resident activist and society matron Penelope had told her about. Wilma Jones was apparently a very valuable person to know in the Fredericksburg community.

Megan was not sure she would have spotted the woman's importance if Penelope hadn't pointed it out. Certainly Wilma was not dressed like a society powerhouse. She had on a simple flowered dress, conservative enough for her busty frame but a little bit old-fashioned, and her hair was short and curled in a decidedly nondescript style.

The only giveaway might have been the set of wedding rings on her left hand. It looked like three, covered with sizeable diamonds, with one large square one dominating. On Wilma's sturdy fingers they looked proportionate, but Megan had no doubt they would have looked the size of car batteries on a daintier hand.

"I'd like everyone to welcome our newest member of the board," Wilma said, smiling at Megan. "Megan Rose has taken over Rose's Animal Hospital, replacing her father, who is now retired. Thank you for joining us."

Megan smiled, pleased that Mrs. Jones had referenced her father without a trace of irony, and looked around the table, nodding a greeting at the other board members. She wondered which one was Sutter's sister. The group was composed of about a dozen people, all but two of them women, who sat with various file folders, coffee cups and soda cans. Most of them smiled back at her.

"I'd also like everyone to welcome Arnetta Suggs," Wilma continued. "She comes to us by way of Liz Foley, who couldn't make it tonight. Arnetta is *Sutter Foley's* personal assistant." She put an emphasis on Sutter's name as if it were very impressive. Which it was.

The entire table turned to look at the woman sent by the man more famous than George Washington.

The thin, graying woman sat tall in her chair and her eyes darted around as if she were the target of a rude joke and was unsure whether she should laugh along or slink away.

"Liz had asked her brother to come," Wilma continued, brows raised as if to say *Wouldn't* that *have been special?* "But he was understandably too busy to attend, so he sent Ms. Suggs to us as his ambassador. Thank you so much for your time."

Ms. Suggs blushed to the roots of her hair and glanced around the table. "Oh it's no trouble. And I wouldn't *dare* not do something Mr. Foley asked anyway."

Silence greeted this admission, but to Megan's eyes Arnetta Suggs appeared oblivious to her implication that she would not be here if it weren't for the fact that Mr. Foley might fire her otherwise.

Wilma recovered first. "Well, thank you anyway."

Arnetta continued, like a panicked bull in a china shop, "I don't know much about the SBCA—"

"That's S-PEE-CA, dear," Wilma corrected, growing noticeably cooler.

"Right, oh, sorry. Anyway, I don't know much but Franklin Ward says getting involved in community activities can be a great way to make contacts outside the job. Networking is what he calls it. So I'm glad to be here."

Wilma frowned. "Yes, well, community works can be socially rewarding, but we're here for the animals, primarily."

Ms. Suggs's face brightened. "Right, the animals. Mr. Foley had some ideas about that."

The room waited breathlessly.

"Well," Wilma said with a smile at the other members, "let's jump right in then, shall we? What are Mr. Foley's ideas?" She sat down as Ms. Suggs straightened importantly in her chair.

"He said I should tell you that you ought to look to *save* money before you ask people for more . . ." She hooked one finger around the other as if trying to remember the exact order of his instructions. Hooking the next finger, she continued, "And that if you just killed the animals a day or two earlier—put them out of their misery—he said," she giggled like a teenager. "Sorry, I'm not very good at an English accent. Anyway, he said that'd probably be more, um, 'cost effective' than begging door-to-door."

If the rest of the room was anything like Megan, they were sitting with their mouths dropped open, feeling as if they'd just been slapped. Megan finally wrenched her eyes from Arnetta Suggs to find that she was right, they were all in a momentary state of shock.

"And that if that didn't work," Ms. Suggs hooked a third finger, "then you should just let them all go because somebody would probably pick them up."

The silence broke all at once. Everyone started talking.

"That's *preposterous*," a man with a bald pate said, standing up to emphasize his point. "The man should be arrested for animal cruelty!"

A thin woman in riding jodhpurs piped up, saying, "I say we go to his house and confront him with this."

Megan pictured her with a riding crop and might have feared for Sutter's well being if she weren't ready to do the same thing herself.

"Who does he think he *is?*" another woman demanded.

"What the hell—?"

"He must be joking—"

"That's just like those rich—"

Megan watched them all, wanting to stand up

and proclaim that he couldn't possibly have said such a thing, but in the back of her mind she feared maybe he had. Maybe she didn't know him at all. Well *obviously* she didn't know him at all. She'd only kissed him.

Wilma got them all firmly in hand at last, pounding on the table and calling for quiet. When they'd settled down and the balding man had sat back in his seat, she took a deep breath and addressed Ms. Suggs.

"I'm going to hope in my heart that anyone related to Liz Foley would not have said something so vile," Wilma said through stiff lips, "but as I have no intention of calling you, Ms. Suggs, a liar, I'd appreciate it if you sent the board's unanimous disapproval of his ideas back to Mr. Foley."

"Well, I'm going to go further than that," the bald man said, dropping a fist hard onto the table and shaking everyone's soda cans. "I'm going to write him a letter and tell him exactly what I think of his *cost-effective* ideas. He may be a billionaire, but he won't get far in life being that cruel to God's living creatures."

Megan figured he'd probably gotten far enough in life already not to have to give God's living creatures a second thought.

"You can also tell him we're already a no-kill shelter," jodhpur woman said. "That means never. Not even to save a few bucks."

Arnetta Suggs, for her part, looked stunned by

the outburst and chewed her bottom lip as Wilma spoke.

"I certainly will pass along all you've said," she said, kneading her hands together and looking toward the door. "I didn't mean to offend everyone. I thought—that is, *he* thought, I think—that it would just be helpful, you know, to think about other ways to save. That a couple days really wouldn't make much diff—"

"*Thank* you, Ms. Suggs," Wilma said, overriding the woman's words. "We really have heard quite enough."

Megan looked at the shy, mortified woman who had delivered Sutter's supposed words and had a hard time believing Ms. Suggs was not repeating something she had actually been told. She just didn't seem the type to come up with such a thing—to come up with *anything*, really—on her own, much less make something up and attribute it to someone else.

Megan's heart thundered in her chest to think that Sutter might have been serious, and only played a gentler role with her in order to . . . what? Kiss her in the park?

It seemed ridiculous, but still, he didn't know she'd be here at this meeting. Certainly the first time she'd met him he'd made no bones about his feelings toward dogs. He'd even said something about setting Baywatch—that is, Twister—free in some field where no one would have to bother with her anymore. But then he had *named* the dog—no wait, his cook had done that, hadn't he said? Well, he'd brought the pup to the park, she knew that. But then, she'd been there and he'd kissed her. What did that mean?

Megan was so confused and upset by the exchange that she missed most of what was said at the rest of the meeting, though she did notice Ms. Suggs taking copious notes as the other members tried to collect themselves and speak to the issues. She was pretty sure everyone else was in the same state of shock and anger when the meeting broke up shortly thereafter with an agreement to meet in two weeks to discuss the gala ball they were planning.

"Heavens!" Penelope said as they left the library. "Can you imagine anyone saying such a thing? You've spoken to him lately, did he seem so heartless to you? So cruel and uncompromising? I have to say, though I'd always thought of him as kind of a cold fish, he must really be an obnoxious jerk!"

"If he really said all that, jerk is putting it mildly," Megan said, smiling at Penelope's primness. She herself would have called him an outright asshole if she could get her mind around his actually having said such things. "I just wonder if Ms. Suggs got it right. It seems anyone with a brain would know not to say something like that to the SPCA, of all people."

Penelope was frowning. "Maybe. I don't know. You don't get to be a billionaire without stepping on a lot of people. And animals are easier to step on than people."

"Maybe, but less productive. It's not like you get ahead by killing pets," Megan pointed out.

"It's a mindset," Penelope clarified. "You just get used to expediency."

Megan had to admit this had the ring of truth. And nobody would dispute that Sutter was a genius, at least in his area of expertise. And you really didn't get ahead without being somewhat ruthless, that much had been clear to Megan for years. She clung to it, in fact, as a reason she was still broke.

"But to answer your question, no, he didn't seem like he'd say something like that." She thought again of that kiss in the park, of the way he'd looked at her—with such *heat*. Surely she couldn't fall for someone, even physically, who was so heartless.

"That mousy assistant of his didn't seem like the type to lie," Penelope said as she unlocked the Mercedes. The two got in.

"No, she didn't. But she also didn't seem like the sharpest tool in the shed." Megan pushed the button to roll down her window, letting the fragrant night air in. "Maybe she got it wrong, somehow."

Penelope shook her head. "I don't know . . ."

"I don't either. And I sure would like to." Megan wondered if she should call him up and ask him. But aside from the fact that she didn't have his phone number, and most likely wouldn't be able to get it, a confrontational call out of the blue would be a difficult thing to pull off. Especially after that kiss.

Maybe a casual visit would be better . . .

"He always seemed pretty aloof to me," Penelope said, a *tsk* in her voice. "But maybe she did get it wrong. He could be a great contributor, even just a great name to use to solicit other corporate donations, if he had an ounce of human compassion for the plight of these animals. Which it sure sounds like he doesn't."

Megan nodded. A contributor . . . she could go see him on the pretext of getting his support . . . She shook her head sharply. She never needed *pretexts* to say what she wanted to say before and now would be a bad time to start. She wasn't going to be either intimidated or lured by his money. She was just going to speak her mind.

Penelope eyed her. "Are you okay?"

"I'm fine. I'm just thinking . . . maybe I should pay Sutter Foley a visit." She glanced at the clock. It was only 7:45 and the evening was still balmy and beautiful, not even quite dark. She could walk Peyton up to check on Twister. A play date. She half grinned, half grimaced to herself. A play date was certainly what *she* wanted, but maybe it wasn't the best thing to have during this conversation.

"And ask him about tonight?" Penelope asked, casting worried glances at her from behind the wheel.

"Yes, why not? When he denies he said such a thing—which he surely must do—I can hit him up for a donation."

"Oh Megan, that would be *great*," Penelope breathed. "Having Sutter Foley behind our cause would be such wonderful P.R. But do you think . . . that is, do you feel comfortable paying him a visit? He's so notoriously private."

Megan shrugged. "I've been to the house before."

Not to mention that she'd felt his tongue with hers, surely that got her some visiting rights.

"Besides," she added, "somebody needs to figure out the real story here. If his solutions really are that draconian he should be called to the mat for them. And I'm just the person to do it."

Sutter was just sitting down to a meal of grilled swordfish with summer squash over a saffron risotto and a lovely white Bordeaux when the doorbell rang. He heard Martina bustle to the door just as Berkley came out of the kitchen to ask how everything was.

"Ace," Sutter said. "Another brilliant feat of simplicity."

"Someday you're going to let me go wild and show you how brilliant complexity can be, but perhaps that's better suited to fall anyway." He wiped his hands on a dishrag and threw it over his shoulder just as Martina entered the dining room.

"A miss want to see you, señor," she said, tilting her head back to the door. "Miss Megan Rose?"

The way she said the name it sounded exotic, Sutter thought, that's the only reason his nerves jumped when he heard it.

Sutter looked back at Berkley and gestured with his chin toward the kitchen. "Is there enough in there for another plate?"

"Sure. Just take me a minute to grill another filet," he said.

"Great, bring that out and another glass of wine, would you? Then you can go. And thanks." Sutter calmly put his fork down and stood just as Megan entered the room.

"Oh." She glanced from the table to the door through which Berkley had disappeared. "I'm so sorry to interrupt. The, uh, your maid?" She moved her hand in the direction Martina had just disappeared. "She didn't tell me you were eating."

"It's not a problem," he said mildly, hoping his face didn't show his apprehension at her visit. Could this have something to do with that disastrously impulsive kiss on Saturday? "Won't you have a seat?"

She shook her head. "I can come back later, really. I'm sorry."

Berkley reappeared with a second plate and Megan managed to look further mortified.

"Oh no, and you've got company too. I'll just come back." She started backing out of the room.

Sutter laughed. "The plate is for you, Dr. Rose, if you'd like it. You're my company."

At that she stopped and gave him that look that clearly showed the devilish spark in her eye. The look that made him think she got a joke that he wasn't even aware of.

She glanced at Berkley. He placed the food on a placemat and produced some silverware from his apron pocket, which he situated around the plate. Then, with a flourish, he lifted the wine bottle from the cooler and filled up her glass.

"Well, who could resist this?" She held her hand out to Berkley. "Hi, my name's Megan Rose. I'm the new vet at Rose's Animal Hospital."

Sutter smiled to himself. Good business sense, he thought, always mentioning the animal hospital.

"Berkley Lambert, at your service," his chef said, grinning through his moustache at Megan. The two shook hands and Megan turned to sit down. Berkley helped with her chair and gave Sutter what could only be called a conspiratorial smile.

"Thank you," Megan said, looking at her plate as she put her napkin in her lap.

"Will there be anything else, sir?" Berkley asked.

"No. Thank you, Berkley. You can go." Sutter picked up his wine glass and brought his gaze to Megan's. Her brow was furrowed and she regarded him as if he'd just insulted someone. "What? What is it now?"

She looked surprised. "Nothing." She clearly thought better of that answer, though, and after glancing behind her, apparently to see that Berkley had gone, added, "No, okay, I was just thinking how natural it is for you to give orders. You're waited on in your own home and you don't seem the least bit awkward about it. I feel funny when the guy at the grocery store helps load the bags into my car."

"I don't understand." He put his wine down. "He's my employee, whom, I might add, I pay extremely well."

"Of course yes, I'm sure you do. I just . . . think I'd feel funny about it, that's all." She smoothed the napkin in her lap, then looked back up at him. "Though I wonder . . . were you as nonchalant in giving your orders to Ms. Suggs before she took your place at the SPCA board meeting tonight?"

Sutter, who had picked up his glass again, froze midway in bringing it to his lips. "I asked Arnetta to go to the meeting and take notes. Good lord, she didn't speak, did she?"

Was he the new donor of a million-dollar facility, he wondered. Had Arnetta suggested he'd adopt a few hundred more pets? What had she done? He contemplated the possibilities with dread, for he was sure it was something he would absolutely not want to do.

"Oh yes, she spoke, all right," Megan said. She paused a moment to sip her wine, started to speak again, then stopped and looked at the glass. "Wow. That's delicious."

"I'll give you a case before you go," he said dismissively, his eyes not leaving her. "What did Arnetta say?"

Megan tilted her head and regarded him steadily. "She said you suggested killing all the animals a couple of days earlier than usual, to save money."

Sutter closed his eyes, laying the fingertips of one hand on his forehead.

She continued, "Or, alternately, she said you proposed letting them all go. An idea, I might add, you suggested to me about Twister."

A look of horror crossed her face and she looked swiftly around.

"Where *is* Twister?" she asked, glaring at him.

He opened his eyes, dropped his hand and glared back at her. "At a farm, in the country, romping with the angels," he said. "Where do you think she is? She's in that cage so that I can eat my meal in peace."

Megan sagged in her seat. "Oh thank God," she muttered.

He looked at her in astonishment. Had she really thought he'd just do away with the dog?

"I apologize for my assistant's tactlessness," he said stiffly. "I of course did not intend for her to repeat any such thing."

"Well, I can tell you right now nobody knows what you intended," she said, looking at him speculatively. "They all think you're evil. The question is, did you really say those things?"

"I believe you've already made up your mind that I did." Sutter studied her face and wished for the life of him that he had *not* said those very things. Leave it to Arnetta to miss the point of his cynical joke and repeat his frustrated ravings as if he'd meant them.

"I am merely reporting back what happened," she said, putting her fork down carefully on her plate. "I thought you might want to repair the considerable damage done by those words with people such as Wilma Jones, who you may not have known heads the SPCA board."

For some reason she looked as if she thought she'd scored rather high with that one.

Sutter was confused. It was all well and good for her to get on her high horse about this. He wasn't forcing her to adopt something that she had never desired and didn't like. Between her and Lizzy he felt as if not only the dog, but the whole animal community was suddenly being crammed down his throat.

"I'm sorry, I don't know any Wilma Jones," he said, his tone more defensive than he'd intended, "but I appreciate your effort to help me clear my good name."

"Are you being sarcastic?" Her mouth dropped open. "Do you not know what impression this kind of attitude makes on people? They were ready to string you up! They couldn't have been madder if the devil himself had shown up and stolen all their souls."

He might have chuckled at that description had he not known how disastrously she would misinterpret even that.

"I was not being sarcastic," he said deliberately. "And I regret the misunderstanding—"

"Are you sure it *was* a misunderstanding?" She looked almost hopeful.

"Of course it was."

"Then you didn't say any of those things."

He took a deep breath. "In Arnetta's defense, I may have said something similar to her—in jest—but I had no intention of it being repeated to the board members of the SPCA."

"Well," she said, looking disappointed, "it *was* repeated. And now they all think you're evil incarnate."

"Including you?" he asked, and he couldn't help the edge in his voice.

How many times had he been accused, turned on, eviscerated by people he *thought* were friends, or at least amiable acquaintances, when he declined to support the cause of their choice? How many times had he been asked to give money to this group, or that group, regardless of whether he had any interest in or dealing with extraterrestrials, or retired racehorses, or library periodicals, or what have you? He could spend his life throwing money at every cause that came by and go broke doing it. Which is why he'd set up a private foundation for just this kind of charity. They screened applicants and gave grants to the most worthy without his ever having to get involved, beyond giving the money, that was.

But what pained him most about this was that he had thought her—Megan Rose—above this kind of thing.

This is just what you got when you kissed someone for no reason, he thought.

Her eyes flashed up to him. "Does it matter what I think?"

He chuckled once, mirthlessly. "Forgive me if I'm wrong, Dr. Rose, but I would not be surprised to learn that you were the angriest one there."

"What? Why would *I* be the angriest one there?"

He sat back and regarded her. "Women are generally at their most passionate when they believe themselves to have been wronged."

She stared at him, then said in a very cold voice, "And how have I been wronged?"

He sighed. "Perhaps you felt personally betrayed. Even though, I must add, I made no effort to hide my true feelings on this subject from our first meeting."

Color rose to her cheeks. "What I think is not the point—"

"Really?" he asked.

She pressed her lips together, her face still glowing with outrage. "Really. What are you trying to say?"

He leaned forward, pinning her with his eyes. "Only that had we not kissed the other day, we would most likely not be having this conversation and I would be eating my meal while it was still hot."

She looked at him, aghast, for a full ten seconds. Then she rose so quickly her chair fell over behind her. She merely blinked at the sound of it hitting the floor. "I—I—this is unbelievable."

He remained calmly seated. "Do you deny it?"

"Not only do I deny it," she said through clenched teeth, "but I'm not even going to dignify the idea by staying here to talk about it. Your ego is obviously much bigger than I imagined. So thank you for . . ." She waved her hand around the untouched dinner. "And good night."

She spun on her heel and headed for the door.

Sutter grappled with a sudden feeling of having maybe not hit the nail quite on the head. He was fairly certain he was right about the kiss being behind all of this, but had no idea how to undo the ugly mess that had come of it.

"Dr. Rose," he called in his most forbidding tone. He rose from his seat and strode through the living room, relieved to see she had stopped at his command. "Megan."

"Yes?" Her hands were on her hips, her color still high and her eyes still dark and flashing with anger. But her voice was cool.

"I'm sorry you've gotten the wrong idea." He took a deep breath.

"Oh I *hate* that kind of apology," she said, raking her hands through her hair.

"I am not apologizing—"

"Then you might not want to use the words, 'I'm sorry'."

"Megan, I'm trying to tell you I'm sorry for how this conversation has gone. Clearly I was mistaken and you—"

She crossed her arms over her chest. "Did you, or did you not, say those things to your assistant?"

"Wouldn't you rather know if I meant them?" he asked.

She spread her hands. "If you're willing to admit it."

He paused. Was it not better for her to believe him a heartless bastard than for him to exonerate himself? He did not want her thinking well of him. Didn't want her thinking of him at all.

Of course, his thinking about her was another matter entirely.

"It doesn't matter," he said finally. "I can see your mind is made up about me."

"Honestly, Sutter, I don't know *what* to think about you. And for the record, that kiss had nothing to do with my outrage about your proposal to kill animals instead of—what was it?—oh yes, 'begging door-to-door' on their behalf."

"I never said 'door-to-door,'" he said, wishing he could fire Arnetta from a cannon. Although, if she hadn't muddled what he'd said, Megan Rose would not be standing in his foyer looking impassioned in a way that was, he hated to admit it, quite stimulating.

She gave him that appalled look again and barked a simple, "*Hah!*" before turning toward the door again.

Despite himself, he reached out for her elbow, caught it and felt a wave of desire swamp him. "I'm sorry," he said quickly, but he didn't—couldn't—drop her arm.

"You keep saying that. So what are you sorry for?" she asked, one brow arched.

"I may have been insensitive but it was, I *thought*, in the privacy of my own office. It was not a proposal I expected to be taken seriously. Taken anywhere at all, really."

She didn't say anything, just stood looking at him, her angry breath filling and emptying her chest rapidly.

Sutter loosened his grip on her arm, but he did not let go and she did not break free.

Her skin was warm and soft under his fingers, her muscles taut.

He should let go, he thought. Let her walk out the door still angry at him. It was the only way he would not feel compelled to see her again.

And yet, here she was, pausing under his touch, looking at him with those wide, forthright eyes.

He recalled the kiss in the park, the way she'd given herself right over to him. It had been so effortless . . .

"Megan . . ." He exerted the smallest of pressures on her arm, pulled her slightly toward him.

The next thing he knew they were kissing.

Eight

Sutter's hands gripped her shoulders as his lips crushed hers. Megan wasn't quite sure how it happened, all she knew was that all the energy she had poured into her anger had mutated instantaneously and without her accord into a desire so strong she could not resist it.

The kiss was dizzying, hot and sensual. Sutter's lips were skillful, his tongue deft. Their bodies pressed into each other as if longing to occupy the same space. Megan's very skin seemed to be crying out for his, reveling in the strength and demand of his arms.

This kiss was different than the one in the park. That one was exploratory, sweet, almost innocent. Not this one. Not while the bedroom was right up those stairs. And her body knew it, too.

Desire turned to molten heat in her abdomen. Her hips pressed forward into his, her need finding his. She felt his excitement hard against her, and moaned softly into his mouth.

His hands rose to her face and cupped it. He pulled back a fraction. "Let's go upstairs."

She hesitated, and he captured her lips once again. A plea and a promise. An irresistible temptation. Her blood sang, her knees went weak, and she screamed in her head, *Yes! Yes! Let's go upstairs!*

He backed off again, their lips parting with a soft *smack*, and he gave her a look that nearly melted her bones. Then he bent slightly and—literally—swept her off her feet.

With a tiny squeal, she put her arms around his neck. He strode across the foyer and took the stairs two at a time, so quickly Megan barely had time to form the fear that they might both go tumbling down the steps under her weight. He reached the top and turned swiftly, heading straight into a darkened room and kicking the door shut behind him.

Then he laid her on the bed. She spread her arms and let herself sink farther onto its surface, feeling the downy softness beneath her, a cool duvet, a limitless mattress.

His voice came out of the darkness, from the tall silhouette of a man unbuttoning his own shirt. "I don't mean to take advantage. If you wish to leave I shan't stop you."

Shan't. She sighed. What kind of man used the word *shan't*? If she closed her eyes she could imagine she was in a fairy tale.

With a man who killed pets, her mind cut in.

She shut it off and sat up, reaching for him. It had been too damn long, she thought, and he was just too damn much to resist.

Her fingers found his belt loop and she pulled him toward her. "I don't wish to leave," she said in a voice so husky she barely recognized it as her own. "And I do mean to take advantage."

She pulled on his belt and released it from the buckle. His hands moved to her hair as she pulled down his zipper, slid his pants, boxers and all, over his lean hips, and found the evidence of his passion.

He groaned softly as she took it in her hands. The silken sweet hardness filled her palm. She guided it slowly into her mouth.

"Oh Jesus," he uttered, so softly she almost didn't hear it.

Pulling his hips toward her, she held to the firm rounds of his buttocks. His taut stomach touched her forehead as she drew him in, then let him so far out he almost escaped her, then drew him in again. His hands gripped her hair and his breathing quickened.

He swore and pulled himself from her mouth,

then pushed her down on the bed. He lifted the skirt of her sundress and grasped her panties, sliding them over her legs and off her feet. She arched her back as he unzipped the dress and lifted it over her head. Dress gone, his hands ran up the sides of her body to her bra, then snaked around her back and undid the clasp with a deft flick of his fingers.

She sighed. He brought his lips to her breast, finding the nipple of the other with his fingers. The sensation was exquisite.

"Sutter," she breathed, satisfied with how the name slid out from between her teeth, barely rustling the air.

He lifted himself and settled over her, his arms on either side of her head. He dipped his head and caught her mouth with his. Reaching down with one hand, he touched his fingers to her thigh, then between them, then slid them along the wet folds of her desire.

Megan nearly gasped as he immediately found the spot. The man was mystical in his lovemaking, instinctively going to the most intimate, desirous places, satisfying every inch that called out to him.

Her hand reached down and rounded him again, gently grazing upward and back. He let out a deeply satisfied sigh.

She shifted her hips as he stroked her, moaning into the side of his neck, feeling his body tremble as her hands worked on him.

With a burst of starfire, she came, and before she had a moment to return from the heavens he rolled on top and plunged inside of her. She pulsed around him as he pumped inside of her. Adrenaline surging, she grabbed at his body, his back, his legs, his buttocks, moving with him, blinded by physical rapture, throbbing as he hit home again and again with his perfect hardness.

Just when she thought she could sustain the orgasm no longer, he exhaled hard and impaled her with a final thrust. Then he shuddered beneath her hands and melted alongside her, their bodies still joined, her arms around his shoulders.

At 10:04 P.M., the phone rang. Megan opened her eyes at the unfamiliar ring, caught sight of the digital clock, and saw the masculine taupe walls with the black accents, the plasma TV and the original Chagall painting, and knew she was not at home. Then she felt the mattress dip and turned her head to see Sutter's lean naked back as he sat up and reached for a sleek cordless phone.

"Yes," he said into it, sounding for all the world as if he had not just roused himself from an unbelievable roll in the sheets.

Megan's limbs felt like sacks of cement. Coccooned in the sheets, beneath the thick down comforter, she snuggled into the pillow, looking at the back of Sutter's tousled hair, and told herself she had to leave. Then she wondered if they couldn't maybe . . . just once more . . . it had, after all, been a very long time for her.

A second later, she knew she had to get out of there.

"I apologize. I know I said I'd call and I intended to. I got . . . distracted. Something came up."

Megan could tell from the way his spine had gone straight that this was the tabloid woman, the one with the diamond earrings. She could also tell by the way he stood and strode swiftly to the bathroom with the phone, not even looking over his shoulder at her, only leaving her with the image of his Greek god's body burned onto her retinas by the bathroom light, that he was having to do some undesirable placating. He did not sound soft—on the contrary—he sounded irked. Was that how he treated the women in his life?

She sat up quickly, paused, felt momentarily dizzy, then located her underwear in the tangle of sheets. All the blood must have pooled in her body as she'd wallowed languorously in his huge warm bed after their lovemaking.

Not so now. She swung her legs over the side of the mattress and pulled on her panties. Then she stood, her feet seeming to sink deep into the plush carpet, and rounded the bed to find her sundress in a passion-strewn heap on the floor, next to Sutter's pants, shirt, and socks.

This can't happen again, she thought. He was attached and was way too high profile for her anyway. She'd had sex buddies before, guys who weren't seeing anyone at the same time she wasn't, but they were usually very close friends who agreed on the temporary nature of the arrangement. This . . . this inferno of passion would not be good for any kind of duration. It would burn itself out as quickly as it had flared and then they could be left with a very public mess on their hands.

No, she was certain this had to be a one-time thing.

Better for her, and better for him.

She'd just pulled on her dress when Sutter emerged from the bathroom. The light blinded her again before he closed the door on it.

He stopped, naked, but for the phone in his hand, when he caught sight of her.

Her knees went weak again. God, but he was beautiful.

"Are you leaving?" he asked.

He sounded surprised, which surprised her, considering he'd just been on the phone with his girlfriend.

Not that she was mad. She understood about these things. Tonight had surprised them both. Monogamy was unnatural, she knew. What she felt for him was physical passion, and that was all. This was the way she liked it, she told herself. Sex with a trusted partner, without all the work and worry of a relationship.

For a moment she wondered what it would be like to be in a relationship with Sutter Foley. Had she sold herself too short by jumping into bed with him? Not that she felt like she'd had much choice. She'd been overcome by desire in a way she didn't remember ever feeling before.

No, she wasn't going to feel bad about this. They had about as much chance of ending up in a relationship as she did of becoming president of the United States. Tonight had been a fluke. A happy accident. An incredible experience. And they were consenting adults. There was nothing to regret and much to relish.

She just had to make sure it didn't happen again or, she felt certain, her heart could definitely wind up at risk.

"Yes. I should go. This was . . . unexpected," she said with a low chuckle.

"Yes. Yes it was." He moved to the bedside table and replaced the phone in its cradle. For someone who seemed so uptight, he certainly was comfortable with his own nudity, she noted. Of course, it probably helped that he could not have been sculpted finer by Michelangelo.

When he turned back from the table, she was in front of him, her hands on his ribcage. She stood on her toes and gave him a kiss. He responded ardently, his hands pulling her in, the kiss deepening immediately into something dangerously . . . what had he said? . . . distracting.

She pulled away, smiling. "I've got to go. This was nice."

"Nice," he repeated, and she thought she saw an ironic glint in his eye, but it was hard to tell with only the vestiges of bathroom light to go by.

"Very nice," she corrected. Her hands played lightly over his skin and she felt his fingers tighten on her back, as if to draw her in to him again. "Besides," the devil in her added, "it sounds like you've got a call to return."

His hands stilled.

She laughed and turned out of his grasp. One more second and she would have ripped her own dress off again.

She looked around for her purse as he pulled on his pants.

"It's downstairs," he said and she glanced at him. "Your bag. It's in the front hall. It landed on my foot as we, ah . . ."

She started to smile, then remembered the argument they'd been having when passion suddenly overcame them.

He was buttoning his shirt when their eyes met and they looked at each other a long moment with great seriousness. "This . . . probably shouldn't continue," he said finally.

Despite herself, despite the fact that she'd had the *very same thought*, she colored and felt a wrenching near her solar plexus. "I know." She nodded, still looking at his face, at the shadow of stubble on his cheek, at the sandy lashes and green eyes. What would it be like to touch that face every day, to kiss him good morning and walk hand-in-hand to bed every night? What would it be like to have him look at her with love, and not just desire?

She swallowed. "Don't worry. I won't say anything."

The moment she said it, she felt cheap. As if she'd seduced a married man. She'd only meant to reassure him that she wasn't a gossip, that this wouldn't get back to his girlfriend, that she hadn't done it because he was famous or rich or anything other than electrifyingly attractive to her. And that had more to do with his touch, really, than his looks, though it *was* hard to separate the two.

She turned swiftly and headed for the door.

"Megan," he said.

She stopped and looked back.

He tipped his head almost imperceptibly and said, "Thank you," with a slight lift at the end. A question?

Without knowing what else to do, she darted a quick smile at him, and left.

* * *

"They have blues in that litter," Georgia was saying to Penelope as Megan approached them in the dog park the next morning. She was snapping Sage's leash in her hands and glaring at Penelope.

"Honey, can't any litter have blues—?"

"No, not any litter. Just ones that are composed of the right recessive genes. And there are *four* in this litter, Penelope. Four." She snapped the leash some more, making Megan's eyes blink every time she did it. "Tell me, Megan, how likely is it that a harlequin and a black will have *four blues* in a litter of six?"

"Well, they'd each have to have blues in their backgrounds. I'd have to see the pedigrees," Megan said carefully.

Georgia was as mad as Megan had ever seen a woman. Her blue eyes stood out like ice shards beneath her heavy black lashes.

"I know there are blues in Gretyl's background but I'd bet everythin' I own there are *none* in Danny's," she growled. "They used Sage's sperm. I know it."

"Did you ask at the . . . what do they call it? A sperm bank?" Penelope gave Megan a worried *do something* look. "Maybe they can tell you if anyone's, uh, checked anything out."

Megan returned a helpless look and unhooked Peyton's leash, gave her a hearty scrub behind the ears, then slapped her on the rump as she ran off toward Wimbledon, Penelope's big black lab.

"It's a canine semen bank," Georgia said, "but since we're still goin' through the legalities about that it's supposed to be off limits to both of us." She turned suddenly to Megan, startling her. "Megan," she said, "how hard is it to do a DNA test?"

Megan's eyes darted to Penelope's and back to Georgia's intense gaze. "Not hard. What are you thinking?"

"If I could get one of those puppies I could find out for sure if Sage's the sire."

"But what would you do if he is?" Penelope asked.

"Sue for custody, of course!" Georgia flung her arms out wide. "I have legal recourse. It's only a matter of time until we have it all in writin'. *That sperm is mine!*"

Megan glanced over to see several people stop dead as this sentence rang out into the cool morning air.

"But Georgia," Penelope protested, moving closer and using a quieter voice, "Clifford's never going to let you take one of those puppies. Especially if he knows, or suspects, why you've asked for one. I think you need to let this go. Start looking for a bitch to breed him to yourself."

Georgia laughed cruelly. "Oh, I'm not goin' to ask Clifford anythin'. I'm gettin' one of those puppies and I'm provin' what a scandalous liar he is. He had a buddy worked at that sperm bank, that's why we used that one, and I just bet that snake let him have a vial of Sage's frozen semen. There's no way that harlequin sired those blues. In fact, I bet I could get a copy of his pedigree and *see* how many blues were in his background." With one last snap of the leash Georgia called to Sage and clicked the leash on him. "Don't forget about next week. My place? Drinks?"

"What?" Megan asked.

"Oh, Pen will fill you in," Georgia said with a wave of her hand. "I've got to go. See you later!"

Megan and Penelope stood looking after her, silent a moment. Then Penelope turned to Megan and said, "I think she's lost her mind."

Megan shrugged. "Maybe. Then again, sounds like it's possible Clifford actually did do something underhanded."

"Well, yeah, *that's* possible," Penelope agreed with a cynical chuckle. "He's not exactly a pillar of morality. I heard recently he's been cheating on the new wife."

"You're kidding. How do you hear this stuff?" If Penelope was a big purveyor of gossip, Megan really needed to know. She was dying to talk about the situation with Sutter, but not to someone who might spill it to everyone she knew.

"People in the shop." She shook her head. "You

wouldn't believe the things women will tell you while trying on jewelry. And I don't even ask!"

"Do they—" Megan paused, not wanting to sound insulting. "Are they, uh, at all concerned about its confidentiality?"

Penelope laughed. "I don't know. If they speak up in the middle of a busy shop, then I have to believe they're not too worried about who knows. It's not as if any of them ever asked me to keep it quiet, either. They don't seem to care."

Megan sighed, relieved.

"So, how did your visit with Sutter Foley go last night?" Penelope asked, as if reading Megan's mind. "I was going to call you last night but I played a doubles match that lasted forever."

Megan took a deep breath. "Well, it started out all right. I caught him in the middle of dinner and he invited me to join him."

"Ooh." Penelope's brows rose. "What was he having?"

"Swordfish. The chef himself served it."

"I've heard about his chef. Was it fabulous?"

Megan shifted, hesitant. "I, actually, I don't know. We ended up sort of arguing."

"You and the chef?" Penelope's eyes widened.

Megan laughed. "No. Me and Sutter."

"Ohhhh," she nodded, "so he did say that awful stuff. I might have known."

"I don't know, exactly, but he didn't deny it! And he was being a real jerk about me even asking about it. Like I should have had some kind of faith in him, God knows why."

Despite the confident words, she wondered if she *should* have had some faith. Something about Sutter screamed "misunderstood" to her every time they met. It was one reason she'd thought he needed the dog. He was quiet, kept to himself, but when he spoke he had an air of honesty. Indeed, something that seemed to say lying was so far beneath him it was not worth bothering with. Still . . . it wasn't as if she knew him well.

Penelope drew her head back, her brow furrowed. "Hm. That's weird. Why would he think you should have faith in him? Unless he's one of those men who thinks he's a gentleman and should therefore be above reproach. No matter what awful things he does or says."

Megan looked around the park, noting there were only four or five other people, then waved Penelope over to a corner where there were a couple of white plastic chairs. They were covered with dried mud and teeth marks, but seemed acceptably clean in the sunshine. They sat.

"What is it?" Pen asked, leaning forward, looking concerned. "He wasn't mean, was he? What did he do, throw you out of the house?"

Megan laughed again, remembering how he'd swept her up in his arms and actually carried her up the stairs to the bedroom. She'd felt like something out of an old movie, though the sex had hardly been old-fashioned.

"Not exactly," she smirked. "Well, first, let me tell you what happened the other day. And please, this can't go any further than the two of us."

Penelope sat up straight. "Of course!" Then understanding dawned. "Oh, I see. I swear I only pass along the gossip that was broadcast to me in public to begin with. I hope you didn't think I was betraying anyone's confidence!"

Penelope's fingers fidgeted in her lap and Megan leaned over to put her hand on top of them. "Penelope, don't be offended. When you hear what I have to tell you, you'll understand my paranoia. I didn't really doubt *you*."

Penelope's brows lowered along with her voice. "What is it?"

"Last Saturday, after you guys left the park here and the rain came down?"

Penelope nodded.

"Sutter Foley showed up, with that puppy he's got. You know, the one his groundskeeper had adopted."

"He *kept* it?" Penelope asked.

"Well, I talked him into it." Megan shrugged. "I thought it would do them both good. Now . . . I don't know. Anyway, he showed up and we got to talking and . . . one thing led to another and . . ." She hesitated. Was it a betrayal of Sutter to tell?

But it was her story too, and if she needed to talk about it . . .

"*And . . . ?*" Penelope asked, actually leaning forward in her seat, her hands now clasped tightly together as her elbows rested on her knees.

"Well, he kissed me."

Penelope gasped and sat up. Then she leaned forward again. "He *kissed* you? Is that what you said? Sutter Foley *kissed* you? In, you know, *that way*?"

Megan laughed. "It wasn't anything close to a chaste kiss, if that's what you mean."

Penelope burst out a laugh, then put a hand over her face. "Oh my God." She dropped the hand and pinned Megan with her eyes. "This is huge. *Huge.* Sutter Foley doesn't do things lightly."

Megan began shaking her head. "Maybe not lightly, but he's not immune to impulse. Besides, that's not all. I still have to tell you about last night . . ."

Today, Aunt Edna's hair was neatly curled, with a small red bow on one side, and she sat with her hands in her lap in the sitting room off her bedroom. She wore red lipstick and two patches of subtle pink glowed on her cheeks.

She beamed at Sutter as he entered.

"Sutter! How lovely to see you. Come sit." She indicated the wing chair across from hers. "Are those for me?"

"Of course," he said, handing her the lilies she so adored. Their perfumey scent was enough to suffocate him but he almost always brought a bouquet of them to her. He couldn't resist seeing her light up like that.

Despite the summer temperatures outside, a fire blazed in the fireplace, and he cast the aide a questioning look as he handed his aunt the flowers.

"I know, Mr. Foley, it's hot as Hades in here, but she insisted. She was chilly, she said." The petite black woman shook her head but smiled. "And you know there's just no arguing with her."

"Now, Lucy, don't go telling on me," Aunt Edna said, handing her the flowers. "Be a dear and put these in some water, would you, love?"

"Sure thing, Miss Foley," Lucy said, and left them alone.

Aunt Edna turned back to Sutter and smiled warmly. "Now, tell me all about you. I haven't seen you for at least a couple of weeks now. Are you still seeing that lovely woman from the newspapers? The one who's moving to town for you?"

Sutter loved it when his aunt was like this. After his mother died, when he was eleven and Lizzy thirteen, Aunt Edna had been the one they had gone to for comfort and shelter when their father had come home drunk and knocked them about. She'd understood—after all, she'd grown up with the man—but at the time there was not much she could do about it. They were all living in one of the poorest parts of London, where getting drunk and beating your wife and children was about as commonplace as hanging your washing out to dry.

"Briana? Yes, I still see her," he said, taking off his suit jacket and laying it on the sofa. "But she's not moving to town for me. She got a job here that she'd been wanting."

"In this little town?" His aunt looked at him skeptically. "Trust me, dear, she's coming here for you."

"No, no." He waved her words away. "It's not like that. We're not that serious. She's coming only for the job, she told me so herself."

Aunt Edna sighed. "Oh Sutter. Are you never going to get married again? I've been waiting years for either you or Lizzy to have children and both of you seem determined to disappoint me."

He sat in the wing chair across from her and loosened his tie. "Believe me, I'm not trying to thwart you. It's simply not easy to know when you've found the right woman."

For a moment, he thought of Megan Rose, of how perfectly her body had fitted his, and how incredibly well he had slept that night they had been together. It was as if some huge burden had been lifted from him for the night and he'd not only finally slept, but relaxed in a way he hadn't for months. Years, maybe.

"Now what is that expression all about?" Aunt

Edna said, her eyes sharp. "You can't tell me this Briana isn't serious if she makes you look like that, Sutter Foley."

He smiled ruefully. "I wasn't thinking about Briana."

"Well, who was it then? I see potential there." She gave him a cheeky grin.

"It's no one. Tell me about you. How has your week been?"

Her brow darkened and she gave him a piercing look, the one that reminded him that she was, after all, related to his father. While her temper didn't come out as abuse the way his did, she was able to singe you with her tongue like nobody he'd ever known when she was of a mind to.

"Don't you try to pull the wool over my eyes, young man. I may be old but I'm not stupid. Nor blind."

"Aunt Edna, the last thing I would ever call you is stupid. I was actually thinking about a woman who gave me a dog. A kind of a golden-retriever type dog. Can you believe it? I've actually got a pet."

"She must be quite a special woman to have talked you into that." Aunt Edna's eyes twinkled.

"She's . . . interesting, I must admit. But she's not right for me."

"Whyever not?"

He laughed dryly. "A bit like Bitsy, if you must know. Not the type to put up with my lifestyle. But

172 ❖

I think she might be a friend," he said contemplatively, thinking that even aside from their unbelievable night of passion, what he enjoyed most about her was her utter confidence to say whatever was on her mind. Even if she ended up taking it back a moment later.

She was impulsive and candid, and laughed as freely as a child. It was . . . refreshing.

"A friend is always good," Aunt Edna said, watching him.

"I think so." He smiled at her. "You would like her, actually. She's very genuine."

"And what about the other woman, Briana?"

"I suppose she's genuine too, but they're different." He laughed and shook his head. "Like night and day, really. Megan is . . . bright and sunny. And she has these eyes . . . you just fall right into them if you're not careful. She's so open." He took a deep breath and shook off more thoughts of the lovely vet. "Briana, on the other hand," he said, leaning back in the chair and smiling at his aunt. "She's dark and unfathomable. Mysterious."

"Women are only mysteries to men who don't want to understand them," his aunt said tersely.

"That's not really true. With Briana, she's not asking to be understood. In fact she's almost easier to be around because she's so reserved and independent. I believe she likes being untouchable."

"Humph," Aunt Edna snorted delicately. "Sounds dull."

He chuckled. "No, not really. Just self-contained."

"Like you," Aunt Edna said. "Sounds to me like this other woman would be better for you. Two self-contained people make for one awfully dull marriage, if you ask me."

"Me? Self-contained?" Sutter put a hand to his chest in mock surprise. "How can you say that? I'm spilling my guts to you here, Aunt Edna."

"Oh I do hate that phrase. It's so American. But as long as you're at it, tell me, do you 'fall into' this Briana's eyes as you do the other woman's? What was her name—Megan?"

"Yes, Megan." Despite himself, Megan's face appeared in his mind's eye and he knew for a fact he did not fall into Briana's eyes they way he did hers. "She's not right for me, Aunt Edna. And she knows it, too. In fact we agreed on it, last time we met."

Aunt Edna's gaze went shrewd. "Ah, so you've been rejected by her. I see."

"Rejected?" He frowned. "No, there was no rejection." *Was there?* "We just have very different lives, that's all. They're not compatible."

"I see," his aunt said, and nodded, clearly unconvinced.

"Truly, Aunt Edna."

"I understand." She gave him a smile, but he

could tell it was her "I know better than anything you could tell me" smile.

He sat back in the chair, but he wasn't as comfortable in it as he had been a minute ago.

Had Megan rejected him?

Why didn't he fall into Briana's eyes?

What was so great about falling anyway?

He heaved a great sigh and had the feeling he would not be sleeping so well tonight.

Nine

The following weekend Sutter found himself pacing the house. Martina was off, Berkley had dropped off frozen meals in the morning because he was taking a week's vacation, work did not seem as imperative as it usually did, and Sutter was alone. Utterly and completely alone. A state he usually liked to be in.

Not today.

Today he could not help thinking about his visit with Aunt Edna and the thoughts it had stirred up about the incredible night with Megan Rose.

He couldn't say he was surprised by her passion. Couldn't even say he'd been surprised by his. She'd tweaked his interest since the day she'd shown up on the doorstep with that damn dog. Even then, he'd found himself with feelings he knew he should not have for a woman like her. Not with Briana moving to town. Briana, who'd been groomed for the life he now lived and who, if he were honest with himself, he knew to be eager to live it with him.

But he'd been telling his aunt the truth. He had made no commitments to Briana and had kept his conscience clear by telling her she should not be moving to town because of him.

She had scoffed at the notion, asking him if he thought she didn't have better things to do than to chase a man from New York to Virginia. The job was the reason, she told him. The unique opportunity to raise funds for the Washington House—an organization that saved historic properties from development.

She swore his being there was just an extra benefit, but he suspected otherwise.

He shouldn't complain. He could certainly do much worse than Briana. She was sharp and undeniably beautiful.

He spent about half a minute thinking about her dark fathomless eyes before his mind strayed to another pair of dark eyes . . . these with laughter and daring in them, intelligence and excitement.

But free-spirited Megan was not the kind of woman he needed. He needed Briana, who was cool and sophisticated, mature and diplomatic. She would grace every table, be an asset at business functions, run his home the way he ran his company—efficiently, with taste and class.

And she had her own money. This was important. While he was certain that he'd be able to spot a gold digger if one tried to seduce him, he'd seen many a smart man fall to those types before, and every single one of them would have said the same thing. Sutter was not so arrogant that he believed he was immune to the blindness that came with not being able to see beyond the end of one's . . . whatever.

Still, he knew Megan wasn't a gold digger. He'd wager his fortune on it, but she also wasn't the intelligent choice for a partner in the enterprise of this life he'd made. For one thing, it would be grossly unfair to her.

She'd just been the most incredible shag of his life. Which was exactly what the gold diggers started out as.

Finding himself pacing through the sunroom for the third time, indulging the same circular thoughts on each circuit, he glanced out into the garden and realized that he was not, actually, alone. He had that blasted dog. The one that probably needed to be let out by now. It wouldn't kill him to spend a moment or two with it, he told himself. He could watch it run, maybe give it a treat.

He went into the mud room, which was just off the kitchen, and found Twister in her crate. She awoke at his arrival and her wagging tail banged against the plastic sides of her crib, as Megan had called it. He bent over and looked in. A large doggy grin greeted him.

He smiled reluctantly. It was kind of a cute thing, especially while it was locked up and doing no harm. He opened the door to the crate and she was out like a shot.

Berkley had let her out this morning, he knew for a fact because he'd seen them coming back in, but that had been several hours ago. For a moment he felt bad for his negligence. Sunday was the only time this dog was his responsibility, surely he could muster the energy to do it right.

From the top of the crate he picked up a box of dog biscuits. Twister charged back into the room at the sound. Standing before him, tail whipping the whole rear end of her body back and forth, she looked up at him expectantly.

He held the treat out. "Sit," he said experimentally.

The dog sat. Sutter grinned and gave it the treat. This was rather fun.

He got out another treat and looked at the dog. "Lie down," he said. The dog sat there, looking at him. "No, *lie down*," he said again, this time bringing the treat to the floor in front of her. She slid to the floor and he let go of the treat.

Berkley must be working with her, he thought, watching her consume the treat.

The phone rang. Sutter rose and pointed at the dog. "Wait there."

He picked up the phone in the next room. It was Montgomery. Of course. A weekend couldn't go by without her calling or coming by or making the point in some other way that she was working, sacrificing a personal life for the advancement of the company—and her career, of course. He appreciated that kind of dedication, he really did. He just hated the way it imposed on *him* every weekend. He'd already spent half a lifetime of weekends getting his business off the ground.

Half an hour later, after he'd sorted Montgomery out, he went looking for Twister. He found her in his bedroom closet, wrestling with a pair of jeans he'd worn yesterday.

"No!" he bellowed, causing her to jump and run over to him, a denim thread hanging from the side of her mouth. "Bad dog," he added, picking up the jeans and examining the chewed hem of one leg. Twister crouched at his tone, ears back, the very picture of submission.

Underneath the pants was his wallet, now adorned with tooth marks and drool spots on the fine chocolate leather. A sopping twenty-dollar bill and half a five were near that and next to a saliva-soaked sock was what was left of his driver's license.

"Dammit," he said, glaring at the dog who was

now plastered to the floor next to him, just the tip of her tail wagging. "You just had two treats."

She watched him as if she'd thought he might be pleased with her handiwork, but was now getting the feeling he was unhappy with the situation.

"Bad dog," he said again, wiping his hand on his pants after putting the wet twenty back in the wallet. "Evil bloody mutt."

She dropped her head to the floor, looking up at him with the most pathetic eyes he'd ever seen. White-rimmed at the bottom, the pseudo-eyebrows lifted, the snout between the paws. She was dejection incarnate.

With a sigh he reached out and patted the top of her head.

"All right," he said, standing up. She jumped up and stood next to him, watchful and wagging, accepting his forgiveness with unencumbered joy. "Let's get you outside before I have something even more unpleasant to discover."

They went downstairs, Sutter following her ex-uberant progress down the steps, around the corner of the marbled foyer, where Twister paddled excitedly on the slick surface with nails and paws before gaining purchase and shooting like something out of a slingshot toward the back door.

He let her out and followed her into the sunny morning.

The dog tore across the low deck and leapt into the grass, making a lap around the entire back garden, weaving in and out of boxwoods, clearing tall flower beds in a single bound, and turning on a dime around trees and shrubs. Her body was agile and quick, the release of energy powerful, her exuberance a paean to liberation. Sutter felt a little thrill of exultation himself just watching her go and found himself thinking about the last time he'd felt that relief from care, that freedom.

He realized, with wonderment more than surprise, that it was something very close to this he'd felt last week with Megan.

Freedom, acceptance, joy—it had all seemed so simple, so gratifying, so . . . comfortable.

Before, of course, Briana had called.

He ran a hand through his hair and sat on the step of the deck, his eyes on Twister, who had slowed and was sniffing around the birdbath.

While he and Briana had never agreed to be exclusive, up until Megan there had been no reason to think they were otherwise. Even if it had been three months since they'd been together.

It was dodgy territory, to be sure.

Should he think about it now? Should he consider committing to Briana if only to keep himself from screwing up Megan's life—and, he had to face it, probably his own—by dallying with someone so clearly unsuited for, not to mention averse to, the spotlight?

He pictured Megan's long slim body as it had looked sprawled out in his bed. Lithe, relaxed, lovely. Yes, she'd been uninhibited, but she was definitely not the type to want to live in the public eye.

Not that he was thinking of living with her. Cor, he barely knew the girl, even if he did remember every inch of her body with a fondness bordering on something dangerous.

No, he was going to retain his independence. It would not be fair to commit to Briana just to keep him from Megan. Nor did he need that kind of policing. He had strength of will—that stubbornness Bitsy had pointed out—he would just stay away from Dr. Rose, that was all.

Decision made.

Twister had apparently figured out all she was going to from a thorough examination of the birdbath and its immediate environs. She trotted over to where he was and sat in front of him. When he did nothing more than look at her, wondering if that had been enough exercise or if he owed her something more, she lay her head on his knee and gazed up at him.

He couldn't help it, he chuckled. He could not be immune to such tactics, he thought, try though he might.

At the sound of his laugh, the dog lifted her head and seemed to smile in return. Then she got up, trotted up onto the deck and sat right next to him, her body leaning against his shoulder.

Despite himself, Sutter felt a deep, demandless

camaraderie descend upon him. This creature was never going to turn on him, he thought. It would never gossip about him, sell its story to the *National Tattler*, or take advantage of his trust. And it certainly wasn't interested in his money. Except maybe the other half of that five.

This animal only wanted his company. His. Just him.

"All right, then," he said, standing up. Twister popped to her feet. "Let's you and I go for a walk, shall we?"

He found the leash on a hook next to her crate in the mud room. Twister danced around at the sight of it. He snapped it on the collar and was immediately dragged to the front door.

Perhaps predictably, though it surprised him, Sutter eventually found himself on Sophia Street, coming up slowly on the animal hospital. Slowly, because Twister apparently had to urinate on every other thing she smelled, making Sutter wonder just how much liquid one dog could contain.

He paused to let Twister examine the base of a no-parking sign on Sophia Street for much longer than he'd let her dwell on anything else and gazed at the animal hospital. It was Sunday, so the place was closed, but he wouldn't have been surprised if Megan was in there. Her house, which was right next door, was equally dark-looking, the way all houses were during the day, and he wondered if wandering around out here was too obvious. Even if his reasons for being here weren't obvious to him.

Twister finished and they walked on, past the animal hospital in the direction of the city dock. They came upon Brock's restaurant and Sutter noticed the busy deck overlooking the river, an idea coming to him.

He enjoyed Megan. In her company he felt released from his famous—or infamous—role. What if they agreed to be friends? He could explain to her that he was unable to commit to anyone right now, or even in the near future, and that he simply wanted her companionship, her friendship. She struck him as the type to take him up on that.

And he would enjoy having one friend who was not overawed by his celebrity, as she certainly did not seem to be.

He walked back toward the animal hospital. As if on cue—or perhaps, as she might say, directed by the unseen hand of the universe—Megan and her dog emerged from the side door of the animal hospital. Her dog caught sight of them first and froze into a stance of alertness. Megan noticed and looked over at them. For a second, she too froze, then he saw her smile.

Sutter gave a short wave and followed behind Twister's sled-dog desire to reach them.

"Well, hello," she said with that amused smile.

"We decided not to come in the dog door this time." Sutter smiled in return. Though he'd worried that seeing her after their night together might be awkward, he felt nothing but gladness at this moment. This was going to be easy.

"I appreciate that. It's tough on a girl to wake up with a stranger." She glanced down at Twister, who was gnawing at Megan's dog's neck. "Just out walking the dog?"

He shrugged. "She insisted. And I am nothing but a pawn in her world." He glanced up at the sky. "Besides, it seemed a nice day for a walk."

"And it's not even raining." She grinned.

He chuckled. "Yes, perhaps I'm not as noticeable as I'd feared."

"Welcome to my world." She stepped over her dog's leash, which was threatening to entangle her feet, as the two animals lunged and wrestled and growled playfully between them. "It is a beautiful day, isn't it? Less humid than yesterday."

"I suppose so," he looked around. Should he worry that they were talking about the weather? Should he be bringing up something more . . . pertinent?

Then again, it *was* a nice day. He could not remember the last time he'd taken a walk, or done anything outdoors other than move from the car to the office and back again. Whatever hobbies he'd enjoyed in the past had disappeared with the creation of SFSolutions.

Today, however, in a small part of his mind he remembered what it was like to simply enjoy a summer day. And to enjoy it with a pretty, uncomplicated woman.

"Listen I was just walking past Brock's, down the way, and they've got a nice deck . . ." He gestured behind him toward the restaurant.

Megan raised her brows, obviously not planning to help him out with the invitation.

"Have you eaten?" he asked. Then, kicking himself for cowardice, added, "Would you like to go to lunch?"

Her smile was like a dam breaking, shedding warmth all over him. "Sure," she said, then looked down at her dog. "Think we should bring the kids?"

"The deck was awfully inviting. I'm sure they'd settle down." He was sure of no such thing, but he had the feeling this answer would please her. And—what the hell—since he was here he might as well be agreeable.

She beamed at him. "Great. Let me just grab my purse."

She handed him her dog's leash and disappeared into her house. Sutter knew a moment of panic. He looked at the two dogs wrangling in front of him. Dogs. He was handling dogs. He was, technically, the *owner* of one of them. And he was taking the young, spunky, unsuitable owner of the other to lunch.

Was this really the best plan? What had gotten into him?

Whatever it was, he didn't think about it for long. She came back out, hair brushed and wearing a different shirt—a soft white tank top that made her tawny skin and dark hair positively Mediterranean in their warmth. They talked easily all the way to the restaurant, then to their table. They discussed everything, moving well beyond the weather with an ease that surprised him. Dogs first, of course. Then books. Movies. She asked about software, even operating systems, revealing a basic knowledge he was impressed by. He bored her to death with the answers, he was sure, but with the sun on his back and her smile in his face he felt lighthearted and engaging and fun for the first time in years. *Years.*

Somehow the subject of Briana never came up. In fact, he didn't think once about her. And while he couldn't say he didn't think about his night with Megan last week—it was all he could do not to touch her smooth skin, her graceful hands—for some reason it didn't seem important to exhume it, explain it, or excuse it.

After nearly two hours the check came—the waiter obviously was getting off his shift—and Sutter reached for his wallet. Megan went for her purse too and after stifling a chuckle just in time, he waved her off.

"This is mine. I invited you." He flipped through his partially chewed wallet.

"Thank you very much," she said, reaching down to pet her dog, who lay not at her feet so much as on them, he'd noted earlier.

Miraculously, Twister was lying quietly next to his chair. Maybe it was the heat, or the hope of another French fry, but whatever it was, he was grateful for it.

"I love the sound of the trains," Megan said as another one rumbled by. "Living so close to the tracks I thought I'd be bothered by the noise, but it's such a romantic sound. I don't even wake up when they blow their whistles at night anymore."

"I can hear them where I am too," he said, flipping back through his wallet a second time. He knew his American Express card was in here somewhere. "Reminds me of where I grew up."

"Really?" her voice was intrigued.

He glanced up with a wry smile. "But that was considerably closer to the tracks than you are. It wasn't the whistles we were concerned with sleeping through, it was the pictures crashing down off the walls."

He loved the way her eyes laughed when she smiled.

"I'd think that wouldn't happen more than once, would it?" She grinned. "I mean, how many trains does it take to learn not to hang them back up again?"

He laughed, but it disappeared as he searched

the wallet once more. "I can't believe it," he murmured.

"What? No money, Mr. Billionaire?" She plopped her elbows on the table and watched him with those laughing eyes.

He couldn't answer. This was mortifying. His card wasn't there and all he had was that dog-slobbered twenty and half a five-dollar bill. The check was close to twenty-four dollars, and that didn't include the tip.

"My AmEx," he said, going through the billfold *again*. "It's . . . not here."

He looked up to see her brows rise incredulously. She didn't look angry, she looked . . . amazed.

"Are you kidding?" A smile spread across her lips, revealing those delicate pearly whites. "You don't have enough money to pay for lunch?" She started laughing, a sound that moments later had escalated to what he would call full-blown belly-laughing. "This is so great!"

He tried to smile too, though he felt an uncharacteristic heat rise to his cheeks at the same time. This was utterly humiliating.

"Let me speak with the server. I'm sure he'll let me come back—"

"Don't be silly!" She reached for her purse, wiping her eyes and trying to contain her mirth. "Let me treat you. It'll be a power trip for me, saving the rich guy from washing dishes."

He sent her a truly rueful look. "You're enjoying this, aren't you?"

"Tremendously." She pulled out a Visa and put it on top of the check. Almost immediately the hovering waiter descended upon them and disappeared with it.

"I do apologize," he said, his face still burning. "This is most humiliating."

"Oh please. I think it's hilarious, really." She sipped her water, eyeing him with obvious amusement.

He felt like leaning over and kissing her. Nothing was a big deal for her. The world—the complicated, demanding, taxing world—was simple when he was with her. Better than simple, it was fun.

A second after the waiter deposited the bill for her to sign, Twister stood up and began making an extremely unpleasant sound. It started out like someone tapping on a bongo drum, a hollow rumbling from the area of her stomach, but then her back hunched and her head dropped. A second later the sound went deeper, was accompanied by a guttural choking and a steady, rhythmic retching.

Sutter stood up, looking down at the animal in horror. "Good lord."

Megan leaned over to look at the dog. "Oh no."

"What on earth is wrong with her?" Sutter stepped back, glaring at the distorted creature, uncertain what to do but pretty sure hauling her off the deck by the neck would not be proper.

"She's throwing up," Megan said. "Poor thing."

They stood there a long moment while the dog worked up whatever it had in its stomach.

Seconds later she heaved and, along with a couple of French fries and a lot of disgusting bile, up came pieces, some quite large, of his black American Express card.

Megan returned home to find her father sitting at the kitchen table. She took Peyton off her lead and went to the refrigerator to put her doggy bag away. She hadn't been able to finish all of her pasta so she'd brought the rest home. It was one doggy bag her doggy wasn't getting anywhere near.

She was still glowing from lunch, and the feeling that she and Sutter had crossed some important line. They'd established, she felt strongly, that they could be friends. Conversation had come easily and they'd had many similar views about books they'd read and political situations.

He'd even laughed at all of her jokes. That, more than anything else, made her feel as if they viewed the world the same way. You couldn't maintain a stress-free life if you didn't let yourself see the world through a joke's eyes, she'd often thought.

"Hey, doll. So who was that?" her father asked, jerking his head toward the window through which he'd obviously seen her and Sutter as they'd parted.

"Who was what?" It was a lame dodge.

"That fellow who walked you home?"

Megan shrugged, taking out a bottle of water from the refrigerator. "Nobody. Just a client."

Her father's eyes narrowed. "Pretty good looker."

She grinned. "I'll tell him you said so. But I'm pretty sure he likes girls."

Her father guffawed. "You didn't get that kind of joke from your mom. He live in town?"

"Yeah." She tilted her head. "So what's this, Dad? Parental intervention? Feeling like you missed out on the shotgun years?"

He chuckled again. "Got me. Guess I don't want my girl going out with anyone unworthy."

She snorted. "If you want to talk *worth* . . ."

"He take you to a nice lunch?"

"As a matter of fact, I took him." She was inordinately pleased at the truth of this.

The phone rang.

"I'll get it." She went into the living room to get the portable. "Hello?"

"Megan Rose?" an unfamiliar voice asked. It didn't sound like a telemarketer, however, so she didn't hang up.

"That's right. Who's this?"

"This is Tanner Pierce," the male voice said, then added something unintelligible, maybe where he was calling from. "Wasn't that Sutter Foley you were just having lunch with?"

"I beg your pardon?" A chill crept up her spine. Had somebody been *watching* them?

"At lunch, you and Sutter Foley. Is he still seeing Briana Ellis or have you replaced her? I've gotta say, in my opinion he traded up." The voice laughed in a way that sounded friendly.

"Who did you say you were?"

"Tanner Pierce. With *NatTat*."

"What's nat tat?"

"The *National Tattler*," he said, as if she should actually be happy to hear it. "So what can you tell me about Sutter Foley? Is he in love with you?"

She laughed once, truly amused. "You *wish*. That would be quite a story, wouldn't it? Billionaire dumps heiress for poor veterinarian."

"So that's how it is, is it? Good for you! Anything else you can tell me about him? It would really help me out, my deadline's tonight. Is he as nice a guy as they say?"

"That's *not* how it is." An inkling of how dangerous this conversation could be edged into her mind.

"He's not nice? Ohhh, used you, eh? Not breaking it off with Briana? Well, you know how those rich people are. They stick together."

"No, that's not what I meant. He's very nice. But we're not an item and there is no news here, Mr. Pierce."

"Oh please. Call me Tanner."

"No." She put a hand on her hip. "And don't call me anything."

"Okay, but you did have lunch with Sutter Foley. I mean, I saw that much."

She thought a moment, her mind spinning. What should she say that would cut this guy off? Should she hang up or would that just make him mad? And wouldn't an angry journalist be the worst kind to have at your throat?

"Okay, we did have lunch." That had to be safe. He obviously already knew it anyway. "So what? We're just friends."

"Friends, huh? Was that your car at his house the other night?"

"What other night? When?" God, had he seen her at his house after the SPCA meeting? Had he seen what time she'd left? And how she'd *looked*? Fresh from his bed . . .

Could he have had a camera?

"I mean, it *could* have been your car. It was late, so I couldn't see the tags."

"What kind of car?" she asked, feeling better about her own caginess.

"Ahh, okay, so you left there late one night . . ."

He was fishing. Good God, and she'd fed right into it.

"Listen, there's nothing going on here," she said in her calmest voice. "Briana Ellis is not threatened, for God's sake. She's gorgeous, rich and exactly his type. I'm nobody. Go bark up some other tree."

He chuckled. "Must be upsetting, huh? Sure, Briana's not threatened. The rich never are by people like you and me. Sucks to be used, though, huh?"

"I was *not* used. I—we're just friends. Goodbye, Mr. Pierce."

"One last thing," he said, and for God knows what reason she didn't hang up, "is he good in bed?"

"Oh my God!" she gasped.

She looked at the phone as if it had groped her and punched the *off* button so hard the receiver dropped out of her hand. She wished she could slam it in the cradle.

Her heart hammered in her chest and her palms were wet with sweat. The whole conversation had lasted only minutes and yet she had totally lost control of it. What had she said? Would he print something about it? He'd seen them having lunch—could he have taken pictures?

That wouldn't be as bad as her having said something, though. And she hadn't given him much, if anything, had she? Certainly not enough for an article . . . ?

She turned around and sat heavily on the couch, pushing her hands into her hair and leaning her elbows on her knees. "Oh my God."

"Who was it?" her father asked, startling her.

She looked up.

His arms were folded across his chest and he leaned on the door jamb to the kitchen. "Someone asking about your lunch with Sutter Foley?"

Ten

"If you knew who he was, why did you ask?"

"Just wondered what you'd say." Her father gave her a self-satisfied grin.

Megan blushed, caught. "What I said was true. He is a client."

"But he's not nobody." Her father regarded her steadily. His eyes may have been bloodshot but they were keen. "Was he the one you were out with so late last week?"

She thought about that night after the SPCA meeting. That incredible night. The sex had been unbelievable, rocket-powered, earth-moving, sunspot-generating, ecstasy-inducing, and wildly indulgent. But how high of a price was Sutter going to pay for it? How high of a price was *she* going to pay?

She'd thought they could keep the episode

quiet. She may not have known much about him, but she was fairly sure Sutter was not one to take sex with the spontaneous attitude it deserved. Even so, that didn't mean it deserved to be splashed on the cover of a tabloid.

As for Megan, it had never occurred to her that being in the sphere of a billionaire might make her a person of interest to sleazy journalists.

If she hadn't been sure before, she certainly was now. That night could not be repeated. She imagined them discovering her father on one of his drunken binges. Worse, finding him passed out on the floor among the shelled peanuts at the Rendevous, as she had done one night on one of her long-ago visits. She could see it now, pictures of her disheveled father with the headlines screaming that Sutter was playing with the daughter of trailer trash while planning to marry classy and monied Briana Ellis.

Which would be nothing to Sutter, as he was probably used to showing up in rags like that, but it could kill her business among the conservative gentry of Fredericksburg.

She stood up and headed back into the kitchen. Her father stepped aside as she passed him.

"What night I was out late?" She made her voice as casual as she could.

"Last Monday." He turned and watched her open the refrigerator door.

"Last Monday?"

He rubbed a stubbled cheek with one hand and she could tell by the look in his eyes that he hadn't been awake long. Didn't seem to be hindering his deductive reasoning any, however. "Yeah, last Monday. The only night you've come home late since you moved here."

She sighed. "Oh that. I went to an SPCA meeting. They asked me to be on the board." She opened and peered into the refrigerator, plucked out a bottle of water.

"Did they now?" Her father's voice was intrigued. "Awfully late for a board meeting."

Megan didn't answer, as it wasn't a direct question, and it paid off.

"They never asked me to join the board," he mused, successfully deflected from the topic at hand.

"Maybe they didn't have any openings until now." She drank from the fresh bottle of water, then with dismay noticed the bottle of water she'd already opened minutes before on the kitchen counter.

Her father laughed. "Your mom raised you nice, young lady, you know that?" He shook his head and returned to his coffee at the kitchen table. "No, I was never *their type*, those board members. They'd have sooner put Genghis Khan on that board before me. But I don't care. It's not like I want to plan a bunch of bake sales."

"So how did you even know I wasn't around,

huh? Slow night at the Eagle's Club?" She was starting to breathe easier. Either he was taking pity on her or he'd forgotten the line of questioning he'd started with. The last thing she needed was to be interrogated about Sutter by him too. She'd just shown quite clearly she wasn't up to the task of diverting interest with that wretched reporter.

"Hey, your old man might be young enough to go out some of the time, but not seven days a week. Even I've got to get a little shut-eye every once in a while." He took a sip of his coffee and glanced at the newspaper. "You know, I always thought all the area vets should be on that board, not just a select few. Who better to promote protection of animals, I ask you."

"Too many vets for that," she said. "Besides, most of them are probably too busy to attend. They probably asked me because I'm new, and not exactly swamped with clients."

"Sure, sure, you're probably right. In my heyday I was real busy."

Megan sensed that beneath his bravado there might be a modicum of hurt, or at least dented, pride. "Hey, what do you think the chances are of a harlequin Great Dane and a black having a litter with four blue puppies?"

Her father cleared his throat and straightened slightly, rousing at the mention of animals. "Not great. I've known a few Great Dane breeders and

I think the harlequins aren't supposed to carry any blue in their pedigrees. If the harlequin was badly bred to begin with, though, maybe. Seems like they'd have known that before they bred 'em anyway."

"It's a husband and wife, breeding their dogs to each other," Megan explained.

"What, do they think someone else got in on the breeding? Didn't get what they expected?"

"Actually, it's my friend Georgia's ex-husband." Megan twisted open the water bottle again and took another sip. Swallowing, she said, "She's afraid they used some of her dog's frozen semen for the breeding and not his new wife's harlequin."

Her father was scratching his head again, looking at her speculatively. "Georgia Darling?"

"Yes. Her ex, Clifford, and his new wife are the ones with the litter. I think the new wife was their old show handler. Monique or Mona somebody."

Her father's white head bobbed slowly up and down. "Mona Gibbons. I remember her. She used to have a huge harlequin with a nasty disposition. Vicious. I think it killed, or nearly killed, a dog in the ring once."

"No kidding." Megan wondered why anyone would breed a dog like that, unless it was just too perfectly conformed. "How'd it look? Good-looking animal, I mean?" She screwed the top back on her water bottle.

Her father shrugged and made a distasteful face. "A little short in the forequarters. She said it had a bad angle to the shoulder blade, too, which was one reason she wanted it neutered."

Megan stopped. "Neutered? You neutered that dog? When?"

"Oh," he looked at the ceiling, "two years ago? I remember because she ordered the largest size Neuticles they offered. Didn't want anyone knowing the boy'd been altered, is my guess. But hey, I just do what they ask me."

"She bought *Neuticles?* Did she continue to show him? *Did Georgia know about this?*" she asked, though she hadn't really meant to, out loud.

"How the hell should I know? This was before her divorce, anyway, I think. 'Cause I remember wondering why their handler didn't take her dog to Fredericksburg Animal Hospital, like the Darlings did. And I have no idea if she continued to show the animal. They're not claiming *that's* the dog they're breeding, are they?"

"They just might be. Georgia said the one Mona had before this was a blue and she'd always been jealous of her Sage."

Megan's heartbeat accelerated. This could be just the ammunition Georgia needed—so would it be better to give it to her or not? She needed to check the records, make sure her father was remembering correctly. Make sure it was the same dog. Then she'd think about spilling the beans.

"You don't by any chance remember the dog's name, do you?" she asked.

He scoffed. "Naw. That kind of thing doesn't even register for me. I can tell you breed, color, and age, mostly. That Dane was around two at the time, as I recall."

"So it'd be about four now, which I think is about right." Megan shook her head. "This is bad."

She certainly didn't want to be the reason Georgia got any more furious with her ex-husband, but still, you couldn't just steal some-one's, uh, fertilizer.

"The dog I saw'll be in the records," her father said, then agreed, "it is awfully fishy."

"It is," Megan said slowly. "Somehow I have to check, make sure it's the same dog. I think Georgia even said something about its conformation, that bad front angle, though." She frowned, not relishing the idea of finding the ugly truth. "But surely not. Why would they say they'd bred that dog when it was obviously neutered?"

"Don't forget the Neuticles," her father said. "Those things are damn good substitutes. No-body'd be able to tell by looking at him. Or feeling him, for that matter, like they do in the ring. And she brought the dog to me, one of the smaller prac-tices in town."

Megan uncapped the bottle again, took another swallow and wondered what the right thing to do would be. If Georgia's ex-husband had stolen that sperm, he should certainly be brought to justice. She just wondered what sort of justice Georgia might mete out before the courts had a chance.

"What on earth are Neuticles?" Penelope asked, pulling out of Megan's driveway later that week.

Megan and Penelope were riding together for drinks at Georgia's, since Pen knew where Georgia lived, and Megan decided to get Penelope's opinion on what Georgia's reaction to the news would be.

"They're basically fake testicles," Megan said. "After we neuter a dog, we can implant Neuticles so nobody can tell."

"And Monique had that done to her dog? Are you sure?" Penelope cast her a quick, appalled glance.

"Apparently. I found the records. She told my father the dog's name was King but I checked on the Internet, and her dog Danny's show name is Danny's King of Hearts. The rest looks the same. Age, markings, etc."

"That's pretty damning," she said. "So, are these fake testicle things allowed in the show ring?"

"Absolutely not," Megan said. "Those dogs are supposed to be unaltered, but it's very difficult to tell the real thing from the fake. I imagine Mona could get into a lot of trouble if this were discovered."

"So why would she do it?"

"To calm the dog down. Rumor has it he had quite a problem with aggressiveness."

"So that's why they market these things?"

"Well, technically they're not marketing them to show people. Mostly it's for people who have to neuter their pets for behavioral or health problems, but like the way their dogs look with balls." Megan shrugged and Penelope laughed.

"*Men*," they said together.

Georgia's house was a large colonial on four acres of land in a subdivision just outside of town. She used to live in town, a few blocks away from Sutter, as a matter of fact, but after her divorce moved to this wooded lot with plenty of room for Sage to run. And plenty of room for a Great Dane was *plenty of room*.

They were just pulling into the driveway when Penelope turned to her and said, "Oh I almost forgot! Did you hear? About Sutter and the SPCA?"

Dread filled Megan's stomach. Had he said something else to piss them all off? Surely he'd told that secretary of his to stay away from them . . .

"No," she said warily.

"He sent Wilma Jones a check for ten thousand dollars!" Penelope announced, her eyes wide and laughing.

Megan choked over the news, inhaling wrong and causing her throat to catch and her body to convulse with coughing.

Her eyes were still watering when they reached Georgia's door.

The house was spotless—sandblasted weekly by a team of maids, according to Georgia, as she led them into the kitchen. A large pitcher of margaritas sat on the counter with three glasses and a saucer of salt.

"Hope you girls are thirsty!" she crowed, picking up the pitcher.

Megan grinned. "After what I just heard, hand me the pitcher. I'm not driving."

Penelope pouted.

"Now, now," Megan said, "I'll spring for the cab for both of us, if we need it, okay?"

They filled Georgia in on Sutter's gift, then Penelope picked up a glass. "Fill 'er up! I've had the day from hell." And she proceeded to tell them about the number of friends of her mother's who had come into the shop and the number of times she had to hear the latest about Glenn. "It was Mrs. Newman who really got to me. Instead of just passing on the news, 'Glenn is dating somebody now, did you know?'" She imitated the woman in a haughty falsetto. "She had to add, 'You were a fool to let that one go, my dear. He'll be snapped up in no time!' I could have slapped her. Honestly, my palm actually itched to give her a good hard wallop."

Georgia laughed and escorted them all through the sunroom to the deck. "Honey, if you'd just get a good hard somethin' else none of this would be a problem. Glenn could put his johnson in everythin' that moved if you had somebody servicin' you properly."

"*Georgia!*" Penelope objected, then laughed. "Servicing me properly. Oh my lord, how you *talk*!"

"It's the truth," Georgia said, crossing herself with her margarita while lounging in a deck chair under the warm lowering sun. Her smile was at its most pointed and devilish. "Take me, for example. I was lonesome and horny after Clifford and I split, until I found . . ." She lowered her eyelids a fraction and along with them her voice. "Now you all can't tell *a soul* about this. We've kept it secret nearly a year now, but I thought I could tell you two."

Penelope leaned forward. "Who? Who have you found? Is he here? In Fredericksburg? Am I the *only one* who can't find someone new?" she wailed.

Georgia looked at Megan. "Is she the only one?"

"Never mind." Penelope collected herself. "Sorry, go ahead. Who did you find?"

Georgia gave her Cheshire smile. "Peter Linton."

Penelope gasped.

Megan sat up. "Who's Peter Linton?"

"The *mayor!*" Penelope said. Then, turning back to Georgia, added, "The *married* mayor."

Georgia lifted her glass, toastlike, and leaned back on her chaise. "Not everyone can be single." She took a sip of her margarita.

"Oh Georgia," Penelope said, in her most disappointed tone.

Georgia swallowed and pointed a red manicured finger at Penelope. "Honey, he's *nearly* divorced. He told me. They haven't slept together in years, he lives in the basement, for pity's sake. Poor man."

Penelope snorted. "Poor man. *Huh*. Out screwing the town's most notorious woman . . ."

"Why Penelope," Georgia cooed, "*thank you*."

Megan sat back in her chair and took a long swig of her margarita, feeling it course down her esophagus and stimulate all of her nerve endings in the most relaxing, delightful way.

Then she remembered her news. Georgia was looking pretty relaxed and pleased with herself, so Megan took a deep breath and dove in.

"So Georgia, I was having a talk with my father the other day, and I asked him about your blue Dane problem," she said.

"You mean Clifford's blue Dane problem, don't you, hon?" Georgia said, her eyes freezing over. "It's up to him to prove those puppies are legitimate, as far as I'm concerned."

Megan sent an apprehensive glance at Penelope. "Maybe not."

"Oh I think so," Georgia said. "If he's gonna try and pull—"

"*Georgia*," Penelope interrupted, "listen to Megan."

Georgia's expression grew immediately alert, and she turned to Megan. "You know something."

In for a penny, in for a pounding, Megan thought. "My father neutered a harlequin dane for Mona Gibbons two years ago. Said it had nearly killed another dog in the ring. And she requested Neuticles."

Georgia sat bolt upright in the chaise, spilling her drink over her arm. She placed the glass on the table next to her, barely noticing her drenched hand. "Have you got records on this?"

"Oh yes." Megan nodded. "The name Mona gave, according to the record, is 'King'—"

"But Danny's show name is Danny's King of Hearts," Georgia supplied. "Oh, honey. You have earned your place in heaven, let me tell you." She pushed out of the chair and came over to give Megan a big kiss on the cheek. "Thank you for telling me. Your daddy isn't gonna mind, now, is he?"

"He thinks you still need other proof. He wouldn't be able to say it was the same dog without having done an x ray of something unusual or a DNA test, which of course he didn't do, but it's pretty compelling. And if it came to a court battle, I think he'd be behind you."

Georgia sat back in her chair and picked up her glass, taking a long sip. Penelope and Megan exchanged glances.

"I'll have to think about this," she said finally.

"Yes . . . I have to think just how to go about this . . ."

Megan and Penelope watched her, Megan's stomach fluttering a bit nervously. Georgia was scary when she was angry, and Megan was uncomfortable knowing she had handed her the cannon with which to blast her ex-husband's new wife.

Impulsively, Megan said, "So, I had sex recently."

It took a beat but Georgia finally let go of her thoughts and turned an astonished look on her.

"Sex!" Georgia exclaimed. "*With* someone?"

They all burst into laughter.

"With another notorious citizen," she grinned, sharing a look with Penelope. She shouldn't be doing this, not on the heels of that nosy reporter's call, but she had to change the subject and she knew this would do the trick.

Georgia glanced at Penelope too. "Oh, so that's what you meant by you being the *only* one not to find someone. Well, do tell, honey."

"All right, but this absolutely *cannot* go any further than the three of us," she said.

"And the mystery man," Georgia added, "unless you jumped him in his sleep."

"Oh yeah, him." They laughed. Megan, briefly, told the story of going to see Sutter after the SPCA meeting, and how things turned out much differently than either of them had expected.

Georgia, however, instead of relishing the tale and the fame of its leading man, was strangely thoughtful. "You watch out for yourself with that one," she said ominously.

"What do you mean?" Megan asked. "We've already said it can't happen again. And I'm fine with that, really. He's way too high profile for me." She again thought of that uncomfortable call from the reporter. "*Way* too high profile."

"Hm," Georgia said. "I don't know. He's good lookin', and God knows he's rich as the devil, but I don't trust his dealin's with women. Don't you remember, Pen? What did Bitsy say?"

"Oh Bitsy." Penelope waved a hand dismissively. "She was divorcing him, of course she had nothing nice to say."

"Yes but she did say this one thing all along. She said he was amazin' in the sack, but talkin' to him was like beatin' your head against a wall." Georgia tipped her head back, looking at the sky a moment, remembering. "I think she called him 'The Vault,' didn't she, Pen?"

"Oh yeah," Penelope said thoughtfully. "I remember thinking it made him sound like a professional wrestler."

"The Vault?" Megan repeated. She took another sip of margarita. God forbid the tequila wore off in the middle of this conversation.

"Yes, you could put stuff in there, and it'd be safe . . ." Georgia licked the salted rim of her glass slowly, thinking.

"That's right, I remember this," Penelope

added. "But you couldn't get anything out that wasn't yours." She turned to Megan. "But I already told you that. He's an emotional cripple."

"You also said he didn't like dogs," Megan pointed out, "but he's kept Twister. And he brought her to the park that day. *And* he was walking her the day we had lunch."

"That is odd," Penelope acknowledged.

"He's obviously after you, girl," Georgia said. "He kissed you in the park, threw you in his bed, then ended up skulking around your house to take you to lunch."

Megan pointed her glass in Georgia's direction. "Not all in the same day. And the second time I came to him."

"Yes, darlin', we heard." Georgia gave a lewd cackle.

"I *meant*—"

"Oh I know, I'm just raggin' on you. All I'm sayin' is, you keep whatever this is just physical and you'll be fine. More than fine, really, if the rest of what Bitsy said was true." She laughed her big boisterous laugh and when Megan glanced at Penelope she saw her blushing scarlet and grinning.

Megan chuckled. "Poor Sutter. He doesn't know how little privacy he's really protecting. Speaking of which . . ."

She told them about the call from the reporter at *NatTat.*

"Oh, that sleazy, sleazy man!" Penelope protested.

Georgia shook her head. "You got nothin' but more a that to look forward to if you keep bangin' the billionaire, honey. The moment he steps out in public they're all over him like flies on shit."

Penelope sighed. "It's true. Ever since he and Bitsy divorced and he landed on all those most eligible bachelor lists, they can't get enough of him."

"Kind of like Donald Trump. With better hair." Georgia polished off her margarita. "Who wants another one?"

Two and a half hours later Megan and Penelope poured themselves into a cab in Georgia's driveway. Georgia, teetering in the doorway, waved one hand at them while clutching the doorjamb with the other.

"Bye y'all! See you first thing in the mornin' at the park!" And with that she shrieked with laughter and fell backwards into her front hall. She continued to wave. "I'm all right! I'm all right!"

The cab pulled out and Megan and Penelope slumped down on the vinyl seat.

"Oh my God, I'm going to be *so sorry* tomorrow morning," Penelope said with her hands over her face. "I'm supposed to play tennis at seven A.M.!"

Megan stretched languorously. "Oooh, that'll be fun. Me, I'm just glad I don't have any clients or

I'd probably have surgeries scheduled in the morning. Guess there are benefits to failing. I sure do feel good right now, though."

They dropped Penelope off first, since she lived on the way, and then Megan directed the cabby down Washington Avenue. She just wanted to see if Sutter was awake. She looked at her watch, but couldn't see it in the dark of the back seat.

"Okay, slow down," she directed the driver as they neared Sutter's house. She leaned toward the window. Several lights were on, including the one in his bedroom, the location of which she now happened to know. Just thinking about that night caused her insides to quiver.

"Slower," she said and her breath briefly fogged the window.

"Uh, miss, I don't feel right about this," the cabby said, "Are you spyin' on Mistah Fo—on whoever lives in that there house?"

Megan giggled. "You can say it, I know it's Sutter Foley's house. But don't worry. I'm a friend of his." She laughed at herself again. "Sort of."

"I don't know," the cabby said. "What kind a friend are you?"

She turned to look at him. What had he heard? "What do you mean?" she asked, her senses alert the way only a drunk's can be.

"My friends don't creep 'round past my house in their cars. They either knock on the door or go on by." He pressed harder on the accelerator.

"Wait just a minute," Megan said, feeling as if he'd called her a liar. She wasn't a liar. She did know Sutter Foley. And if you defined a friend as someone you knew intimately on some level, then she most certainly was a friend. She bet he had lifelong friends who couldn't tell you he had freckles from the sun on his shoulders, or the palest, tightest ass she'd ever seen.

The cabby was still accelerating. "Where do you live, miss?"

"Take me back to that house," Megan said, suddenly sure she had to prove something to this man. It didn't hurt either that the margaritas had made her feel as if taking her clothes off and being touched all over would be about the best thing she could do right now.

Besides, she figured, with perhaps slightly impaired reasoning, that without her car to leave near his house this was a golden opportunity to avoid the notice of any nosy reporters.

"Are you sure?" the cabby asked.

"Yes, I'm sure. I'm going to visit my friend. He took me to lunch the other day, you know." *Shut up*, she told herself. This is exactly the kind of indiscretion that makes you juicy game for journalists.

She pulled her purse into her lap and dug through it first for some money, then for her hairbrush. After whipping the brush through her hair, she tossed it back in the bag and zipped it up.

The cab pulled slowly up in front of the house.

"How do I look?" she asked the man.

He turned in his seat and glanced over her with a wary eye. "Like a pretty girl who gone and had too much to drink."

She made a face. "That obvious, huh?"

He shrugged, nodded.

She made a decision. "That's okay. I need to see him. He'll understand."

"You want me to wait?"

She laughed and handed him the money. "I don't think so."

The cabby took it and shook his head.

Megan took a minute searching for the door handle, finding it only when the cabby lit the overhead light.

"Okay, thanks," she said, getting out into the warm night air.

She shut the door of the cab and walked up to the front door of Sutter Foley's house. She felt fine, not drunk at all. She felt great, in fact. And wasn't it fate that Sutter was up in the middle of the night just like she was? Yes, absolutely, she answered herself. It was fate that she even knew Sutter Foley at all. How could his dog coming through her dog door be anything else?

She rang the bell.

For a long time nothing happened.

From the corner of her eye, she noticed that the cabby had stopped again one house down. He clearly didn't think she was going to gain entry.

She hefted her purse higher on her shoulder and shook her hair back.

She knocked again and minutes later the door opened.

Sutter Foley stood before her barefoot, in worn khaki shorts, with a wrinkled white business shirt open to the chest.

He looked delicious.

Eleven

 "Hi!" she said buoyantly. "I hope I'm not in-terrupting anything."

He looked amused. "No, actually, you're not. I just got home from work."

"From work! In the middle of the night?"

"Megan, it's ..." He looked at his watch. "Nine-twenty."

"*Nine*—?"

"That's right."

"Oh my God, I'm so sorry, I thought it was like midnight."

He looked puzzled. "You're sorry it's not mid-night?"

"Well, no. I meant ..." She meant it would have been more obvious fate had had a hand in his being awake at this hour if it had been later, but one of the three un-alcohol-drenched cells left in her brain told her not to get into that. "Can I come in?"

He stepped back and she entered. He started to close the door behind her. Before it latched she said, "Oh, wait wait." Then she bent one eye to the crack between the door and the jamb to watch the cabby drive off. With a triumphant laugh she closed it all the way and turned back to Sutter.

"Megan . . . have you been drinking?"

She grinned. "Well, yes, a little. I only wanted to see the cab drive off. He didn't believe I knew you, see. I think he thought I wouldn't get in the door."

His eyes narrowed. "Did you have some sort of wager with him?"

Her face fell. "No. Shoot. You're right, I *should* have put some money on it. He was totally sure I was one of your computer geek groupies."

Sutter's brows rose.

"Not that that would be so bad," she amended quickly. "I just . . . don't know much about computers. And I'm not a groupie."

One corner of his mouth twitched upward. "What are you, then?"

"Well, I'm glad you asked. I decided in the cab," she threw a hand toward the door to the street, illustrating where the cab had been, "that I was a friend. Because friends are people who know each other intimately, in some way. And you and I . . . well, that is I . . ." Too late, she saw where she herself was heading, and a blush hit her cheeks, hard.

To her surprise, he laughed. Deep dimples lined each side of his mouth and those green eyes actually sparkled. She found herself smiling in return.

"So where's Twister?" she asked.

He crossed his arms over his chest. "I wondered how long it would be before you asked. She's in the yard. She likes it out there, even if the new gardener doesn't."

"She doesn't stay out there all the time?" She frowned.

He scoffed. "Hardly. Any more than an hour or two and she'd actually reach China."

Megan laughed, putting a hand to her mouth, and momentarily lost her balance. Sutter reached a hand out but she righted herself before he could help her. She was afraid with just one touch she'd feel compelled to jump him.

"Can I get you some coffee?" he asked, with a slight but solicitous bow.

She took a deep breath, put a hand to her blush-hot forehead and said, "That would be great."

She followed him into the most gorgeous kitchen she'd ever seen. It took up the whole back side of the house and had every kind of stainless-steel appliance invented. Despite that, it was cozy, with dark wood beams, a wooden pot rack suspended over the stove, deep ochre walls and warm amber granite counter tops. She loved it instantly.

"Do you even know how to make coffee?" she teased, watching him pull an espresso maker from against the wall.

He slid her a look. "Oh ye of little faith. I am a master coffee maker."

Sure enough, he served up a cup of French roast and even steamed the cream so it resembled a latte. "Sugar?" he asked, holding up a sugar pot.

"Thanks, honey," she grinned, reaching for it.

He narrowed his eyes but a chuckle escaped.

To her delight, he sat down across from her at the thick, country kitchen table, folded his hands together on the surface in front of him, and they chatted. About nothing, about everything. About his gift to the SPCA. "Just a little cleanup PR," he said sheepishly.

Before she knew it she felt relatively sober, but could not stop looking at the turn of his lips when he smiled, the fine crows' feet that spread from the corners of his eyes, and the sexy way his hair was slightly disheveled.

She also couldn't keep her eyes from his hands. She remembered so well how they'd touched her most private places, how skilled they were in manipulating every nerve ending in her body. Square and large-knuckled, they were strong hands, yet deft. She imagined one of them sliding down her hip to her thigh, then over to her moist, hot arousal . . . she remembered how he'd kissed her, then taken her nipple between those sculpted lips and pulled, creating torrents of fire and light and energy and thrill along every single pore of her skin.

Thinking about it she almost couldn't breathe, and she found herself taking a sharp inhale when his tongue brushed out briefly to wet his lips.

"Megan."

Her eyes shot up to his. They seemed to glow in the dim light of the cozy kitchen.

"Are you all right?" he asked, leaning forward a bit onto his elbows.

"Yes," she murmured, gazing squarely into those mossy green eyes. Her own dropped to his mouth, and she rose up on her feet, put her hands in the middle of the table, and leaned toward him.

He stood and met her halfway, their lips colliding over the sugar pot. Their tongues sought each other and whirled together, deepening the kiss, drawing their mouths even closer, seeming to make their breath, their faces, their thoughts, one.

Megan put one knee on the table and pushed closer, until she was kneeling on the surface, pressing her body against his. His arms came around her tightly and the warmth of his body radiated through his thin cotton shirt. His hands, those strong, square hands skimmed under her skimpy tee shirt and slid up her back. She sighed into his mouth. She *knew* it would feel good to be touched. She knew what she'd needed was this, skin on skin, breath on breath, desire on desire.

And what she needed now was him inside of her.

She sank lower on her knees and pulled him down with her. Placing one hand on the table, she felt the sugar pot overturn and decided to ignore it. A second later he was putting a knee onto the table himself and pushing his hands into her hair as he laid her down on her back and kissed her thoroughly.

Her fingers went for the buttons of his shirt and nimbly undid them. He began to pull up her tee and she arched for him to pull it to her shoulders, then raised her head as he swung it off. God only knew where it landed.

His hands cupped her breasts in their lace cups, let them fill his palms and looked at them, his eyes glowing. "You are . . ." he murmured, leaning down to run his tongue along her cleavage, "incredible." He reached around her back, she arched again, and he unclasped the bra, sending it off with the shirt.

She pushed his shirt along his arms and down his back. "Your turn," she said, her eyes raking his chest, well-defined pecs, trim stomach, with that sandy line of hair pointed downward . . .

Then she went for his shorts. They came off easily, as did her little cotton skirt, and then they were naked on top of the table. Megan could feel sugar sticking to her back and her upper arms like sand and had a thrilling *From Here to Eternity* moment.

He leaned over her, kissed her once, then smiled down. "Don't you look delicious," he said mildly, "here on my kitchen table."

"Hope you're not watching your sweets." She ran one finger through the scattered white granules on the table and held it up to him.

He took it in his mouth and she gasped at the sensation. She grabbed the back of his head. He tasted of sugar when she kissed him.

"Do I need . . . ?" He paused, kissed her again. "I have protection."

She pulled him down and kissed him deeply. "It's all right," she whispered against his lips, moving her head so that her lips brushed lightly along his. "Don't worry."

Their tongues twined again, and just as she'd imagined he ran one hand down her side, then between her thighs to part the hair that was so damp with desire. His fingers caressed her and she sighed, lifting her hips into his hand. When his lips found her breast at the same time, she thought she'd died and gone to heaven.

But she hadn't seen nothin' yet. His mouth made its way down her body, over her belly button and down . . . lower . . . then lower still. He flicked her with his tongue, then sucked, and Megan's hips rose high, her body electric with the sensations.

Minutes later, just as she was on the verge of spiraling out of control, he pulled himself away and slid her gently to the end of the table. Sugar grated beneath her and made her giggle. He sucked one shoulder and murmured close in her ear, "So sweet."

Parting her legs around him, he ran the head of his rock-hardness along her desire. So ready for him, it was all she could do not to grab him and envelop him with her heat.

She crossed her ankles behind his back and pulled him gently with her legs. He smiled, his eyes smoky, and lay his hands on her hips. Then he pulled, ever so slowly, until she covered him completely. He gave a low moan.

She exhaled and arched her head back. "Oh lord."

He pulled back a little, then pushed in again, deeper. She felt as if he were touching her soul, so deep was he inside of her. She opened her eyes and found him looking at her face. Reaching down, she took his hands in hers. They clasped, fingers intertwined, and he leaned over her, looking into her eyes, as he thrust, slowly at first, into and out of her. Her hands, still in his, were pinned next to her on the table.

His rhythm increased. Megan's heart slammed against her ribcage in time with it. The cords stood out on his neck and she felt his hands tighten, then crush hers in their grip. She squeezed back just as hard, with her hands, with her legs, with her very core.

Thrust for thrust they met each other's hips,

their lips parted, their eyes locked together, until Megan felt her world blitz apart and she closed her eyes with the overwhelming sensation.

A second later, Sutter pushed one last time, exhaling long and hard, his body trembling above her.

They went upstairs to shower together, licking the sugar off each other's skin as they bumped against one another on the steps. She never thought she'd be able to actually giggle with this man, but here they both were, getting punchier as the night went on in the darkened house.

His shower had six heads, something she could not get over and found a thousand jokes for. But they soaped each other up with care, and rinsed each other off with relish. He even shampooed her hair. She felt as if she'd been massaged inside and out.

When they stepped out of the steamy stall, he handed her a thick white robe and wrapped a towel around his waist.

"Will you be staying the night?" he asked, polite as a bellhop.

Megan smiled, wondering if she should, doubting it would be wise. She could get too comfortable here and forget all about The Vault. She started to shake her head slowly. "I can't. I've got Peyton to let out and I can't show up late for work. Bad example, you know."

Their eyes met and Sutter looked as if he understood something. Megan wasn't quite sure what, but resisted an impulse to correct him. Let him think it was she who was holding back, she thought. *For God's sake, for once keep your mouth shut and not be the one whose heart gets taken for granted.*

He nodded and she moved into the bedroom. "I guess my clothes are somewhere in the kitchen."

"Somewhere . . ." He smiled slyly, then added, "Let me get dressed and I'll give you a ride home."

She waved a hand. "No, no, that's all right. I like the walk." She needed it to clear her head, if nothing else.

"Don't be silly, Megan, it's late. You can't walk home alone."

She laughed. "Sutter, it's perfectly safe. It's a few blocks through," she spread her arms, "the *best* neighborhood. I'll be fine." She went to him and kissed him softly on the lips. "But thank you."

"You are a stubborn one, aren't you," he murmured, holding her a moment too long before letting her go.

"Sometimes." She slipped away and started for the door before she could change her mind.

"Megan," he stopped her.

She turned, brows raised.

"This is . . . well, it's not brilliant timing, but I was wondering . . ." He looked disconcerted, which intrigued her. She came back toward him. "About birth control. I didn't think," he shrugged haplessly, "last time, and only at the last minute this time. When you said 'don't worry' you meant . . . ?"

Despite herself, something inside of her stilled.

"I meant there's no danger. I've been tested and I . . . can't get pregnant." She took a deep breath before adding, "I can't have children."

Then she turned and headed out the door.

In the end, though he protested a little more, and even tried humorously to keep her from gathering her clothes, she left.

And she hadn't seen him since.

That had been over a week ago. Did he think about her at all, she wondered. And if he did, was it because of anything other than sex? Surely he thought about that night. It had been so incredible for her, she had to believe it was at least good for him.

But maybe he did that kind of thing frequently. Perhaps with some of the more understanding and less whacko groupies.

For the thousandth time she thought about that moment he'd asked her if she were staying and wondered what might have happened if she had. Would he have made her breakfast in the morning? Would they have reached some other conclusion than this eight-days-going-on-forever silence? Would it have felt more emotional this time simply to sleep with him, to climb into bed sated and warm from the shower, to curl up and be held by him? Would it have felt less like sex and more like l—

"Dr. Rose?"

Megan glanced up to see Allison standing in her office door.

"Mrs. Walters is still waiting," Allison said, flipping her hair back and looking hassled at having to tell her again. "With Hildy? Her cat?"

"I'll be there in just a minute." She straightened. "I just need to finish this. Ask her to wait one more second."

Allison sighed. "All right."

Megan looked down at the paper in front of her, where she'd drawn a series of curlicued Ss and Fs instead of paying the stack of bills beside her. She was losing it. She'd done just exactly what Georgia had warned her not to. She'd fallen for The Vault. Thinking back on their lunch, and even their companionable chat that night in the kitchen—the specifics of which were mostly lost in a tequila haze—she didn't remember things getting very personal. Except, of course, for the physically personal part.

But then there was that moment when she'd told him she couldn't have children. A sinking feeling returned to her stomach at the memory. Something had flashed across his face. Something like pity, or disappointment. Or had she just imagined it? Though she strove with all of her being not to believe it, she wondered if she had blown whatever small chance she might have had with him by revealing that inadequacy.

Not, she reassured herself, that she considered it an *inadequacy*. She was who she was, her body was built the way it was built, and that was life. Just . . . she couldn't help acknowledging the fact that to someone who really wanted to start a family, who'd perhaps looked forward their whole life to having children, *heirs*, maybe even to creating a dynasty to quote the *National Tattler*, it would certainly be a relationship inadequacy. A flaw.

A deal breaker.

She sighed. This was silly. She was trying to interpret his feelings without knowing or even asking what they were. Surely she owed it to the situation to find out what was in his head, even if it was not her. She wasn't asking for a commitment, she wasn't looking to pin him down, she wasn't even asking what he thought was in their future. She just wanted to know if he ever wanted to see her again. Didn't she owe it to herself to ask? Maybe she even owed it to him.

With a burst of conviction, she pulled the phone book out of the bottom desk drawer. She knew she wouldn't be able to find his home number but SF-Solutions should be listed. Sure enough, she found it in seconds flat. Before she could change her mind she dialed.

"Good morning!" a loud, chipper voice said,

"SFSolutions, Arnetta speaking, how may I help you?"

"Good morning," Megan said, wishing she'd thought a moment about what she intended to say. But sometimes impulse dictated the most honest conversations, and she firmly believed that honesty was never a mistake. "Is Sutter Foley in? This is Megan Rose calling."

"I'm sorry, Mr. Foley isn't in. Can I take a message?" the amplified voice asked. Megan actually had to hold the phone a little away from her ear when the woman spoke. She wondered briefly if this was the woman who'd come to the SPCA meeting.

"Yes, please. Let him know I called and . . ." She thought quickly. "And . . . that I'd like to see him again, if he'd like it. No pressure, though." She laughed.

"Oh, I've got it. Anything else?"

"No, that'll be all, I guess," Megan said.

But her emotions screamed otherwise. *Yes! Tell him I miss him inexplicably; tell him that, even though I resisted, I feel something for him; and tell him I'm wondering if he feels anything for me, even just plain desire.* But she couldn't ask that. Not, at least, through his secretary.

Voicemail! Megan thought.

"All righty, then, thank you for calling!" the woman chirped and hung up.

"Damn," she said out loud to the dead phone

line. Should she call back? Or let the message stand? It did say, basically, what she wanted.

She sighed again. She couldn't think about this any longer. She had to work, for pity's sake.

She rose to her feet. Hildy the cat, she thought, Hildy the cat. What was her problem again?

Of course, she thought, looking at the chart. The cat was pregnant.

Sutter leaned back in the wing chair and stared briefly up at the ceiling of Aunt Edna's sitting room. She was in the restroom with Lucy and would be out in a minute, which was good. It gave him a moment more to collect himself.

He'd arrived at Sunrise Hills irritated. Just before leaving the office, Arnetta had handed him another handful of incomprehensible messages. Someone wanted to see him if he wanted to see them but Arnetta had put no name on the "From" line; someone claiming to be a "Mr. Smith" was interested in a breakfast meeting but she'd written nothing about why or what company he was with; and someone else, improbably named Frosty, had called for no discernible reason at all.

He could probably blame his sleeping problems on Arnetta alone, though he'd also been having trouble getting work done since Megan's visit last week. He truly believed if he could just get some consistent sleep he would be able to stop thinking about Megan in inappropriate ways.

Unfortunately, it seemed to take having sex with Megan to cure his sleeping problems. Once again, the last time they'd been together he'd had the best night's sleep in days.

And though he knew he shouldn't, he'd been hoping she would stop by again just about every night since the last time she'd come, the night she'd been out with her friends. For some reason he was able to justify their trysts if she came to him. If he were to go to her, however, he would feel as if he were leading her on.

Or himself. One or the other.

Aunt Edna emerged from the bathroom with Lucy behind her and he was glad to see that she was dressed properly and wore makeup—a sure sign that this was another "good" day.

He and Lucy exchanged pleasantries before the aide left the room and Aunt Edna fixed him with her most piercing gaze.

"So, how is the young woman into whose eyes you so unwillingly fall?" she asked, a devilish look on her face.

"Bad news," he said, trying to be light and failing. "You won't be rooting for her when I tell you what she told me the last time we met."

"What is it?" She looked concerned.

"It was quite personal, actually. I don't feel at liberty to say, exactly," he said, wondering what had gotten into him to want to be so open with another person's private information.

"So you're getting closer to her," Aunt Edna said, a note of satisfaction in her voice. "You've developed that friendship you said you wanted."

He leaned forward in his chair, his elbows on his knees, and looked down at the floor. "I suppose so. But . . . I'm not sure I can handle it." He looked up at his aunt, the one person on earth who knew him better than anyone else. Better than Bitsy. Better than Lizzy, even.

"What do you mean? Of course you can handle it," she said indignantly. "You're the strongest, most caring and loyal man in the world, Sutter Foley. Don't let this blooming fame you're so unhappy with make you second guess yourself."

He chuckled softly. "It's not the fame. It's just . . . when she told me this personal thing I felt . . . I felt almost hurt, on her behalf."

Aunt Edna hesitated, then said, "Well, isn't it something you could help her with?"

He shook his head. "I don't believe so. I don't even know how I'd offer, frankly. But I have to say I was moved by it. And daunted that she would confide in me. It was . . . a tragedy, I believe."

"I see."

But she couldn't see, he thought. Not unless she'd seen the pain in Megan's eyes the way he had in that instant after she'd told him she couldn't have children. She could have answered his question differently. Could have told him she was on the pill, or had taken care of contraception some other way, but she'd just laid it out there. She could not have children. And he'd never before met someone who he thought would make a better mother.

"Are you sorry she told you?" Aunt Edna asked.

"No. I'm more . . . I'm amazed by it. She hasn't a dishonest bone in her body. Not even to protect her own privacy." He tented his fingers together in front of him and lowered his forehead to the index fingers. "While I . . ."

"While you what?" his aunt prompted.

He raised his head, dropping his hands. "I give away nothing, confide in no one. No one but you, that is." He smiled at her wryly. "But I've been accused of being selfish with my thoughts. Perhaps a bit obsessive about my privacy."

"Don't be daft, Sutter, you have dozens more intrusions on yours," his aunt objected. "You've got to be protective. She chose to confide in you and that's a wonderful thing. You're being a friend, just as you wanted to be. You should feel good about that."

"She only confided because I asked. She didn't volunteer it."

Aunt Edna paused. "But it was her choice. She could have said nothing."

He smiled and shook his head. "Not Megan."

Another week had passed since Megan left Sutter that message and she was now convinced she'd made a terrible and foolish mistake. One she shouldn't have made at this stage in her life.

He wasn't interested. He'd just taken what she'd offered—freely, she reminded herself—and then he'd had enough. His girlfriend had moved to town and she, Megan, was history.

"Maybe he didn't get the message," Penelope said. "Things like that happen all the time."

Megan smiled at her wanly, her fingers playing with one of Peyton's silken ears. The dog's muzzle rested against her knee.

"Maybe," she said skeptically.

They were sitting under the trees at the dog park, a humid breeze blowing over them like air out of a convection oven. Even the dogs were lethargic. Penelope's Wimbledon was sprawled in some mud a few feet away. Only two other people were in the park and their dogs, a golden and some kind of beagle mix, were walking slowly around the fenceline with their tongues lolling.

"But even if he didn't get the message," Megan continued, "he hasn't called me anyway. And if he wanted to see me, he would call. That's Dating 101."

Penelope sighed. "He might feel bad. I mean, that woman did just move to town, supposedly because of him. That Briana person. Maybe he needs time to break up with her before calling you."

Megan let go of Peyton's ear and the dog shifted so that she lay along Megan's thigh. She pulled away an inch. A hot furry animal was not what you needed up against you in ninety-eight-degree weather.

"Why in the world would he break up with her?" Megan asked, anger at the situation tingeing her voice. "She's beautiful and classy and rich—"

"He couldn't possibly care that she's rich," Penelope interjected. "Or that you're not. He's got more money than God."

"Okay," Megan said, "but she's still beautiful and classy. And she's still in his league. Unlike me. I'm just . . . I'm nobody."

"Now, Megan—"

Megan shook her head and held up a hand. "No, Penelope. I appreciate your trying to make me feel better about this, but let's call a spade a spade. Okay, I know I'm not *really* a nobody, not in the vast scheme of things, but let's face it, in Sutter Foley's world I am definitely one of the little people. And the bottom line is, if he wanted one of the little people he'd have a lot more choices than just me."

Penelope patted her hand. "But he couldn't do better than you."

"Oh please, he used to be married to Bitsy Powell, and she was rich and beautiful too, right?"

Penelope admitted it, reluctantly.

"So there's no question that wealthy women are his type." Megan pushed her sandals off and ran her feet through the grass.

"We're talking about two women," Penelope

said. "That's not much of a sampling. Who knows who else he's dated in his life? Besides, rich women are probably the only kind he meets anymore."

"Well, regardless," Megan continued. "Whatever list he has of desirable qualities, they obviously aren't the ones I have or he'd have called. No, I did this to myself. I went after him. I made it easy for him. I was fun and available and discreet." She laughed cynically. "I let him have the milk for free. Can you believe how right our mothers always turn out to be?"

"And always at the worst times," Penelope agreed. "Although, my mother wasn't right when she said Glenn and I would have beautiful children together."

Megan gave her a sympathetic look. "You'd have beautiful children with anybody, Pen. I mean that."

Penelope smiled at her. "And you, Megan, will find someone who loves the cow even more than the milk. I'm sure of that."

Megan laughed. "That's right. There's got to be someone better for *me* out there, too, right? I mean, I may not be the right woman for him but he's not perfect for me either. He doesn't love animals, for one thing."

"That's right!" Penelope said, jumping into the game. "And he's a workaholic. Day and night and weekends. You'd never see him."

"Talk about an unbalanced life! I can't be with someone who doesn't know how to play. *And* he's a terrible communicator. Doesn't know his own emotions from a hole in the ground," Megan added.

"Let alone care about yours!" Penelope jabbed her finger decisively toward Megan. "That would drive you crazy, wouldn't it?"

"Of course it would! And he's—he's aloof, and weird about his privacy." Which she could understand, but still. As long as she was thinking Perfect Soulmate she could add it to the list.

"He'd never let your friends come over, if you lived with him," Penelope added, nodding. "You'd be a prisoner in that mansion."

Megan couldn't imagine letting that happen, but went with the flow. "Right. And he's a snob."

"Right." Penelope sat back in her chair and gathered her hair in one hand, sighing. "Okay. So now we know what we have to do."

Megan had tired of the diversion too, finding her mind coming up with arguments for every point. "What's that?"

Penelope smiled and gave her a sideways glance. "Find someone who wants to buy a cow!"

Twelve

 "Miss Montgomery is here." Arnetta's voice over the intercom was accompanied by something that sounded like marbles spilling onto the floor in the background.

"Send her in," Sutter said, even though he was in the middle of a document and Montgomery was early. They had a meeting in Washington they had to leave for in forty-five minutes, to ink a new contract with a large multinational company needing software support. He was just putting the finishing touches on a memo to human resources about what positions would need to be filled for the new work. The project was a coup, snatched from the near-victorious grasp of a larger software company, and Sutter was anxious to get them signed on the dotted line.

Montgomery entered the office with her briefcase in one hand and a newspaper under her arm. Forty-five minutes early was taking enthusiasm to absurd heights, in his opinion, but Montgomery was nothing if not gung-ho.

"Have a seat," he said, not slowing his typing, "we've got some time before we have to leave."

"Yes, I know," Montgomery said, taking a seat across the desk from him.

As he focused on the document in front of him, he became dimly aware that Montgomery had unfolded her paper and put it in the center of his desk. Ten minutes later he finished his on-screen thought and turned to her.

"What's this?" He picked it up and instantly felt annoyed. The *National Tattler*. He nearly threw it back on the desk, but she had obviously brought it for a reason. Instead of looking at it, he opted to look at Montgomery. "Let's cut to the chase. What's in it?"

Montgomery, her face a mask of trepidation, said, "I'd rather not paraphrase, sir. It's referenced on the front page, but the article's on page three."

Sutter sighed and studied the tabloid. In the top right-hand corner was a picture of himself and another person sitting at a table. Upon closer inspection he saw who it was and nearly groaned aloud. It was Megan Rose, sitting with him on the deck at Brock's.

He snapped open the paper to page three.

BILLIONAIRE DUMPS HEIRESS
FOR POOR VETERINARIAN
By Tanner Pierce

He closed his eyes and felt fatigue wash over him. How did they get away with making this stuff up? His lawyer counseled him repeatedly that a lawsuit would only make things worse. It would draw attention to the article by coverage of the civil action in mainstream news sources and therefore reach people who would not otherwise be concerned with or even aware of the *National Tattler*'s speculations.

Still, it was infuriating. And there'd be hell to pay with Briana, who was becoming increasingly insistent about defining their relationship anyway. No doubt that was because he'd been holding her at bay since she'd moved to town. He had to get over his abnormal backwards guilt about Megan before he could figure out his feelings for Briana.

He read on.

FREDERICKSBURG, Va.—With Briana Ellis still unpacking boxes in her newly rented home just yards from Sutter Foley's Fredericksburg, Va., estate, the handsome billionaire Foley was seen in a cozy lunchtime tete-a-tete with hometown beauty Megan Rose. Rose, a local veterinarian, when reached for comment said, "Yes, we did have lunch. And he's very nice. We're . . . friends."

Sutter stopped and read that sentence over. "Rose, a local veterinarian, when reached for comment . . ." He looked up at Montgomery, appalled. "She was *reached for comment?*"

"Apparently," Montgomery said.

"What the bloody hell is she doing talking to these people?" He nearly threw the paper on the ground, but he had to see what else she'd said. "Doesn't everyone know not to talk to the *Tattler*?"

"I would think anyone with even half a brain would know, sir." Montgomery kept her expression bland.

Sutter continued to read.

Lunch is not all they've been sharing, however. Rose's car has been spotted at Foley's estate late in the evening, prompting speculation about the exact nature of their relationship. When suggested to Rose that things might be more friendly than she was letting on, she laughed coyly and said, "That would be quite a story, wouldn't it?"

Indeed it would. And this reporter is on it.

In characterizing her relationship with Foley, Rose suggested with some pride that this article be titled, "Billionaire dumps heiress for poor veterinarian!"

Rose, however, was not completely without sympathy for her competition. Acknowledging how hard the news would be for the heiress to take, Rose lamented on her rival's behalf, "Briana is gorgeous, rich and exactly his type. I'm nobody." In other words, she believed that news of Rose's relationship with Foley was bound to be very upsetting for Ms. Ellis.

Foley biographer and *CelebRiches* magazine writer Drew Martin commented, "Megan Rose obviously has high hopes for this relationship, casting herself, rightly or wrongly, ahead of Briana Ellis in the contest to win Mr. Foley's heart. And checkbook."

Foley, having been burned by love once already and still, according to reports, grieving the loss of his first wife, does not seem likely to make a decision between the two quickly.

Martin continued, "If I had to bet, I'd put Ellis in the lead, with Rose coming in a distant second. Despite her delusions of grandeur, she's just a bit of small-town entertainment on the side."

Still, with regard to her late nights at the Foley mansion, Rose was not above exulting in her perceived triumph. When asked how Foley was in bed, she exclaimed ecstatically, "Oh my God!"

Sutter put the paper down slowly. They'd seen her car at his place. They'd photographed them lunching. They knew that something was going on and if he hadn't been such an idiot and *let* something go on this would just be one more harmless lie the paper had concocted.

Instead, the cat was struggling to get out of the bag.

It was his own damn fault. He'd dragged Megan Rose into this cauldron himself and discovered that he didn't know her at all. This proved it. She was an accident. An impulse. Anyone looking at it objectively would call her a pickup, even if it hadn't exactly felt that way.

He hadn't intended to have an affair with her. And he certainly hadn't thought it would lead anywhere. And now, here she was, talking to the *Tattler* as if they'd agreed they had a future.

"Do you think she's trying to force your hand, sir?" Montgomery offered.

Sutter slowly focused on his VP's face. "Force my hand?"

"That Rose woman." Montgomery nodded toward the paper. "If she makes a stir, causes Briana to break up with you . . . maybe she thinks something will happen between you."

Sutter studied her a long moment. "You don't believe what's written here?" It almost wasn't a question, and part of him hated that his tone misconstrued the truth of the situation.

"Of course not." She looked indignant at having been asked. "I mean, I know you've had dealings with her, because of that dog. And you obviously went to lunch. But that does not translate to the billionaire dumping the heiress to me." She frowned. "You're worried about Briana's reaction to this, aren't you?"

He stared at the paper. "Among other things."

"I'm sure she'll understand," Montgomery said. "But you may want to see a little less of this Rose woman."

Sutter's eyes darted to Montgomery's. "The day I start altering my behavior because of a bloody rag like this one is the day I have my head examined," he said sharply, his vehemence surprising even himself.

Montgomery's expression was taken aback. "I was thinking more of altering it for Briana, not the *National Tattler*."

"Six of one . . ." he muttered.

"I beg your pardon?"

He looked up to see Montgomery's face as alert as any reporter's.

"I answer to no one, Montgomery," he stated, "least of all those who try to manipulate me."

"Is Briana—?"

"The paper," he said irritably, shaking it once. "Let's leave Briana out of this."

"Of course." Montgomery's gaze dropped to her lap.

The intercom buzzed. Arnetta's voice filled the room. Was it just him or was it abnormally loud? "The car is here for you, Mr. Foley."

Damn. The meeting. Sutter rose. "All right. No time to think about this now." He threw the paper in the trash and grabbed his briefcase. It would be tough shifting mental gears from this revelation but he could do it. He had to. Later, he told himself, he would figure out why the idea of seeing less of Dr. Rose had made him so angry.

Exiting the office, Arnetta got up from her seat, bumping into her desk lamp and sending the chair into the permanently dented file cabinet.

"Good luck, sir," she said, waving as if he were half a mile away.

"Thank you, Arnetta."

"I know it's going to go great. I just feel it," she added. "This is going to be your Waterloo!"

Sutter halted in the doorway and looked back at her. "My Waterloo?"

"Yes, sir!" She beamed.

"Arnetta, you realize that Waterloo was Napoleon's greatest defeat, do you not?"

He didn't have time to quibble about it, but his Waterloo was seeming all too close at hand to let the remark go.

Arnetta looked consternated. "His defeat? Oh, uh, well *somebody* won, right?"

"Wellington."

She brightened. "Right, then. That's what I meant!"

"Darling, that's Fred Carson," Briana leaned toward Sutter and breathed her low words into his ear, "he writes for *InStyle* magazine. Let's invite him over, shall we?"

Sutter sighed. "You know how I feel about that, Bri. And don't you think we owe it to your other guests to maintain some privacy?"

He nodded toward her friends across and

down the table, a group of six he'd met a couple of times before who appeared regularly in New York's society pages. He had little hope of gaining support from them in this matter but it was worth a try.

Briana gave him an arch look. "You know they won't mind. Besides, *InStyle* isn't like that rag that's been after you and your little *flirtation*."

Her words were pointed and it was the first inkling Sutter had gotten that Briana had seen the *Tattler* article. He'd debated telling her about it, but as they were not even sleeping together these days—and she'd been rumored to have been tete-a-teting with a famous real estate mogul in New York last month anyway; a man he knew she liked to socialize with mostly because of the press he garnered—he decided the conversation would be inappropriate. Not to mention that he did not want to start explaining himself at every cock of the shutter.

He lifted one eyebrow at her.

She shifted her gaze, uncomfortable. "Besides, they are very respectful," she continued. "Every time I've appeared in their mag they've made me look my very best."

Sutter shook his head. "Briana, I don't want them here. It's bad enough they're even in this restaurant. In this *town*. They're only here to intrude."

"They won't be intruding if we invite them over," she hissed, her glance darting back to Carson, obviously hoping to catch his eye. "It's been weeks since anyone's reported on the two of us, Sutter. They virtually ignored my move to Fredericksburg."

Sutter sat back and gazed at her. "What of it? Do you want your new address nationally known?"

"Darling, I'm only thinking of you," she crooned. "This kind of publicity can help your business. As a stockholder, I can tell you I don't think you use your celebrity nearly enough for the good of the company." She sat up straighter and looked across the fancy dining room toward the press. "Look, I think he's dining with Maria Sandoval. She's that divine photographer who covered my beach party last year."

"Bri, honey," her friend Bibi called less than discreetly across the table, "isn't that *InStyle* mag sitting over there? Let's invite them over."

"Well, I thought we should," she said, sliding a hurt look toward Sutter. "What do the rest of you think?"

Below the chorus of "why not" and "sure" from the inebriated group, Sutter leaned toward her and said, "Briana, if you invite them over here I'm leaving. I've had enough of the media in all forms for one month."

Briana held out a hand toward the rest of the group. "But they want—Oh, Fred!" she called suddenly, her hand darting into the air in a fluttery wave, as the man in question rose from his table.

He glanced over and gave a wide smile, for all the world as if he hadn't realized they were here. "Briana, hello!"

Sutter shook his head.

"And is that Maria with you?" Briana asked, her own smile muted and pretty, the way it usually was in photos. "Why don't you two join us?"

Fred and Maria made the move as quickly as two people could possibly switch tables, leaving behind drinks, napkins, appetizers—but not notepad and camera.

"And Sutter Foley too," Fred said jovially. "Looks like we've hit the jackpot tonight. Bibi, Tom . . ." He nodded to the two others he recognized.

While they were looking for a second chair for Fred, Sutter rose from his own.

"Take my seat, Fred, I've got to leave early this evening anyway." He answered Briana's brittle smile with a cool kiss on the cheek. "Goodnight, darling," he said, his tone icy. "I'll ring you sometime."

"I hope it wasn't something we said," Fred laughed, shaking Sutter's hand goodnight.

In truth, Fred Carson wasn't bad as journalists went, but Sutter had had enough of the limelight, and was especially annoyed that Briana couldn't keep herself out of it for once at his request. Usually he indulged her in her desire for coverage, knowing she usually managed to keep it tasteful. But tonight he'd just wanted to relax.

He bid the rest of the group goodnight and made his exit.

Outside, he decided to walk. It was late, the restaurant they were in about the only one in town that stayed open long enough to accommodate Briana's continental dining demands, and there were few people out. But it was warm and Sutter needed to calm down. He decided to walk home and send someone for the car in the morning.

He was about to pass La Petite when two men stumbled out the front door in front of him. One was white-haired and slightly overweight, the other was younger and slim.

"Easy, there, doc," the younger one laughed, holding up the other. "I thought you said you were going to have another drink."

"Well, I *was*, 'till that overgrown gorilla in there told me I had enough," the older man slurred.

"I guess as a vet you'd know an overgrown gorilla when you saw one," the first man said.

At that, Sutter slowed just enough to keep the two men within earshot. They hadn't noticed him yet, even though the younger man seemed considerably more sober than the other.

"Damn straight I know 'em," the white-haired man said. "He's kicked me outta there before, the bastard. But it ain't like I was buying the drinks this time, thank you very much."

He nodded at the other man, then shook his head, making himself dizzy enough to stumble. The other man held him up.

"That sonofabitch," he continued. "He oughta start treatin' me better, and he will, goddamnit. He will when he realizes who I am."

"Will he?" the young man said. "Why's that, doc?"

"Ah, ah, ah," the older man said, wagging a finger at his companion. "You been tryin' to get stuff outta me all night long but I'm too smart for that. Who my daughter's dating ain't no business of yours, mister."

"You mean Sutter Foley?"

The older man stopped at the mouth of an alley between two buildings. "Hang on, hang on," he said, belching a little. He pointed into the alley. "I gotta see a man about a dog," he added and began laughing, fumbling at his belt buckle and moving into the darkened space.

The younger man waited a moment before pulling a slim camera out of his front pocket and training on the man in the alley.

"Smile, doc!" he laughed. "You're next month's cover model!"

Sutter reached him in four strides, knocking the camera out of his hands and pushing him up against the brick wall.

"You bloody tosser," he growled, gripping the man's shirt so tightly he gave a little cough. "I know who you work for. Do they actually pay you to get your subjects pissed before you humiliate them with photos?"

"Well, if it isn't the man himself," the reporter choked over the hold Sutter had on him. "Care to comment on Doc Rose's assertion that you're dating his daughter? Or maybe I should just say *shagging*."

Sutter dragged the man off the wall and threw him to the ground. Then he turned and picked the camera up off the floor of the alley.

"Hey, what's going on?" Doc Rose said, zipping up and looking at the man on the ground.

"I'll tell you what I'll comment on," Sutter said. "I'll comment on the fact that if I see one word printed about this evening or this gentleman I'm going to buy your bleeding paper and the first person I'm going to fire is *you*, Tanner Pierce."

"Hey, you two know each other!" Doc Rose crowed. "You wouldn't be Sutter Foley, would you now?" he asked, giving Sutter a delighted look. "My daughter speaks real high of you, you know." He held out a hand to Sutter and swayed on his feet.

Sutter popped the memory card out of the small digital camera and put it in his pocket. Then, after double-checking the internal memory, he handed the camera to the man picking himself up off the ground.

He turned to the older man and shook his hand, pulling him gently toward the mouth of the alley.

"Come with me now, Dr. Rose," he said quietly, eyeing the reporter to make sure he didn't follow. "And let me get you a cab home."

From: "Elizabeth Powell" Bitsy@worldnet.net
To: <SF@SFSolutions.com>
Date: Wed, 9 Aug 16:01:01
Subject: Re: Escapades

Darling! You've become international news. And I couldn't be more shocked at the reason. Imagine my surprise at seeing you in the *National Tattler*. I had to laugh at the "pining for his first wife" part. But are you actually reconsidering the elegant Miss Ellis? I have to say, I think it's a good idea. It is said in circles over here that she never met a photographer she didn't like. Though I imagine the one who snapped that shot of you and the veterinarian is no favorite. But Sutter, two women at once! And one of them an indigent. You may not want to hang on to Briana, but the insolvent one is no doubt after your money (though darling, I don't mean to say you wouldn't make it *fun* for the poor girl). Still, where in the world are you finding the time? As I recall you barely had time for a wife, let alone a girlfriend and a tart on the side.

I suppose times change. Got to run. Have meditation at six, followed by cocktails at the embassy. And I still have to see Henri about my hair!

Ciao, darling,
Bitsy

From: "Sutter Foley" <SF@SFSolutions.com>
To: "Elizabeth Powell" Bitsy@worldnet.net
Date: Thu, 10 Aug 08:37:42
Subject: Re: Escapades

Surprised you would read that rag at all. Has your gossip network deteriorated so completely that you must now rely on materials printed for the masses?

—S.

From: "Elizabeth Powell" Bitsy@worldnet.net
To: "Sutter Foley" <SF@SFSolutions.com>
Date: Thu, 10 Aug 13:27:02
Subject: Re: Gossip

Sutter, when it comes to you I have always had to rely on outside sources for information. You are hopelessly uninformative. Am I to believe, then, that this isn't true? My gossip network, as you so sensitively referred to my friends, tells me Miss Ellis is in a funk. Who is this Megan Rose person? Tell me she's not related to that disgusting little man who used to try to pick me up at La Petite. If she is, perhaps the *Tattler* got it right. They seem to be an oversexed lot.

Massage at 2, must run.

Ciao,
Bitsy

From: "Sutter Foley" <SF@SFsolutions.com>
To: "Elizabeth Powell" Bitsy@worldnet.net
Date: Fri, 11 Aug 08:04:12
Subject: Re: Gossip

Megan Rose is a friend. Miss Ellis is unhappy with me for other reasons.

Be honest, Bits, how bad of a husband was I?

—S.

From: "Elizabeth Powell" Bitsy@worldnet.net
To: "Sutter Foley" <SF@SFSolutions.com>
Date: Fri, 11 Aug 23:44:17
Subject: Re: Marriage

You were a wonderful husband, when you wanted to be. Impenetrable when you didn't. It was all up to you, dearest.

Why? Who are you planning to marry?
Bedtime awaits.

A bientot,
Bitsy

From: "Sutter Foley" <SF@SFSolutions.com>
To: "Elizabeth Powell" Bitsy@worldnet.net
Date: Sat, 12 Aug 04:24:57
Subject: Re: Marriage

Sutter stopped typing and stared at the blinking cursor. Had he made a decision? Or was he just reacting to events of the last week?

Not that he had any doubts. No, the last week had opened his eyes considerably. He was not a fool, not if he trusted his intellect. It had never once let him down. Even when Bitsy had left him and he thought his heart would turn to stone, he'd known that it was for the best. And it had been. He couldn't imagine being married to Bitsy now.

No, at least one path was clear. He had made his decision and it was the right one.

He put his hands on the keyboard and typed:

If I were planning to marry, don't you think I would tell my good friends at the *National Tattler* first?

—S.

* * *

"We have to get out," Penelope said on the phone, "and we need to go where the quality people are, not some bar."

"The quality people, huh?" Megan said.

"Yes, you know, the ones who can afford to buy a cow," Penelope said.

Megan laughed. It hadn't taken her long to realize that Penelope had more than a little of the debutante inside her. Not that she was a snob, not at all. She just had no intention of ending up with someone unsuitable—and by unsuitable she seemed to mean "poor." Considering that Megan had not only married, but before that, dated many an unsuitable man, it couldn't hurt to ride along on Penelope's coattails and see what a "quality" man might be like.

She tried to ignore the fact that the only man she thought of when it came to the subject of dating, not to mention "quality," was Sutter. Talk about unsuitable. Aside from the fact that he hadn't called her in a month, he was the type of man who was clearly unobtainable to someone like her. She was a fool to have ever entertained any kind of romantic thoughts about him.

But she had. And unfortunately even now she thought of him far more than she knew she should. Especially since that horrible article had come out in the *National Tattler*. She could just kill that Tanner Pierce for twisting her words so disastrously. And the way he'd written the article made it sound as if half the things he said were her thoughts too. She came across like an egomaniacal idiot. If Sutter had seen it she would just have to move, that's all there was to it. He'd think she was a fool. Beyond that, a . . . a Jezebel.

"And where do the quality men hang out?" Megan asked.

"That's just the point. They don't "hang out." They go to *events*. Benefits, fund-raisers, balls, that kind of thing."

"Balls?" Megan repeated, picturing a bunch of animated Prince Charmings. "Do people really still have *balls*?"

"Of course. Charity balls and things like that. But that's not what I have in mind."

Megan squelched an urge to say "uh-oh." She heard paper shifting in the background over the phone. "What do you have in mind?"

"Here it is. A chamber music concert. At St. George's Episcopal church. Reception to follow."

"Chamber music, huh?"

"It's great. I went last year. The church is historic and the acoustics are lovely, and all the best people in town go."

Megan had to smile. *All the best people.* "Well, okay, sure. What the heck."

"Really?" Delight was evident in Penelope's voice. "Oh, I'm *so* glad. I always had to drag Glenn out to these things, but this'll be fun. Just you and me. I can't wait!"

The event was the following weekend, Sunday evening, and Penelope had Megan join her for a little shopping foray the Thursday before. Megan couldn't afford or justify buying a new dress for the occasion but she really didn't want to show up to an event with "all the best people" wearing one of her cotton sundresses. She chalked it up to advertising costs—an attempt to get the best people to bring the best pets to her for the best care.

She was exhausted the night they went shopping but sucked it up in the name of new friendship. Work had picked up, which was great, but as the only vet she was run ragged by the end of the day. Still, she and Penelope had a good time. And Penelope talked Megan into buying an amazing red halter dress that, according to Pen, covered all the Ss, making her look shapely, stylish, and sexy.

Megan didn't know about any of that, but she did know when she looked in the mirror she barely recognized the girl looking back at her.

Penelope had picked out a black and white party dress for herself, spaghetti-strapped and cinched at the waist with a dancing skirt, that looked gorgeous on her. Simple yet sophisticated, a look Megan would have envied if she had not been so mesmerized by her own classic yet vampish look.

The concert was packed. They parked several blocks away and when Megan saw the crowd, she felt fatigue wash over her again. Maybe she wasn't up for this. Maybe she was more of a "some of the pretty good people" type person. Seeing so many men in tuxes and women in little black dresses suddenly made her feel conspicuous in her candy-apple red.

"I don't know about this, Pen," she said, slowing her walk from the car toward the church. She knew she couldn't back out now, but something was making her more nervous than normal. Her usual bravado was for some reason not kicking in.

Penelope slowed too and looked at her, worried. "What do you mean?"

Megan shook her head. Was this a premonition? Or was she just tired? "I don't feel right about this. Like, I don't know, I don't belong. What if these people have seen that stupid article?"

"Oh please," Penelope said, "Nobody believes anything said in those tabloids."

"That's because they don't know the people involved. Gossip about people they've met might be different."

"I doubt they've even seen it. It's not as if it was on the front page and visible in the checkout line at Giant," Penelope protested. "Besides, most of these people wouldn't be caught dead reading anything that wasn't the *Wall Street Journal* or *Town and Country*."

"I don't know . . ." Megan persisted. "Are you sure I don't look like a homewrecker in this dress?"

Penelope looked relieved. "Don't be ridiculous. You look incredible. And Sutter is not even living with that Briana person so there is no home to wreck. Most of these people are old fuddy-duddies anyway. I just thought it would be fun to get dressed up. Besides, I can introduce you to some people you should know."

Megan took a deep breath. "Of course. You're right, I'm sorry. But don't forget I've got that doctor's appointment first thing in the morning so I can't stay out late."

"I know. I want to leave early too. I have tennis tomorrow morning. But your appointment is just a checkup, right? Oh and you're going to see Dr. Lee!" she said, obviously just remembering that she had recommended this doctor to Megan. "I nearly forgot! She won't mind if you sleep while she checks you out."

"I just hope I don't sleep through the alarm," Megan said. "Yesterday I woke up twenty minutes after the clock radio had come on. That never happens to me."

Penelope took her arm. "Don't worry. We'll just go in, mingle a little bit and find a seat. You'll like the music, Megan. There's nothing like a violin to nourish the soul."

"I know. You're right. I don't know what's gotten in to me." She picked up her pace again and they headed for the crowd at the church. It was a sultry evening, and the church was too old to be air conditioned, so many were standing on the front steps, chatting and laughing, holding clear plastic glasses of wine cupped in cocktail napkins.

"Cynthia!" Penelope waved to someone as they neared. "How *are* you? I heard about little Justin's piano recital."

Megan marveled at Penelope's social skill, the details she knew about people's lives were amazing. She was always so enthusiastic, and yet sincere about everything she said.

"You heard?" Cynthia, a polished blonde with an abundance of gold jewelry, exulted. "That he won first place?"

"I certainly did," Penelope said indulgently. "Mrs. Monroe was in Wednesday and told me all about it." She turned to Megan. "Mrs. Monroe is Justin's piano teacher. And doesn't she just love having bragging rights to that!"

Penelope and Cynthia laughed together and Megan thought about slipping inside to find a seat.

"Oh, Cynthia Belton, this is my friend Megan Rose," Penelope said, taking Megan lightly by the arm and drawing her back into their circle of conversation as if reading her thoughts.

"How do you do?" Cynthia said, extending her hand.

"Nice to meet you," Megan said, taking the chilly fingers in her hot ones. She wondered if all the best people exuded a similarly refrigerated air and if her hot paw was what would give her away.

"That's a gorgeous dress you have on, Megan," Cynthia said. "Wherever did you get it? And why haven't we met before?"

"Oh, I took her to Silvio's," Penelope said.

"I just moved to town," Megan said, trying to shake off her uncharacteristic cynicism. "I'm the new vet at Rose's Animal Hospital."

Even as she was looking at her, Megan could swear Cynthia's gaze went glacial. "At Rose's? You aren't—are you *related*?" The question was almost incredulous, and Megan felt the first inkling of dread trip up her spine. Maybe this was why she'd been so reluctant to come tonight.

"Yes, he's my father." Her chin rose a fraction.

"Really?" Cynthia looked at her a moment more—sizing her up, it felt like—then let her eyes slip just past Megan's right shoulder. "Oh, look. There's Charles. Do excuse me, Penelope. I've got to talk to Charles."

And just like that, she was gone.

Megan's blood stalled. This was bad. Never had she been so snubbed before in her life. Never had she felt so *looked down upon*. Surely she hadn't imagined it.

Penelope looked around happily. "Should we get some wine?"

"Penelope," Megan said in a low voice, "didn't you *notice* that?"

Penelope leaned in. "Notice what?"

"That woman." Megan glanced behind her to see Cynthia standing with a tall, white-haired man in a tux. Both of them were looking at her. "Cynthia. She found out who I was—or rather, who my father is—and bolted."

A crease developed between Penelope's brows. "No she didn't. She wanted to talk to Charles." She looked around, saw Cynthia and looked back at Megan. "And she's talking to Charles. Charles Van Dorn. Oh, he's such a nice man. I should introduce you to him, too. He has Irish wolfhounds. You should see them, they're the most amazing animals I've ever seen. I swear, you look in their eyes and you see old souls. Like they've lived many lifetimes before."

Megan sighed, misgivings gnawing at her stomach. Or was it hunger?

"Let's find a seat, okay? The concert starts in a few minutes anyway, doesn't it?" Megan said.

Penelope looked at her diamond-edged watch. "You're right. I can introduce you around afterwards."

They found a seat in a pew about halfway back from where the musicians were set up. Megan, determined to shake off her strange frame of mind, let herself be charmed by the nineteenth-century pews with doors on them, the balcony encircling the nave and the elaborate, stained glass windows that lined the walls.

The music was lovely too, and by the intermission Megan was lulled back into the calm that had been missing earlier. Penelope had been right. There really *was* nothing like violin music to nourish the soul. She almost felt as if she'd been massaged.

At the intermission, Penelope and Megan went back out onto the front stairs and let the warm night air blow gently over them. Megan lifted her hair off the back of her neck and looked up into a clear night sky. Only a few stars were visible, as they were standing near the open lighted doorway, but she thought she could pick out the Big Dipper.

Penelope was talking to a lovely young woman named Blythe, who was married to a Captain Miller who stood nearby in his dress blues. A handsome couple, Megan thought, feeling warmly toward Blythe because she did not recoil when they were introduced.

"Oh my God," Blythe said, grabbing Penelope by the arm and leaning toward both her and Megan. "Did you see that?"

Penelope and Megan gazed in the direction Blythe was looking.

"Sutter Foley," Blythe said, at the same moment Megan caught sight of him.

Maybe it was the tuxedo, maybe it was the stunning, bejeweled woman on his arm, or maybe it was because she hadn't eaten dinner, but Megan's stomach hit the floor and she thought for a moment she might actually be sick.

She hadn't seen him since the night they'd had sex on his kitchen table. She could still feel the sugar on her skin, sticking like sand and scrunching under her body as she'd writhed under his skillful ministrations.

"God, have you ever seen a handsomer billionaire?" Blythe said with a laugh.

"Aren't they *all* handsome?" Penelope quipped.

Blythe laughed. "None more than this guy, I'd be willing to bet. Who's that he's with?"

Penelope sent an apprehensive glance Megan's way. "Briana Ellis. She's from Massachusetts, but she just moved to town a couple weeks ago."

Megan felt the blood drain to her feet. She'd moved to town and Megan hadn't heard from Sutter since. That told that story clear enough, she thought. Between Briana and that wretched tabloid, Sutter was probably determined never to see her again.

As the three of them stared at him, his eyes raked the crowd, coming to rest on Penelope.

She gave a little wave and he nodded back.

Then his gaze shifted to Megan and she felt all the blood leave her head.

The expression in those green eyes could have frozen every drink in the hand of every person between them, and she knew beyond a shadow of a doubt . . .

He'd seen the article.

Thirteen

"Excuse me," Megan said, too abruptly, and turned to push through the crowd, away from Penelope and Blythe.

Away from Sutter's icy gaze.

The restroom, where was the restroom? She should have asked Penelope, but when she turned around to go back, she saw that Sutter was making his way through the crowd toward them. She wheeled and headed back inside. Somebody else could tell her where it was.

She pushed through the people at the door, hearing some hisses of disapproval as she did so less than gently, and asked an elderly woman just inside the door where the ladies' room was. She directed Megan down the stairs.

Precarious on her unfamiliar heels, Megan bee-lined for the steps. She made it down only to find the door was locked, and an old-sounding voice warbled, "Just a minute," when she tried the knob. She leaned against the wall next to the room, one hand on her forehead.

She had to be coming down with something. She felt positively clammy.

A moment later more footsteps sounded on the steps and Megan watched in mounting apprehension as limber tuxedoed legs came into view, leading to a pair of lean hips, a broad chest, then the handsome—if chilly—face of Sutter Foley.

What were the odds, she wondered, that he would be searching for the restrooms at the same time she was?

Between slim and none, she discovered.

He hadn't been looking for the restrooms, she could tell the moment he laid eyes on her.

"Megan," he said. His low voice and polished accent made her name sound like someone else's. The look in his eyes made her wish she *was* someone else. "I need to talk to you."

At the sound of more footsteps coming down the stairs, he glanced around, then took her by the elbow and steered her down a short hall to a darkened Sunday school room.

She went willingly, if only to get out of the glare of the hallway light. She could tell her face was blushing furiously. She knew what was coming and it was the last thing she wanted. He was going to acknowledge the awkwardness of Briana, he would address the undefined nature of their own sexual relationship, and he was going to inform her that her romantic aspirations as outlined by Tanner Pierce in the *National Tattler* were beyond ridiculous.

He was going to assume there were emotions on her side, and no matter how true that turned out to be she didn't want to have to endure his pity. Or more likely his guilt about misleading her, which would feel like pity.

And she didn't want to have to hear about how this Briana person was the chosen one. The one who merited public outings. On the heels of all her discomfort at not belonging in this elite crowd, and in the wake of Cynthia Belton's obvious censure, she did *not* need Sutter Foley's excuses for fucking the nobody while marrying the rich girl.

"Megan," he said again, "what in the world were you thinking, talking to the *National Tattler*?"

"Oh, I was hoping you wouldn't see that. Sutter, I'm sorry. That guy—" she began, but he wasn't finished.

"Hoping I wouldn't see it? Megan, when people I know speak to the press about me, I usually hear about it. And to speak to that blasted tabloid, of all places! They've been after me for weeks, ever since they got hold of those pictures of my house. Looking for dirt or scandal or deception, anything they can pin on me." He looked at her as if fathoming an entirely new person. "And you've fed right into it."

She took a step toward him and stopped. "Sutter, I'm sorry, but you have to understand—"

"No, Megan," he interrupted, his eyes intense, "*you* must understand that these people are devious. You cannot play along. Ever since you've talked to them suddenly everyone I know seems to be reading the sodding rag. Do you know what it's like to have people calling you up, clamoring to know what the hell's going on in your private life?"

"Actually, yes," she said, some heat in her voice.

He gave an ironic smile. "Yes, I suppose you do, now. In a small way. Imagine if that happened to you every day, Megan. *Every bleeding day.* Imagine if every little thing you did, every mistake, every wrong turn, was publicly analyzed by a group of malcontents eager to do you harm."

Megan choked back a sudden lump in her throat. "Are you calling me a wrong turn, Sutter?"

He sighed and ran a hand through his hair. "I don't know what you are, Megan. Just as you're probably wondering what the devil I am to you. This may seem like a lark to you now, seeing your name in print in a celebrity magazine, but for me it's a daily curse. This week alone I've been approached by every bloody gossip magazine there is. The damn phone is ringing off the hook as if I'd announced to the world I was opening up my life for public viewing. And all because you chose to tell them what happened between us. Why,

Megan? Why did you do it? What did you think would happen?"

Megan's heart dropped in her chest. "What do you mean, *what did I think would happen?* I didn't plan that. I was as shocked as you were by that article."

"Are you saying you didn't speak to this Pierce person?"

Megan felt the telltale blush hit her cheeks. "I did, but—"

"No, don't explain," he exhaled heavily and looked at the floor, "I know how they operate. They ambushed you, you didn't know what you were saying, the next thing you knew he'd extracted information you didn't intend—"

"He *twisted* what I said, Sutter. I didn't—"

"I know, you didn't make anything up. And our . . . encounters have been real. But don't you see how important it is to keep them out of the press?"

"Sutter, would you please *listen to what I'm saying?*" Rage thundered through her veins. "I didn't *take* them to the press, as you seem to think. I was tricked into a conversation and my words were twisted. I told him we were friends, and *that's all*. But frankly I'm starting to see that even that isn't true. I haven't a friend alive who would suspect me of doing what you have accused me of tonight."

Sutter looked disconcerted at her vehemence. He glanced toward the door and lowered his voice. "Megan, I haven't accused you of anything. You simply don't understand how careful I must be. Many people I have dealt with have used the press in order to manipulate me—"

"*Manipulate you?*" She felt as if she'd been struck. "Are you saying you think I want to—to *blackmail* you or something?"

"No, of course not. No."

"Okay," she said icily, "what, then? Something worse? You think I wanted to become famous for screwing the rich guy? To ride your coattails onto the illustrious pages of the *National Tattler*?"

"No—Megan, you're missing my point."

"Then enlighten me, please. I'm trying desperately to figure out what your point is."

"Just that you must be careful about talking to reporters about . . . about something as personal as what went on between us."

"Listen, Sutter," she said angrily, her voice dropping as she stalked toward him. "I'll let you in on a little secret. People like me are not accustomed to being approached by reporters for any reason, let alone our sex lives. Especially not sleazy tabloid ambulance-chasers like that *National Tattler* guy. I was shocked and confused when I got that call. And I'll admit that I botched the conversation pretty badly. Then he misconstrued the few things I did say and added a few things of his own." She stopped in front of him, her eyes pinned on his. "Honestly, I thought I hadn't given him anything he could use. It wasn't until the article came out that I realized how dangerous those guys really are. But *you* knew, Sutter. You've just spent the last fifteen minutes telling me how experienced you are with them. So why didn't you warn me?" She crossed her arms over her chest and tilted her head. "And why, I have to ask, are you surprised that they caught you cheating on your girlfriend?"

He took a deep breath. "I was not cheating on my girlfriend. Briana and I have no . . . exclusive arrangement."

Megan didn't bother to quell the scoff that rose within her.

He colored and his eyes hardened. "Regardless, in the past there has never been anything for them to catch. I've never done anything like that, like this, before."

She shook her head, dropping her arms. "Doesn't count. Not in this courtroom," she said, turning away. She couldn't stand that close to him and maintain her objectivity.

"I'm not defending myself," he said. "Neither one of us is on trial, here, Megan."

She turned back and put her hands on her hips. "No? Then why did you come marching down here if not to collar me like I was a criminal with a lot of explaining to do?"

His face was dark, unreadable. "I wanted to know what you were thinking."

"What I was thinking? What *I* was thinking? Oh, that's just great, coming from The Vault."

At that he looked startled. "What did you call me?"

"The Vault. You know, the thing that's impossible to break into? But hey, I'll tell you what *I'm* thinking, like it's ever a mystery. I'm thinking I was crazy to get involved with you in any way. And I'm thinking that it was my own fault. I asked for trouble and got more than I ever anticipated." She took a quick breath. "I have no illusions about us, Sutter. I know people like you end up with people like Briana Ellis. Who, by the way, as long as we're throwing stones, you never seemed terribly concerned about when we were together. So let's just . . . call it even."

Sutter stood silent a long moment, looking at her sadly. Finally he said, "You're right."

She'd been about to give up and turn away, but that stopped her. "I beg your pardon?"

He paused. Then, "I said, you're right. I wasn't thinking. And I forgot what it's like to be caught off guard by a reporter for the first time. I . . . I do owe you an apology."

He looked contrite, damn him. Contrite and guilty, all those awful second-rate emotions she didn't want from him.

"And I should have told you about Briana

sooner, even though that relationship is not as they've characterized it. Hearing about her from a reporter must have been . . . unpleasant." He shook his head, gesturing back upstairs, presumably to the place where she'd seen him with Briana. His eyes glittered in the light from the hall. "This was not right. We should have talked about it. I should have explained before you had to run into us."

"Sutter," she said, sending a desperate wish heavenward that whoever was in the damn bathroom would get the hell out so she could go splash some cold water on her face. "I'm not looking for an apology. At least not for that. I knew about Briana before the reporter called. And maybe I don't need to apologize for the reporter, but there is one thing I would like to say. You and I—whatever you and I were—are *finished*. Clearly I do not fit into your world, nor did I enjoy 'seeing my name in print in a celebrity magazine.'" Her tone as she quoted him was scathing. She took a deep breath and finished more gently. "It was truly nice while it lasted, Sutter, but it's done now. Let's just . . . forget we ever met each other."

His expression was immediately disconcerted and she congratulated herself for her performance.

"Forget we ever met each other?" he repeated.

"That's right." Her heart slammed in her chest and she could hardly believe her own words. But there was no way she could continue this . . . whatever this was between them, if he thought her capable of trying to manipulate him through the press. Her pride had been assaulted tonight, but that was small compared to being thought of as a celebrity hanger-on by the very celebrity she was sleeping with.

"Forget we ever met each other," she repeated, breathing as hard as if she'd just run a mile with the devil on her heels. But she was not far enough away from him yet. "Clearly we've caused nothing but trouble for each other."

At *last* the door to the bathroom opened, and a crooked old woman in a feathered hat emerged. Megan felt the impulse to head for the door, but something stopped her.

The look in Sutter's eyes, the high color in his cheeks, the obvious effort he was making to reconstruct what he thought had happened, all had her wanting to take him by the shoulders and shake him.

What about that night at his house, when he had looked at her so tenderly? What about the laughter they'd shared? What about the incomparable thrill of being together, just the two of them, neither of them famous or poor? *They* were not part of this madness of fame and gossip and wealth, she thought, the madness that contained things like the *National Tattler* and Briana Ellis. Whatever it was between them was something different, something better . . .

But no, she needed to shake *herself*. If nothing else he'd made it perfectly clear tonight that his main concern was keeping whatever was between them a secret. Like something shameful . . . something wrong.

"I've got to go," she said, forcing herself toward the door instead of pulling him into a dark corner like she wanted to. A dark corner where it was just the two of them and they could forget about all of this, forget "all the best people" upstairs, and most of all forget Briana Ellis. But there were some things—well, *many* things—sex couldn't solve.

"Megan, wait. You—" He stopped, dropping the hand he'd reached out toward her. "I have made so many mistakes." He paused. "But I never thought of you as one. Not you," he insisted—to himself?

She forced a smile, maintaining a calm she did not remotely feel. "Until you saw the *National Tattler*."

He stiffened, then swore.

She raised her brows, schooling her voice to sympathy. "Look, I know it must be tough, living in a fishbowl the way you do. I know I wouldn't be able to stand it. That one encounter with the *Tattler* convinced me of that. But in the future, Sutter? Could you just maybe give me the benefit of the doubt?"

He bowed his head once. "Absolutely. I should have been more sympathetic to the effect I had on your life, instead of thinking only about your effect on mine."

She smiled sadly. "I guess I'm glad I had some effect on yours. Even if I was a 'wrong turn.'"

He was quiet a moment, then he approached her and took her arms in his hands. Desire raced along her skin.

"You've got it backwards," he said, looking down at her with eyes so kind it hurt. "It is my road that you don't wish to be on. Trust me."

For a moment she was caught, stuck in the look in his eyes and by an emotion—something even stronger than desire—that pulled at her chest. Before it swallowed her whole, she pulled back from his hands.

She gave a light, thoroughly unconvincing laugh, and said, "Well, no need to get out the hair shirt."

He regarded her steadily, not fooled by her bravado. "I hope I see you again. Not the same way, I understand . . . but . . . well, you know what I mean."

A lump grew in her throat and she felt that dangerous emotion welling to the surface, ready to spill over. She had to stop this. After everything they'd said, she didn't need him thinking she was suffering a broken heart on top of everything else.

"I'm sure we'll see each other around. It's a

small town, right?" she offered, glad that in the dim light her expressions might not be visible.

His voice was gentle. "I'm sorry if I've hurt you."

Oh God, this was the worst. It was torture. She didn't want him to be *sorry*. She wanted him to want her, and if he didn't . . .

"I'm not hurt!" she protested. "You have nothing to be sorry for. I told you, I understood how things were from the beginning. And hey, we all know monogamy is not a natural state."

He stopped, regarding her with puzzlement. "You don't really believe that."

"Of course I do." She threw a hand out with, she hoped, insouciance. "Men and women are sexual beings, and tying ourselves to one person sets up the unreasonable expectation that we can overcome our own biological imperatives. It's simple science."

"Megan—" he started, but she couldn't stop.

"No really." Her voice was rising but she didn't seem to have any control over it. "All you have to do is look around. The proof is everywhere. Fidelity is a fiction. I believe that, I really do."

Why, then, did she feel tears—actual inconvenient, weak, stupid *tears*— pricking her eyelids? She blinked them away and turned toward the stairway.

But Sutter was next to her in a heartbeat. "Megan, you don't have to do this," he said in a low voice.

The same low voice he'd used weeks ago, when they'd been alone in another dark room. *Don't you look delicious, here on my kitchen table . . .*

A breath caught in her throat. "Do what?" she squeaked.

He took her upper arms in his hands and turned her toward him, looking intently into her face, trying too hard to see the truth in the dim light from the hall.

The truth that even Megan was shocked by.

She had fallen for him, head over heels. For all her bold words and bolder actions, for all her determination that she didn't want a relationship, that he was just somebody she desired, she felt emotion as big as a tidal wave threatening to sweep her away.

"Megan," he said gently, and pulled her toward him.

Then a flash blinded them both.

Megan heard Sutter's voice. "What the—?"

A flash went off again. "Gotcha!" a male voice laughed. "What do you suppose Miss Ellis will think of this, Sutter Foley?"

"Bloody hell—"

Belatedly, Megan realized it was a camera. Someone was taking pictures of them. Here, alone, in an empty Sunday school room, with Sutter's hands on her.

She stepped quickly away, squinting toward the door.

Through the retinal echoes of the flash, Megan saw a man in a short-sleeved shirt and jeans, with a camera around his neck and another in his hands, laughing at them.

"One more for the *Tattler!*" the man said.

And she was blinded again.

Megan fled. She pushed past the man with the cameras, the smell of his sweat brushing her nose as his laughter rang in her ears, and she charged up the steps.

The commotion had caused people to gather near the top of the staircase and Megan pushed through them too, oblivious to their questions about what was going on, was everything all right, and was that Sutter Foley?

Megan headed for the door like a horse fleeing a burning stable, only stopping when a hand grabbed her forearm and wouldn't let go.

She whirled to see Penelope's distressed face. "Megan, what is it? Oh my God, you're *crying!*"

Megan pushed the dampness off her cheeks with her fingers. "No, I'm not."

Penelope followed her out the front doors, glancing anxiously behind as if someone might be after them. "What is it? What's wrong? Megan, you're scaring me."

Megan reached the sidewalk and stopped. "I'm sorry. It's nothing. Really, I'm fine." She glanced past Penelope and saw people emerging onto the steps. "I just—got upset so I think I'd better go home. You go on back in and enjoy the rest of the concert."

She started to pull away but Penelope protested. "Megan! I'm not going to just go back inside and *enjoy the concert*, for pity's sake."

Megan stopped, took a deep breath and wondered why on earth she felt so out of control. "I'm sorry," she said again and forced a smile, "but I really have to get out of here."

"Come on then," Penelope said in the most no-nonsense voice Megan had ever heard out of her. "Let's get the car. I'll drive you home and you can tell me what happened."

"Oh my God," Megan moaned once they were in the car. Her head was in her hands and she rocked back and forth. "Oh my God, oh my God, oh my God."

"What *happened?* Did Sutter do something to you?" Penelope started the car and peeled away from the curb as if the cops were hot on their trail. In seconds flat they were pulling up in front of Megan's house, headlights flashing across the darkened animal hospital next door as Penelope turned into the driveway.

Megan recounted the conversation with Sutter for her, every word seeming to have been burned into her memory. She had to stop once or twice to regain control over her voice, or to stem the tide of tears that, having once broken free, now refused to stop for any length of time.

Penelope made soothing sounds and asked soft, encouraging questions, making no judgements, offering no platitudes. She simply rubbed Megan's back whenever she leaned forward to cover her face with her hands and let a few more self-pitying sobs escape her.

Finally, she was talked out.

"You really fell for him, didn't you?" Penelope said softly.

Megan's throat threatened to close up on her again, but she shook her head angrily as if she could will the emotion away. "Oh Pen, I'm such *an idiot*. How could I have fallen for him? That's like falling for Luke Perry when you're fifteen."

"Honey, no," Penelope said. "You're not an idiot. For goodness sake, who *wouldn't* fall for a man like that? He's got everything. Charm, good looks, wealth . . ."

"None of that is what I fell for, though." She looked at Penelope and nearly wilted under her pitying eyes. "I swear, Penelope. There was something else between us and I truly believe he felt it too. We were good together. I felt like . . . like we *knew* each other somehow."

Penelope nodded.

"Oh I know you don't believe me," Megan said, grabbing another Starbuck's napkin from the glove compartment and drying a fresh round of tears. They were just falling out of her eyes now, like water from a leaky faucet. "But it's true.

I will believe it 'til the day I die. There was *something* between Sutter Foley and me. He just didn't want it."

"I believe you," Penelope said. "Though I'm not sure I agree that he doesn't want it."

"It doesn't matter," Megan said, blowing her nose.

"No, I mean it."

Megan looked at her askance.

"When Sutter came through the crowd tonight," Penelope continued, "heading for you, there was a look on his face. Something . . . I'd never seen before. I looked at him, then I looked at you practically running into the church, and I thought . . ."

Megan straightened. "You thought what?"

"I thought, 'He loves her,' " she said simply. "It was all over his face."

Megan's breath caught. "Really?"

Penelope shrugged, looking miserable on her behalf. "That's what I thought."

Megan leaned back in the seat. She was exhausted. She felt like closing her eyes and going to sleep for a week.

"I don't know. He's so hard to read. At first I thought he was livid. Then he was so kind . . . Oh, it's just so confusing." She took a deep breath and sat in silence a moment. "I cut it off, Pen. I told him we should pretend we'd never met. I told him we only caused each other trouble. Do you think that was stupid?"

"Not if that's how you felt," Penelope said.

"But I didn't really. I mean, I know I caused him trouble but he . . . he was no trouble to me."

"Are you sure? That reporter never would have accosted you if not for him."

Megan waved a hand dismissively. "I don't care about that. Who believes those rags, anyway?"

Penelope shrugged.

"In any case, he said he was the wrong road for me to be on anyway. If that's not a kind way of blowing somebody off I don't know what is."

Penelope glanced over at her, opened her mouth, then closed it again without speaking.

They sat in silence for several minutes. Finally Megan sighed, reaching for the door handle. "Thank you so much, Pen. I don't know what I would have done without you tonight."

"You wouldn't have been there at all," she said ruefully.

"Then it would have happened somewhere else, somewhere along the line. I did enjoy the concert, though." Megan smiled. "What I saw of it."

"Well, that's something. Call me tomor . . ." The word dwindled off her lips as they both watched a Lincoln Navigator pull into the parking lot of the animal hospital next door. It turned off its headlights and continued around the building to the back side, the one they couldn't see from where they were parked.

"That's Georgia's car," Penelope said.

"What in the world is she doing here?" Megan said, watching the next-door building as if she could see the car through it. "Surely she's not . . ." She looked at Penelope, and a giggle escaped her. "You don't think she and the mayor . . . ?"

Penelope gasped and a hand flew to her mouth. Then she, too, giggled. "Oh my God—they're probably necking!"

"Necking! Pen, you crack me up. Who says 'necking' anymore?" Megan said, laughter making her feel whole again the way nothing else could have. "We should go sneak up on them."

"Oh we *should*. We could scare them to death!" Penelope launched into a whole new round of laughter.

Then a light came on in the animal hospital.

"Wait a minute." Megan leaned forward in the car seat.

Penelope quieted and leaned forward too.

"What's she doing in there?" Megan murmured, then glanced at Penelope. "I wonder if this has anything to do with Danny and those puppies . . ."

Penelope opened the car door. "Come on. Let's find out."

Megan stuffed the tear-damp napkins in her purse and got out, and the two of them slipped noiselessly across the grass in the warm summer air.

Fourteen

Penelope and Megan rounded the corner of the animal hospital to see Georgia's huge Lincoln Navigator parked by the back door. The engine ticked as it cooled.

Megan pushed open the back door and stepped in. Voices carried from the middle exam area, so she and Penelope crept past the bags of food, the cat litter, the extra crates and supplies, to look into the brightly lit area.

Georgia, her dog Sage, and Megan's father clustered around the examination table.

Megan and Penelope exchanged knowing looks.

With a fortifying breath, Megan straightened her shoulders and strode into the room. "What's going on?"

Everyone jumped and Sage barked, then saw

her and began wagging his tail. Her father turned around, a puppy cradled in his arms.

"Oh thank God," Georgia breathed. "I thought you were Clifford."

"It's not nice to sneak up on people," her father said, trying on a parental frown.

Megan stopped next to them and stroked Sage on the head. He sat slowly and leaned his entire body weight against her. She braced herself with a foot and crossed her arms over her chest.

Penelope stopped just behind her. "Oh my God, is that one of Clifford's puppies?"

"Looks like I'm not the only one who's been sneaking around tonight," Megan said. "This is disgraceful. Hasn't anybody ever explained the idea of ethics to you?" She nailed her father with a stern look.

"Don't be mad at him." Georgia came around the table to stand next to Megan's father. "I asked Doc to help me—"

"You don't need to explain anything, doll," Megan's father said. "I got a right to break the law, same as anyone else. Megan, honey, I'm just trying to right a terrible wrong. If that's not proper ethics, then I don't want anything to do with them."

"I think we can chalk that up as a given," Megan said. "But stealing seems pretty clearly beyond the bounds."

"We didn't steal this puppy," her father protested. "We're just *borrowing* it."

"Does anyone *know* you're borrowing it?" Megan asked. "Call me picky, but that seems to be what makes 'borrowing' different from 'stealing'."

"*You* know," he offered weakly, then looked at Penelope. "And her. Now."

"I cannot believe you stole a dog," Penelope said, her gaze censuring the two of them.

"Really, y'all, it wasn't stealin'," Georgia said, flipping her hair back with one hand. "These dogs will belong to me, you'll see."

"Besides, we got in through the laundry room window," her father explained, "which was wide open. Puppies were right there. And don't fret, we're going to take it right back after I get enough blood for a DNA test."

"Why didn't you just take the blood while you were there?" Megan asked.

Her father looked dumbfounded. He and Georgia looked at each other, then started laughing.

"Damn, Doc, guess I should've asked Megan in the first place," Georgia said. "She seems to be the criminal mastermind in the family."

"I knew she had some of my genes in her somewhere," he said.

"So now you've got to break in *again* to return the puppy." Megan looked from her father to Georgia and back.

"Sure," Georgia said, reaching out to stroke the puppy in Doc's arms. "But it's okay. I used to live there, remember? I know that house like the back a my own little hand. We'll just slip in, return the pup, and in a coupla weeks I'll have my answer."

"What then?" Megan asked.

"Well, when the test shows Sage is the father, then Clifford's got some talkin' to do." Georgia laughed. "And when he can't explain away Sage's paternity, he's gonna have some testifyin' to do."

"You won't be able to use these tests in court, you know," Megan said. "I've got to believe stolen evidence is inadmissible."

"Doesn't matter," Georgia said, throwing up her hands in triumph. "*He'll* know what the tests showed because he knows he stole the frozen sperm. All I've gotta do is threaten Clifford with a suit, tell him he'll have to subject the litter to DNA testing and next thing you know I'll have me a litter of gorgeous blue Danes. And Clifford's name'll be mud in the show ring."

Megan shook her head again but couldn't help the smile that crept onto her lips. This was absurd, beyond absurd. But it was the perfect ending to this evening.

"We better hurry," Doc said, putting the puppy back on the examination table. "Clifford won't be out all night."

Megan watched as her father took out a hypodermic needle and tried to direct its point at the tiny leg in front of him. His hands were shaking so much he had to start over three times, first prop-ping his elbows on the table, then his wrists, then asking Georgia to hold the dog up.

"I can't watch this," she said finally, stepping over to the counter behind them and pulling out a VetGen swab. "You know you don't even need blood, Dad, don't you? We can just swab the inside of their cheeks and send it by regular mail. No overnighting it chilled or anything."

Her father looked befuddled. "No kidding."

"No kidding," she said. Two minutes later she'd gotten a swab from both the puppy and Sage. Dropping the samples into an envelope, she turned back to the dastardly duo.

"These kids today," her father mumbled. "New fangled thingamajigs . . ." The rest of his lament was lost in a sea of grumbling.

"By the way, I'll be sending this in under your name, Dad," Megan added, "and if it ever comes up, I'm saying I didn't know a thing about it. Georgia, no matter what the outcome of this is, I hope that Rose's Animal Hospital will not enter into any of your discussions about the matter."

"Oh honey, of course not. And thank you!" Georgia rounded the table to give her a big hug. "I knew you were a pal. And I'm sorry to have gotten you involved at all."

"I'm only doing this because I think you've got a good case," she said, hugging Georgia back. The things one had to do these days to make friends.

Georgia pulled back and gave her a hundred-watt smile. "You know it, honey. You just wait. Those tests'll come back a positive match for Sage. Then we'll celebrate."

Megan smiled as they gathered their things and took the dogs back out to the Navigator.

"Be *careful*," Megan said. "And Dad, if you get caught, would you mind using an alias?"

They all laughed and Penelope and Megan watched the thieves drive off.

"Think they'll get caught?" Penelope asked.

Megan shook her head, her eyes on the disappearing taillights and her stomach full of dread. "I don't know. But if they do, you can bet there'll be hell to pay."

The following morning, Megan lay back on Dr. Lee's examination table in exhaustion. The paper covering scrunched beneath her, and the small paper pillow cradled her head. She hadn't gotten much sleep last night after the puppy incident, though she did manage to drift off before her father got in. She woke up again at the crack of dawn and went in to the office to fill out the paperwork for the DNA test. She wanted to get that out the door before the rest of the staff came in.

Pulling the edges of her paper vest together, Megan gazed up at the picture of George Clooney the nurses had taped to the ceiling.

She never liked visiting the doctor, normally, but today it felt so good to lie down she didn't even mind that the table was connected to those awful metal stirrups. To Dr. Lee's credit, however, Megan noted that these had fake-fur coverings that made them look a little less like a medieval torture device.

She closed her eyes as she waited for the doctor, remembering the ruckus at the concert last night. She wished she'd kept her head about her a little more. She'd just been so thrown by Sutter's initial reaction, followed by his tenderness, that she hadn't known which way to jump when the photographer had shown up.

Thinking about it now, it was obvious she would have been *much* better off not racing out like that. No doubt her hasty exit prompted more speculation and gossip than staying there and laughing it off would have. The way she'd bolted, people probably suspected that she and Sutter had been caught *in flagrante delicto* instead of *in discussion detesto*, as was really the case.

She still couldn't believe that when she'd gotten into the car with Penelope she'd actually burst into tears. *Burst!* Into tears! She hadn't done that since her divorce, and at least then she'd known what she was upset about. This had just been some kind of emotional overload.

Okay, that wasn't strictly true. She knew what she was upset about this time, too, but it wasn't as if she'd ever actually believed that she and Sutter Foley would end up together. Was it? Good God, she could still barely believe she even knew the man, let alone had had the most incredible sex of her life with him.

Maybe it had been all that talk about fidelity and monogamy being unnatural. Even though it had been *her* talk, it must have brought back all her feelings about Ray and his profligacy. Yes, that had to be it. It wasn't really because she had fallen in love with Sutter.

Inexplicably, she felt another lump grow in her throat and her mouth contorted downward with the effort not to cry again. An image of his face floated before her closed eyes and she felt her heart wrench.

This was stupid. She had to get a grip.

So maybe she was in love with the man, damn it all to hell. He was funny and handsome and sincere and intelligent and successful—for God's sake, what was there not to love? She'd been an idiot to think she could sleep with him and not want more. Monogamy might be unnatural, but it certainly seemed to be more unnatural for men than it was for women.

A light knock sounded on the door and a small Asian woman with a bright smile entered the room. Megan sat up.

"Megan?" the doctor asked. "I'm Dr. Lee."

"Nice to meet you," Megan said, liking her instantly. She had a kind, friendly face that had

Megan wanting to confide all of her problems to her. She had an air about her that said she could solve them all.

Of course just explaining all that had gone on lately would have taken a week.

They chatted briefly about how Megan had recently moved to town and Megan updated her about what was going on with her since her last checkup.

"Lately it's been mostly fatigue, but that comes with the territory of moving and taking over a business, I guess," Megan said. "Other than that, I've felt pretty good. Healthy."

"Great." Dr. Lee flipped through her chart. "Hm. I see you have some adhesions distorting the fallopian tubes."

"Yes, from endometriosis. Dr. Hill, in Connecticut, said because of it I only had a one in a million chance of ever getting pregnant. That even if the sperm made it to the egg, they'd likely encounter a 'hostile environment' once they got there." Megan chuckled at the phrase, as she always did, sometimes to deflect the pain, sometimes to deflect the pity.

"I see. Okay, let's get started." Dr. Lee called in the nurse, snapped on her latex gloves and Megan lay back down on the table, gazing up into George Clooney's compassionate face. She ought to try to meet him, she thought, closing her eyes against the subtle discomfort of the exam. Heck, if she could get Sutter Foley into bed, maybe George wasn't as impossible as he seemed either.

"Joyce, let me see that chart again, would you?" Dr. Lee asked the nurse.

Joyce took the file folder and held it out to her. Dr. Lee was still palpating Megan's abdomen.

"That's what I thought. Go to that next page," Dr. Lee said.

Megan opened her eyes. Was there a problem?

Dr. Lee was still studying the records. Great, there *was* a problem. On top of everything else she was going to die of cervical cancer or something equally hideous.

"It's been a little while since my last exam, I know," Megan said nervously, as if to explain away any discovery on Dr. Lee's part. "I was really busy that last year before I moved and it just slipped my mind, I'm afraid."

"That's all right," Dr. Lee said, her brow furrowed. "When did you say your last period was, Megan?"

Megan thought back. "It was . . ."

She searched her memory, nervousness making it even more difficult. Ovarian cancer, maybe. That could be in there too. Which would affect her period. Maybe the endometriosis had gotten worse. God, a hysterectomy would be expensive right now. And all she needed was that hormone hell on top of everything else, too.

"I don't keep very good track," Megan confessed. "But I think it was before I moved. Um, God, two months ago? No, three! I've been here almost three months. Oh my gosh, could that be right?"

Dr. Lee stepped back and moved the light away. "It could be right. You can sit up now."

Megan looked at her in trepidation, but the woman didn't look like she was about to impart terminal news. She looked, in fact, cautiously amused.

"We're going to need to do a urine test on you," the doctor said with a smile.

Bladder cancer? Megan thought.

"I don't know if this will come as good news or not, but from your records I see it'll certainly be a surprise. Megan," she said, her eyes seeming to twinkle, "there's a good possibility you're pregnant."

Megan walked out to her car through the sweltering summer heat in a daze. The urinalysis had proved it. She was pregnant. *Pregnant!* She was going to have a baby, be a mother, raise a child. For some reason she thought of all that stuff she'd thrown away when she thought she'd never have any progeny. When she'd believed it was *a million to one shot*. What a fool!

The fluttering of surprise inside her escalated, making her hand shake as she tried to insert the key into the lock. She steadied it with the other one.

A baby. She couldn't believe it. She paused and put her hands to her abdomen, wherein a little person was incubating. A baby, someone with her genes, her blood—it was astonishing!

She looked up to the sky at a flock of passing birds and felt within her rise up the most incredible feeling of happiness. Pure, blossoming euphoria.

She, Megan Rose, was going to have a baby! She was going to grow large and round and maybe waddle and pee too often and get a crib and a mobile and go to the hospital and give birth and go through the rest of her life with another person—a person she will love more than life itself. A little boy. Or a little girl.

It was the most wonderful news she'd ever gotten in her life and she felt as if she could hardly contain herself. Yet at the same time she wanted to keep it quiet, cherish the secret, as if letting it out might damage it somehow, make it not true.

It was a miracle. When she'd protested to Dr. Lee that pregnancy was impossible the woman had simply smiled and said in fact it wasn't. Improbable, yes. But clearly not impossible. She estimated Megan was about two months along.

Two months, Megan thought, opening the car door. That meant it had happened the first time she and Sutter—

She hit the car seat with a hard *plop* as her knees gave out.

Sutter, she thought. Holy shit, Sutter was going

to be a father. The father of her baby. *Her baby*, she thought wildly. Then, with a kind of terror:

Her baby was Sutter Foley's.

Unfortunately, she had three afternoon appointments that were absolutely uncancellable. Her clientele had finally begun to build, and if she started canceling appointments for no reason she could divulge, they wouldn't trust her the next time.

She wasn't sure how she did it but she got through the first two without making an utter ass of herself. Lucky for her one was just a simple checkup and rabies inoculation on a cat, and the other a flea problem for a dog—both no-brainers. And she certainly had no brain.

The last one, though, was the kicker.

"A *sugar glider!*" Allison said, when she came to retrieve Megan from her office for the last appointment. "I've never seen one before in my life and ohmygod it's *the cutest thing!* It's like a squirrel, only smaller. Where do they come from?"

"Australia and Indonesia," Megan said. She'd just been boning up. It had been a long time since she'd had to deal with an exotic that unusual. "They're marsupials."

"Yeah, and so soft!" Allison exclaimed.

Megan laughed. She had never seen her receptionist this animated about anything, but it only proved her belief that everyone was a pet person, it was just a matter of finding the right pet.

"I wanted to hold it," Alison continued, "but she wouldn't let go of it."

"That's because sugar gliders are like tiny flying squirrels. They have the ability to jump and fly good distances and quite quickly. You don't want one of those getting away from you."

"They even have little hands with fingers!"

Megan chuckled, thinking about her baby's little fingers, and went into the exam room.

A short woman in a wrinkled dress with damp hair along her brow—testifying to the sweltering summer day—cradled a little cloth pouch in her hands.

"Hi, I'm Dr. Rose," Megan said, reaching out a hand to the woman. "You must be Doris Fleiger."

"Oh, I'd better not let go," Mrs. Fleiger said. "Jiminy here might get away. He loves to fly, he does."

"I guess that comes with the territory." Megan smiled. "Now what is going on with Jiminy?"

"Well," the woman said, cautiously opening up the little pouch she wore around her neck like a necklace. "He's started to smell kinda bad and I know they're not supposed to have much of a scent. And I'm real good about keeping their cage clean and all."

Out of the pouch came a tiny little creature, about the size of a lemon, that instantly captured Megan's heart. Its large black eyes blinked up at her from under pointed, catlike ears, its face as sweet as any Disney character's.

"Oh my goodness," Megan murmured, reaching out for the little animal.

Mrs. Fleiger held Jiminy out, but before Megan could cup her hand around him he let out an astonishingly loud scream and flew at her chest.

He landed with a thump and stuck like velcro to her shirt front.

Megan couldn't withhold a yelp of surprise and looked down at the tiny beast. As she met its eyes, it pulled its lips back and revealed a mouthful of needle-like teeth.

The devil in pint-sized form.

It screamed again.

"He's very tame at home," Mrs. Fleiger said, a frantic note in her voice as she tried to speak over the chirps and barks the little thing was now emitting. "He just doesn't like strangers much."

Now you tell me, Megan thought, reaching toward the animal on her chest. Despite the ominous teeth, she cupped her hand toward its body. If she didn't get hold of it quickly it would—

It did. It leapt from her chest to the counter beside her. Mrs. Fleiger raced around the examination table, bumping into Megan who in turn bumped into the counter.

The devil sprang to the wall with a fiendish grin and held on to the picture frame. Ironically, a picture of dogs wearing angel wings.

Megan attempted the impossible, diving for an animal without the animal noticing.

Of course it saw her coming and sailed to the floor, dangerously close to the crack under the door. It would take nothing for the animal to disappear through it.

Both she and Mrs. Fleiger lunged for the miniature beast. Megan was acutely aware that she couldn't grab *hard* or things would really get ugly.

They both missed.

Before she knew it the thing was leaping and flying around the room nonstop, a demonic pinball, a cartoon character gone bad, a furry fanged poltergeist.

Megan and Mrs. Fleiger bumped against each other in pursuit, bouncing off the counter and the walls like Keystone cops chasing a superball.

Mrs. Fleiger was screaming, "Jiminy! Jiminy!" freaking out both Megan and the diminutive Jiminy, who at the same time was screaming with his own little voice, no doubt summoning the rest of the tribe in Indonesia.

Footsteps sounded outside the exam room door. "Don't come in!" Megan yelled.

Jiminy leapt off the corner cooler and landed in her hair.

"Oh my God!" she burst out, before she could stop herself. She could feel the wee hands burrowing into her hair. Megan pressed her own hands together in front of her for a quick moment to keep herself from batting the creature from her hair in a panic and flinging it, no doubt to its death, across the room.

"Jiminy!" Mrs. Fleiger shouted again, going for Megan's hair with her frantic and considerably larger paws.

"Are you all right?" Allison called through the door.

"*No!*" Megan ordered Mrs. Fleiger, stepping back away from her.

The door burst open and Allison barreled in. "What's going on?"

"Allison, shut the door," Megan said as calmly as she could.

Mrs. Fleiger fairly twitched in the corner of the room, where she'd retreated at Megan's barked command.

The creature was under a thick lock of her hair, apparently feeling momentarily safe. "Let's calm down, *calm down*, Mrs. Fleiger."

"All right, all right. He's never done this at home. He's perfectly docile at home, even though he's never really liked strangers." She kneaded her hands together. "Oh God."

"I thought you said he was tame." Megan gave her a stern look.

"Well, he is. Except with other people. He's good with me because I've been carrying him around here, during the days." She pointed to her cleavage and the cloth pouch.

Megan remembered that this was standard bonding technique for sugar gliders but Allison looked at Mrs. Fleiger with disgust written all over her face.

"You keep it in your *bra*?" Allison exclaimed.

"Allison, I'll explain later," Megan said. "Please go back out to reception, I just heard the door chimes. Mrs. Fleiger, perhaps you should come over here—*slowly*—and try to get Jiminy out of my hair."

Fifteen

Sutter entered the animal hospital with Twister straining on the leash just in time to hear a shriek come from the exam room. A moment later he heard a series of thumps, as if a struggle were going on. He was about to charge the door when it opened and a petite blond girl emerged.

She had one hand to her hair when she noticed him, startled, and said, "Oh!" Then she glanced at Twister, walked over to the counter and began flipping through the appointment book. "I'm not sure I have you down here. What's your dog's name?"

"Twister, but I'm just looking for Dr. Rose," Sutter said. Twister strained at the leash, sniffing at the exam room door as if she might be able to follow her nose right though it.

Frowning, the girl looked at him critically and asked, "Have you got an appointment?"

"No." He glanced back at the door from which she'd emerged. Things seemed quiet now. "Is everything all right in there?"

She looked up. "Oh yes. It was just a sugar glider got loose. I think they're getting it out of Dr. Rose's hair right now."

"A . . . sugar glider?"

"Because we're closed now," she went on, clearly afraid of having to stay late. "The sugar glider was her last appointment. This isn't an emergency, is it?" She glanced doubtfully at Twister, as if he couldn't possibly claim an emergency with that healthy dog.

"No. I don't need an appointment. I'm only here to see Dr. Rose," he explained.

She gave him a bland look. "That's usually what people make appointments *for* here."

He raised a brow. "That's not what I meant. I'm a friend of hers. This is a social call."

"Oh," she said, her tone full of sudden interest. "I didn't know she had a *friend* in town already. I'll tell her you're here. What's your name?"

"Sutter Foley."

She paused, then her mouth dropped open. "No way."

"I beg your pardon?"

"I mean no *way! You're* Sutter Foley? And you're from *England*, that's right. Oh my God, my boyfriend, like, *worships* you. Or, really, your computer stuff. He's a total geek." She flipped her hair behind her shoulders and tilted her head. "So are you really a billionaire?"

Sutter wondered what it was about himself and Megan that they ended up with assistants like Arnetta and this girl.

He was saved from deflecting the question by the opening of the exam room door. Megan, her hair tousled in a way that made him picture her naked in his bed, emerged with a short, dark-haired woman.

"So I should stop all the vitamins?" the woman asked, coming out of the door sideways and clutching her breasts. She was looking back at Megan.

"Yes," Megan said, looking at a chart and following the woman out, "just for a couple days. Then add them back in slowly, a little at a time, so you can gauge how much they can handle before the smell returns."

"And keep the cat out of that room," the woman said, mentally noting.

"Absolutely. Remember, fear makes the males—" She glanced up and saw Sutter, stopping dead in her tracks.

"Oh sure, I knew that. Males' anal glands smell when they're afraid—" The woman turned to see him too, stopped talking and blushed red.

"Hello, Sutter," Megan said.

Inexplicably, she wore the classic deer-in-the-headlights expression. Sutter wondered if there was any chance of regaining the carefree woman she was on every other meeting until last night and today.

"Oh wow," the shorter woman said. "Are you Sutter Foley? My husband will *die* when I tell him I met you."

"I know!" Allison contributed. "My boyfriend too! Are men, like, all total nerds or what?"

Sutter nodded at her, but returned his gaze to Megan. "I'm sorry to intrude but I assumed you would be closing up. I didn't intend to interrupt your workday."

Megan swallowed and visibly collected herself. "It's all right. I'm just, uh, let me finish here." She turned to the woman and said, "You let me know how that goes. If that doesn't fix the problem, bring him back in and we'll check him out again."

"Yes, and I'll bring the cage next time." The woman giggled and spoke to her bosom. "No more escape tricks, you hear?"

Sutter sincerely hoped it listened.

Allison checked the woman out and Megan invited Sutter through the swinging door into the large back room. The place was filled with equipment and cages for the animals and another exam table. There was a back hall lined with bags of dog food—or maybe it was cat food—and an open door to another room revealed a large waist-high tub with a long sprayer attachment hanging from the ceiling.

Twister checked the place out thoroughly, too, for the six-foot radius she was allowed on the leash.

Megan turned in the center of the room and squatted to greet Twister with an affectionate voice, exclaiming how big she was getting, and body scratches to the writhing delight of the dog, who tried repeatedly to lap her with its tongue.

Finally, she stood and with a deep breath said, "I imagine this visit has to do with last night."

She crossed her arms over her stomach. The expression on her face was as wary as he'd ever seen it. There'd be no falling into Megan Rose's eyes today.

"Yes, I felt the need to follow up. I wanted to apologize," he began, searching her face, but her expression gave nothing away. Perhaps she thought they had covered everything they needed to last night. Perhaps they had. But despite the fact that she had declared them finished last night, he still felt the need to inform her of his plans, just so she wouldn't be surprised when the tabloids got hold of it.

He cleared his throat and continued, "First, to apologize again for leaping to conclusions. I misjudged you about that *Tattler* thing. It was inexcusable."

She dropped her hands from their folded position and clasped them loosely before her. "Yes, that was insulting."

He paused. Smoothing the waters churned up last night was going to be difficult, he'd known that—it was one reason he'd brought Twister, as an ice breaker—but he hadn't expected to find this cool, contained person in place of the open-hearted Megan he'd come to count on.

"You're upset," he said, taking in her shuttered eyes and reserved posture. "And I certainly don't blame you. Last night went from awkward to intolerable in the flash of an eye." He forced a smile, and added, "Or rather, the flash of a camera."

He was congratulating himself on this turn of phrase when she sighed heavily.

"I'm not upset, Sutter," she said, meeting his eyes. "I'm sorry I ran last night, after that photographer showed up. I'm sure that only made things worse. God knows what people are saying about it today. I was just taken by surprise."

"As was I."

"Look, Sutter," she said, moving slowly to the counter and leaning back against it. The move made her just a bit farther away from him. "It seems clear to me that the *Tattler* has it in for us. I mean, obviously they're following you, so your coming here today is probably just adding fuel to the fire."

The implication that he shouldn't have come stung.

"I'm not going to change how I run my life for the bloody *Tattler*," he declared, ready to take a bite out of anyone who said he should. But a second before he continued his rant he noted the look on her face and paused. "But that's not taking into account what it does to you, does it?"

She didn't reply. But he saw her swallow and her eyes didn't leave his. It was as much of an admission as he would get from her, he knew.

He shook his head, running a hand through his hair. "I guess I've blown it again. I'm sorry. I seem to have caused nothing but trouble for you."

He hadn't meant it to sound so self-pitying, but that's how it came out. And hell, perhaps that's how it really was. He felt exiled from her. Cut off not only by the *Tattler*, but by the state of his own life. And he couldn't blame her. Who would willingly sign on for a life of zero privacy and constant media intrusion? She'd said last night that she was not prepared to deal with such things and then she'd told him they were through. Whatever had made him think that she might be interested in his plans with regard to Briana was just sheer hubris.

She wanted nothing to do with him.

He turned around, giving a quick yank to Twister's leash. "I should leave."

"Sutter, wait," she said, as if the words burst from her involuntarily.

He turned around. In fact she did look surprised at having stopped him. "I—I need to tell you . . ." she fumbled.

He couldn't interpret the expression on her face

but the intensity of it concerned him. She looked—urgent. Uncharacteristically grim.

"Yes?" His voice had an edge.

"Just . . ." She swallowed again. "I hope we're ending on a good note." She gave a strained laugh. "I mean, I don't want . . . I understand . . ." She stopped, closed her eyes briefly, and took a breath. "I hope you know how much I treasure the time we had together. And I'll always think of you . . ." She let the sentence trail off without an adverb.

Fondly? he wondered. With affection? As a spineless jerk?

"You speak as if one of us were dying." He wanted to make the comment light, but couldn't. It dropped like a stone between them.

She gave a small smile. "On the contrary." She hesitated, then added, "I think we both know the lives we're supposed to live are . . . not connected."

"That's a bit dramatic, isn't it?" Why was he so irritated? Why was she acting so odd?

This time she did laugh, and he got a glimpse of the old Megan. His heart twisted.

"Maybe so," she said. "But we both also know that you belong in your world and I belong in mine. And the two don't meet so much as collide." She sighed.

He looked at her a long moment and knew that he had to let her go. She was like the butterfly who would die in captivity. For her to remain the woman he loved, she needed to be free of him.

"I understand," he said at last. "But I want you to know that I . . ." How to say what she meant to him in a concise, yet unburdensome way? "I value our friendship. I hope we don't lose all of that."

He could have kicked himself for how incomparably lame that sounded. As he said it he knew the *last* thing he wanted from her was mere friendship. But his life was too complicated. Too inescapable.

"I'm not going to spit on you on the street or anything." Laughter twinkled in her eyes a moment. "But I believe we'll always be . . . friendly."

"I should hope so," he said stiffly. This was getting worse by the minute. He had to get out of here. "All right, then." He turned away again, hoping against reason that she would call him back once more.

He longed to take her in his arms, to feel her soft, willing body burrowing into his, experience at least once more the freedom of their passion.

At this moment it was the one single thing he longed for, the comfort of her uncomplicated love.

Love.

The word startled him, even in his own thoughts.

He glanced back at her when he reached the door to the reception area. She hadn't moved and she definitely hadn't said anything. She was watching him leave, watching him walk out of her life. And yet she said nothing.

"Goodbye, Megan," he said. "I do wish you well."

She lifted her brows and took a deep breath, then slowly exhaled.

And still, she said nothing.

Megan missed her mother so much she could hardly stand it. She had died when Megan was in vet school but whenever times got tough Megan wished more than ever that she could call her. She would have been the one person to whom Megan would have immediately spilled the news about her pregnancy. And she'd also have been the one who would have known just what to do about Sutter.

Megan lay back on her bed. It was only seven o'clock, and she hadn't had dinner, but all she wanted to do was sleep. This day had been too much. Seeing Sutter mere hours after learning about the baby had done her in. She hadn't had a moment to think about how to tell him. She hadn't had a moment to decide if she even *would* tell him.

Her mother would tell her she had to, Megan knew that as surely as if she'd voiced the question and heard her answer. She had a moral obligation to tell the father that he was going to *be* a father.

And for a moment today she had thought so too. As he'd stood in her office she'd almost told him. But then she couldn't, and it didn't seem such a crime to wait until she'd adjusted to the news herself.

But now Megan wasn't sure. She couldn't imagine how he would react. Based on his response to her appearance in the *Tattler*, she was pretty sure he'd think first of all the negatives. Like, was she trying to trap him? Had she lied to him about her inability to have children? Had she done this *on purpose*?

In fact she could not even imagine a positive response from him. For God's sake, he'd thought she was trying to manipulate him by talking to a tabloid. Popping up with his baby would trump that in spades.

And how would that be for the child? For the poor innocent baby—*her* baby—who would only want love?

She put her hands on her belly and tears sprang to her eyes.

If nothing else, pregnancy explained why all of a sudden she was falling into tears wherever she went. It was something of a relief.

Then she thought about Sutter's face at the animal hospital this evening. Yes, he'd sounded tough and irascible, but she had felt strongly that it was because he was conflicted. He didn't want to let her go. And yet . . . he couldn't commit to her either. And the last thing she wanted or needed was him twisting himself around to accommodate this circumstance. If they had any chance at all of having a relationship based on their feelings alone, without her having to wonder for all eternity if he was with her because of the baby, she had to see how things shook out without adding that complication.

He may not ever need to know at all . . . she thought, moments before drifting into a dreamless sleep.

The following morning, Megan shuffled into the kitchen to find her father, freshly dressed and looking nervous.

"What's up, Dad?" she asked, eyeing him as she opened the refrigerator. "You're looking awfully dapper for so early in the morning. Don't tell me you just got in."

She glanced at the clock—7:55—and looked back at her father with questioning eyes.

He hemmed and hawed a minute, making great work of folding the newspaper.

"You might as well know now," he said gruffly, "since I won't be able to hide it from you forever."

He took the folded paper from the table and brought it to her, slapping it down on the kitchen counter.

"It's a con job, I tell you," he said with a self-righteous tone. "Nothing's going to come of it. They're just hard up for stories."

It was folded open to the third page of the A section, and a small headline over a three-paragraph article read, "Local Vet Caught Poaching Puppy."

Megan's heart sank, along with her stomach, and she pushed away the orange juice she'd just poured for herself.

Georgia Darling and Laurence "Doc" Rose, of Rose's Animal Hospital, had been caught in Georgia's ex-husband's home, the article explained, allegedly trying to steal one of a new litter of puppies. Clifford Darling had not yet decided whether or not to press charges.

"It won't stick," her father said. "As soon as those lab reports come back that asshole Clifford will back off faster'n you can say stolen sperm."

"Were you *arrested*?" she asked, scanning the article again. "Oh my God, Dad, it says here 'Dr. Rose, of Rose's Animal Hospital.' People are going to think *I* broke into that house!"

"Hey, it says 'Laurence.'"

"*And* it says '*Rose's Animal Hospital*.'" Megan closed her eyes. "This is going to kill business."

"No it won't," he said, but he didn't sound sure.

"Why not? If people think their vet might like their pet enough to break into their house and steal it, why would they bring their animals to them in the first place?"

"People know I've retired," he said. "Besides, this isn't about you."

"Yes it is, Dad," she said, putting the paper down and giving him a hard look. "You may not be aware of it, and it's been a surprise to me too, but people tend to paint children with the sins of their fathers."

He scoffed. "You don't put any stock in people like that, do you? Why would you want to be friends with someone who couldn't tell the difference between a young woman and an old man? Hell, I didn't even raise you. Your pious mother did all of that."

"It's not my *friends* I'm worried about, Dad. It's my clients. And people I meet. People I run into. Just about everyone who finds out who I am has something to say about you."

"Oh, come on. It's not so bad as all that," he said, not meeting her eyes.

"It wasn't," she said, feeling pity for him, even if he did make his own bed. "Until now."

She couldn't shake the feeling of doom the little article produced in her.

"Well, just you wait, missy," he said, looking tough again. His faded blue eyes met hers and he poked a finger down onto the newspaper. "Those samples will come back and vindicate everyone. *Your* friend Georgia most of all."

She sighed. He was right; he had been helping her friend. And it hadn't seemed that serious the other night, when she'd told them what to do and how to do it.

"How did you avoid getting thrown in jail?" she asked.

He grinned then. "Georgia was great. She made a big show of just wanting to see the puppies, said she was so sad to have lost her Gretyl, the dam, and knew Clifford would never let her hold one. They thought they'd caught us coming in for the *first* time, see. They didn't know we'd already been there and were just returning the pup."

Megan shook her head. "Great, that's just great, Dad. But what if Clifford decides to press charges? What if the results don't come back in time?"

He shook his head, dismissing the idea of failure. "They only take a couple weeks. And Georgia and I are going to see Clifford and his lawyer this morning, tell them what's really going on. We had to wait a day so she could get her lawyer to come with us." He patted her hand. "So don't you worry about your old man, doll. There aren't going to be any charges."

Megan mustered an unconvincing smile, but her concerns were not with her father at all. One of the amazing things she'd learned about him was that he always got out of trouble almost as easily as he got into it.

No, what was bothering her was what this would do to business. *Her* business, now.

Not to mention how unscrupulous by association this would make her look to Sutter. If he'd had any qualms about severing ties with her before, this would surely quiet them.

* * *

"Did you see this?" Montgomery handed him a copy of the *Fredericksburg Daily Times*, and stepped back, her arms crossed over her chest. "It's yesterday's local paper."

Sutter scanned the short article she indicated.

"That Georgia Darling is trouble," he said, handing her back the paper. "I used to tell Bitsy the same thing."

He turned back to the computer, calling up a client email they'd just been talking about.

"Isn't that your Dr. Rose's father?" Montgomery persisted.

He didn't glance up as he scrolled through his inbox. "*My* Dr. Rose?" he inquired mildly.

"Yes, the one you had lunch with. The one who's clearly after you."

Sutter turned back in his chair and looked at her a long moment. Montgomery's eyes were defensive, her short haircut suddenly making her look more childish than tough, as it usually did. "After me, Montgomery? What are you getting at?"

She sighed and rolled her eyes up. "Isn't it obvious, sir? She's in trouble. Her business is in trouble. This is going to do her in." She tapped a short fingernail on the folded paper. "I just think you need to be on guard for the next thing she pulls."

"The *next* thing?" he asked coldly. "What was the last thing she pulled?"

"That *Tattler* article, of course. The woman is diabolical." Montgomery's face reddened as Sutter laughed.

"*Diabolical*? Oh come now, Montgomery."

At his laugh, Twister lifted her head from where she lay beneath his desk. Not sensing a walk, however, she lay back down.

Sutter had begun bringing the dog to work because he liked that she made him get outside a couple times a day. Plus, she wasn't such a wild thing when he got home, either.

Mostly, however, he liked the company. For whatever reason, she made him feel calm.

"I can't believe you don't see what she's doing, sir," Montgomery continued. "That woman is trying her damnedest to squeeze her way into your life. And she's obviously desperate for money."

He sobered, concerned about Montgomery's fervor on his behalf.

"Montgomery, correct me if I'm wrong but you make it sound as if money is the only reason a woman might want to be in my life." He tried to make the comment light, give her a chance to take a hint, but she didn't take it.

"You know I don't mean that. I just know a woman with an agenda when I see one. And if that *Tattler* article didn't convince you of that, I don't know what will. But we'll see. Mark my words, she'll come up with something."

He gave Montgomery a hard look. "She's a

young woman. She's not used to talking to re-porters. If anything, I have been the one infringing on *her* life, not the other way around. Do you think even the Fredericksburg paper would have been interested in this little story if not for the *Tattler*'s bringing Megan Rose to everyone's attention?"

"This was a *robbery*," Montgomery objected. "This is news. And she was involved!"

He glanced at the article again. "No charges have been filed. And she was *not* involved. In fact, it doesn't seem to have anything to do with *Megan Rose*. Only her father."

Montgomery's lips went thin. After all their years of working together, she had to know it was pointless to argue with him.

"I appreciate your watching out for me," he said, his tone making the issue final. "But, believe me, I do not need protecting from Megan Rose, or anyone else. You can stop your worrying."

What he needed, he thought, was protection from himself. He was the one driving himself mad. Mad with desire for a woman he couldn't have.

"I'll try, sir," she said, her chin raised stub-bornly. "But you don't make it easy."

Sixteen

"I can't do it, Aunt Edna," he said to the paja-ma'd woman sitting across from him. She was looking a bit wild-eyed today but she had asked him about Briana so he thought she might be more present than her afternoon dishabille suggested. "I can't continue seeing her. For some reason everything she says has begun to annoy me. And her obsession with the media is threatening to make me a little barmy."

She leaned over and patted his knee with a crooked hand. "I think that's wise, dear. You clearly need to keep seeing that other woman. Talking about her is the only time I see you happy."

"I doubt that's going to happen either." He slouched down in the chair like a kid. Being with Aunt Edna sometimes made him feel as if he were fifteen again, at her kitchen table, telling her about the girls he wanted to ask out and how none of them would go because he didn't have a car, let alone a couple quid to take them out.

He'd tried to engage her in conversation about herself today, asking about Uncle Ted, who'd died after Sutter had come to the States, but she only wanted to hear about him. And Briana. And Megan.

Sutter realized with amusement that his life had become another soap opera for her to follow.

"I don't think she wants to be my friend."

"Why in the world not? You're a delightful friend, Sutter."

He laughed cynically. "Perhaps to you. To her . . . well, it's difficult when you can't keep things . . . strictly friendly."

He thought his aunt would take this as a problem with arguing but a knowing gleam lit her eyes and she nodded. "I see. Well, that does create a problem. When one of you wants friendship and the other wants more."

He shook his head. "She doesn't want more."

"I was talking about you. *You* want more, don't you, Sutter?"

He looked at his aunt, wheels turning in his head.

"I thought you went after what you wanted," she continued. "Isn't that how you got to where you are today?"

"You can't go after someone who doesn't want to be gone after," he protested.

"Let me tell you, young man, you can't say you know a woman's true feelings until you *have* gone after her. Have you asked her about her feelings?"

He remembered how she'd looked in the church basement, how certain she'd seemed that they were through. "I don't know about that, Aunt. She's made them pretty clear . . ."

"What a woman says and what she does are sometimes quite different," Aunt Edna said sagely. "Take that Brittany, for example."

Sutter felt a sinking in his gut. "Brittany?"

"Yes, Brittany Snow. She told Lance she wanted nothing to do with him and now she's mooning about, behaving like a right stroppy cow about his seeing Shannon. Of course we all know Shannon is using him, but still. Communication, Sutter! That's what makes a good relationship."

Sutter wasn't sure he should consider relationship advice based on a soap opera, even though she had a point.

"And what does Lance make of all of this?" he asked, playing along.

"Oh *Lance*." His aunt threw out a hand as if throwing him into a wastebasket. "He's as dense as they come. Doesn't think Brittany loves him, believes everything Shannon says. I've half a mind to tell him what's going on, but I've found it's better if they just work these things out themselves."

"Quite," Sutter said, nodding.

"You can't tell young people a thing these

days," she shook her head, her gray curls quivering with the movement.

He smiled gently. "No, I don't suppose you can . . ."

"You could ruin me with this," Sutter said, watching Briana's motionless face. "You could take it to the tabloids and have me splashed across their pages for months. But you deserve the truth. The who, the what, the where . . . the only thing I can't give you is the why. I don't *know* why, Briana. It just . . . wasn't working."

Her dark eyes were, as always, a mystery as they regarded him beneath aristocratically arched brows. "How much does this have to do with that little veterinarian you've been seeing?" she asked calmly.

He'd dreaded this question for more than a week, since he'd spoken to his aunt. Briana had gone back to Massachusetts to settle some final business, so he had waited until she returned to speak with her. He just couldn't go another day with her thinking their relationship might be going somewhere.

"It has more to do with us, Briana. Surely you can see that we don't want the same things." He shifted on her delicate antique settee, trying not to think about how Megan's emotions would be written across her face and in her eyes, only to come out of her mouth. She did not have an equivocal bone in her body. Her purpose burned bright as a wildfire within her, blown even brighter by hard winds.

But Briana was different. He could not tell what she was thinking, or if she was in the least upset by his revelation.

He was leaving in the morning for a business trip to New York, something he should have done last week, but he couldn't leave without settling things with Briana.

"But you are certain that you don't love me." Briana's voice, smooth as silk, betrayed nothing. She was so placid he wondered if she might not be relieved.

"I'm sorry," he said. "But I am certain."

She was silent a long moment, gazing at her hands.

"I hardly think I could ruin you," she said finally, lifting her eyes to his. She looked as if she were considering just how it might be done and was disappointed that it was not clearer. "Maybe your reputation could be marred, but only for a while. It's not as if anything I had to say would affect your stock prices."

He frowned.

"Regardless," he said steadily, "I leave it in your hands to handle as you see fit. I am happy to play the cad. Either the one who erred, or the one who was left, whatever suits you."

Her eyes frosted over, regarding him coldly. "How kind."

There it was, he thought. She was angry. Not hurt, not heartbroken, not even humiliated. Just angry.

"In any case," he said, "you have always been better at handling the media, so I will leave you to it. I will not speak to the press."

She was quiet again. A clock ticked on the mantel, loud within the hollow shell of their relationship.

Finally, she spoke, her voice quiet. "You do realize how this could make me look, don't you, Sutter? If this is your final decision, you must be prepared for what I might do. How I might characterize this. Not to mention . . . certain players in the drama."

There it was. The threat.

"It is my final decision. And I am sorry about it, Briana. I have no problem with your doing what you will to me," he said, then added, his voice hardening, "but if you bring Megan Rose into this it will change everything."

Her back stiffened and her next words were thrown like rocks. "So it is the little tart. Well, I hope that works out for you because I do not take people back, Sutter. Not ever. If you ask me to forgive your indiscretion now, I will do so. After all, until recently we lived in separate cities. But if you persist in saying we should split, then this *will* be the end of it. Forever."

Sutter met her gaze. "I understand. But my feelings are decided." *Even if my future is not.*

"And so," she said venomously, "are mine. I'll be speaking to the press in the morning."

He stood up then. "Whatever you want. Just remember," he leveled her with a look, "leave Megan out of this. I mean it."

Color hit her cheeks and her nostrils flared. "I can see that. So I'll leave her out of it. She's nothing to me anyway." She gave an elegant shrug. "But you can't blame me for what that tabloid might dig up on you."

He chuckled mirthlessly. "I'll deal with them," he said, and headed for the door. "Goodbye, Briana."

And then he was gone. Out the door, in the car, then on the chopper heading for National Airport, where his jet would take him to New York.

He had a tabloid to buy.

It had been twelve days since Megan had last seen Sutter, but the funk she'd fallen into made it feel like a year.

As she'd feared, business had indeed slacked off since the tiny article in the local newspaper about her father's "puppy poaching" had morphed into national news via the *National Tattler*. "Sutter's Sweetie Daughter of Puppy Poacher!" the headline had read. It was, however, only a sidebar to the bigger story about Megan and Sutter's clandestine meeting in the basement of a church. "Foley Frisky with Feline Physician in Church Basement—Ellis Upstairs!"

Between the two, there was enough bad behavior to offend the citizens of Fredericksburg on every level. The steady growth of new clients had halted abruptly and a few people even called to cancel their appointments. She'd already had to let go two of the three receptionists and one of her vet techs. She was not looking forward to what would have to go next.

Megan's financial future looked bleak.

Georgia had come back to the house to apologize to Megan, after she and Megan's father had met with the lawyers. Clifford wasn't going to press charges until after the tests had been received, she said, as if calling her bluff, but they both knew what those results would show. He was just jerking them around while he had the chance.

Still, she hadn't meant to injure Megan in the process and she was so abjectly sorry that Megan could do nothing but take pity on her and forgive her. Besides, Megan *had* participated a little bit. None of them had anticipated the article's being picked up by the tabloid or the dire effect it would have on her business.

But Georgia didn't know the worst part of the circumstances and Megan wasn't ready to tell her. She didn't want anyone to know about the pregnancy yet, not until she'd figured out how to tell Sutter. Even then the fallout would probably be pretty ugly. Already struggling with the reputation of her father, and the *Tattler*'s subsequent article about Sutter and Megan's tryst in a church basement, of all places, then dealing with the family name's involvement in a dog theft, becoming an unwed mother by the town's most celebrated citizen was going to seal her fate as the town's most notorious. It didn't take much imagination to realize there would be no recovering from that. If she thought she'd been snubbed at the chamber music concert, she hadn't seen anything yet.

But all of that was nothing compared to the total financial devastation she faced. With the costs of doctor bills and prenatal care—covered only partially by her catastrophic health insurance plan—the outlook for Megan's finances recovering from this blow any time soon was grim.

Apart from being robbed of current business, the income from which she could be using to sock away money for her maternity leave, she now had nobody to cover for her at the animal hospital after the baby was born. She couldn't ask her father, not now. He'd sealed his retirement and made it permanent by participating in that ill-conceived plot with Georgia. Even after the results of the DNA tests were received and they were vindicated—*if* they were vindicated—she wasn't sure people would ever trust him again. Not that many of them had to begin with.

Granted, the baby's birth was six months down the line. But six months of little to no income, followed by at least two more of downtime with the baby, and there was no way she could exist for the better part of a year on what she had now.

Of course there was always Sutter. The moment she told him about the baby she knew he would cover the costs. If you could ignore the documentation of your every false step, unguarded word and stupid move by a national tabloid, there were perks to the father of your baby being a billionaire. When she was honest with herself, she conceded that knowing he would help was the only thing keeping her from coming completely apart at the seams.

Because she knew she had to tell him. He had a right to know.

But even though she felt sure he wouldn't let her sink completely, she had hoped he would come around to seeing their potential as a couple first. Now she had to face facts: if he was going to come around he would have done it by now. The best she could hope for was that she and Sutter would be co-parents. And that Briana wouldn't actively sabotage any civility in the relationship.

One plus was now that she knew the cause of her fatigue—not to mention her overemotionality, overeating, and hypersensitivity to everything from smells to sights—she was at peace with it.

She was also at peace with the pregnancy. The only thing marring her complete happiness about it was anticipating the meeting she had to have with Sutter to tell him about his impending fatherhood.

As she sat in her quiet office, alone with an un-ringing phone and empty exam rooms, she contemplated the Herculean task of sitting across from Sutter and telling him she was going to have his baby.

The moment when the words must come out of her mouth was the moment she dreaded more than anything else in her life. But in keeping with a lifelong philosophy, she finally decided that she had to face that moment head-on and as soon as possible. Getting it out of the way, for good or for ill, would at least eliminate the crushing dread she felt at the prospect of it.

She picked up the phone and dialed the number for SFSolutions. She still didn't know his home number. What kind of woman was she that she didn't even know the home phone number for the father of her baby?

"SFSolutions! Arnetta speaking!" the loud, chipper voice exclaimed.

"Yes, may I speak with Sutter Foley, please? This is Megan Rose calling. Please tell him it's important," she said, her voice shaking. She didn't think he'd actually refuse her call, but telling him it was important would at least set him up for something big.

How big, he'd never guess.

Not that she was going to tell him over the phone, of course, but asking for a meeting could be construed many different ways, especially in their case. What she needed to do was set the stage appropriately as early as possible.

"Mr. Foley isn't in," Arnetta said. "If it's important you can reach him at the Palace hotel in New York City. Would you like that number?"

New York?

"Uh, no . . ." What was he doing in New York? And what was this woman doing giving out his number? "Can you tell me how long he'll be gone?"

"Oh yes . . . let's see. He left here last . . . Tuesday. And he'll be back . . . the twenty-ninth. Two weeks from today."

"Two weeks," Megan repeated.

"That's right. He's arriving at National Airport at 8:04 A.M."

Megan suppressed a laugh. It was no wonder the *Tattler* always knew where to find him.

"Well, uh, I guess I'll try him back after that, then," she said. "Thank you. Oh, wait!" She nearly shouted, remembering how fast the woman had hung up last time.

But she didn't want voicemail this time. She had to talk to him in person about this, and there was no sense leaving him a message he couldn't act on until he got home.

No, this time she wanted to know, "Do you have any idea what he's done with Twister? Uh, with his dog, I mean?"

If he'd left Twister in a kennel without asking her to take care of the puppy first she'd kill him. Or worse—he probably left her in the house all alone, depending on his housekeeper or his chef to let her out. Her heart bled just thinking about the poor little thing all alone in that huge place all night . . .

"Twister, sure!" Arnetta boomed. "I know the dog. He took it with him of course."

That stopped her. "He—what?"

"He took the dog with him," Arnetta said more slowly, enunciating each word as if Megan might suddenly have become hard of hearing.

"He took Twister with him. The young retriever mix dog he has," Megan said, as if he might have had some other kind of dog stashed somewhere.

"I guess, yes. Twister, that's the one. She comes to the office with him too. He's real attached to that one. Funny, isn't it? A rich guy like him having a dog that's not even pure bred."

"Yes . . . funny." Megan was floored.

"You'd think he'd have one of those weird kind of dogs," Arnetta continued, "like you see on the television. I watch Animal Planet when they have the dog shows on sometimes. They have some prissy-looking dogs on there. But he's just got this regular mutt. Cute, though."

"Yes, she is. And you say he brings her to work with him?"

"That's right. She just sits there under his desk while he works."

Megan shook her head. She could hardly believe it.

After a few minutes of silence, Arnetta asked, "Will there be anything else, ma'am?"

Megan shook her head again, dazed. "No. No, thank you."

"You're welcome! And thank you for calling SFSolutions!"

Megan expelled a long breath. He'd taken the dog with him. He even took the dog to work! Her plan had worked, and she'd had no idea.

She didn't know the man at all.

And she was carrying his child.

Megan realized she was still holding the phone receiver and gently placed it back in the cradle.

She took a deep breath.

Sutter was in New York for two more weeks. A reprieve. She had two weeks to figure out what to say to him, how to break the news. Two weeks to make a plan for her life and stick to it.

First things first, however. While she had a little bit of money to spare, she had to get a few things for the future. She wasn't sure if she was imagining it or not, but some of her clothes were starting to feel a bit snug around the waist. She was glad the weather was still warm enough for her to wear loose-fitting sundresses, but fall was coming and she would need something bigger soon.

It was time to buy some maternity clothes.

Seventeen

Saturday afternoon Megan set off. She closed the animal hospital at noon, as usual—after a day of no appointments, as was becoming usual again—and went to the mall.

The problem with buying maternity clothes, she discovered, was that you had to go to a maternity shop. And being seen in a maternity shop in a small town was a dicey proposition. She thought up several excuses—like that she was going to a friend's baby shower or was helping out a (fictional) sister—in case someone happened to ask. But the sad fact was that no one *would* ask, they'd just see her and leap to conclusions.

Correct conclusions, as it happened, or it wouldn't matter.

After skulking around outside a shop called Mommy 'N Me for the better part of fifteen min-

338 ❧ Elaine Fox

utes, eyeing every passerby for signs of recognition or familiarity, she decided the best tactic was to look completely confident and walk right in.

With her best I'm-Buying-A-Gift face she entered the store and headed straight for the back. She poked around the sale racks for a while, concentrating on the items farthest from the front and most concealed from the outside world. She plucked a couple of tops from a rack, trying to imagine herself getting big enough to actually wear them, when a saleswoman appeared at her elbow.

"Can I set up a fitting room for you?" the woman smiled. She looked to be in her forties and had a kindly, sympathetic look about her. And she cleary had no idea who Megan was.

"I doubt I'll have any trouble with the fit," Megan said. "Not yet anyway."

The woman laughed. "I know. But trust me, it helps to try them on. You can tell a lot about how the style and color work for you even at this stage. Besides, they have false bellies in the dressing room."

"False bellies?" Megan snickered. "That's really funny."

"Just practical. So can I take those to a room?"

"Okay. Sure." Megan handed her the clothes.

"Is this your first?" the woman asked.

Ridiculously, Megan felt herself blush, as if the pregnancy were something she made up and was now tricking others into believing. "Yes, actually.

I'm only about three months, but I could swear my clothes feel tight."

"Could be. Some people notice the changes quickly, others it takes longer. It's different for everyone. Besides, it makes the pregnancy feel a little more tangible when you start to buy the clothes." She winked.

Megan smiled warmly. There was such a sisterhood to pregnancy, she thought. Embarking on the path of reproduction felt like the first truly selfless thing she'd ever done, even though at the same time she felt as if she'd had very little to do with it occurring. It was a miracle, was all she could think. A lucky, joyous phenomenon that had simply happened.

"You should check out those stretch jeans over there," the woman added. "They look just like regular jeans from the back, but they've got a wonderful soft elastic belly that'll get you almost all the way through the ninth month."

"Oh, okay, thanks," Megan said, drifting toward the jeans.

As the woman disappeared toward the fitting rooms, Megan turned and her eye was caught by a display of baby overalls in fabrics from denim to corduroy, and in prints from boats to trains to teddy bears. They were so tiny and so cute, she could picture a baby boy with green eyes and blond hair tottering around in them amongst a sea of Christmas presents in Sutter's glorious but oh-so-homey living room. She could even imagine the tree, set up in that lovely bay window, of course.

Was there a chance Sutter would be at all excited about the prospect of fatherhood? she wondered. How could he not dote on the sight of his very own son or daughter? She could picture it so easily. As easily as she could picture him telling her he loved her . . . as he lay her down on the kitchen table . . . *don't you look delicious* . . .

"Megan?"

Megan jumped, dropping the autumn-leaf patterned overalls she held, and turned guiltily toward the voice.

"Oh Penelope, thank God!" she gushed, heat searing her face.

Her mind spun frantically to come up with something that would explain her presence in this store, even while she praised the heavens for making this intruder Penelope and not someone else.

"What are you doing here?" Penelope peered with concern into Megan's face. "Are you all right? You look as if I scared you to death."

Megan swallowed and put a hand to her fluttering heart. She bent to pick up the overalls. "You did, actually. I guess that *National Tattler* thing has me paranoid that I'm being followed. Though I know I'm only interesting to them when I'm with Sutter."

"No doubt," Pen said, studying the overalls Megan held. "Those are cute."

"Aren't they? I just love looking at these tiny things." Megan hoped it sounded as if she did it all the time. "What are *you* doing here?" The best defense was a good offense.

Penelope blushed. "Oh . . . I . . . I guess I just like coming in to this store," she said, shrugging. "Just to fantasize, you know?" She glanced at the overalls in Megan's hand again and laughed. "I guess you *do* know."

"Well . . ." Megan hung the overalls back up, unsure what to say. She didn't want to lie outright, but she wasn't sure how to get off the subject of children, especially considering they were surrounded by nothing but baby clothes and maternity wear.

"Oh, honey," Penelope said, surprising Megan by putting an arm around her shoulders and squeezing briefly. "I know just how you feel. I just didn't realize you felt as strongly about it as I do."

"I . . . I didn't always," Megan said. It was tough, sticking to the truth.

"You could always adopt, you know," Penelope said kindly. "It would be just as fun buying those little overalls for a baby you were entrusted with as one you gave birth to yourself. And I think the agencies have gotten fairly liberal about even single women adopting these days. I have a friend who adopted the most beautiful little Guatemalan boy."

Megan swallowed. "I don't know . . ."

"Just think about it," Penelope advised, as they

moved away from the overalls. "When we talked about it before you sounded so resigned and balanced about not having children. I never dreamed I'd find you someplace like this."

Megan stopped at a rack of clothes and flipped through them, unseeing. "I know. I was," she said. "I really was. I thought fate was telling me I had a different path to take, but then . . ." She couldn't finish the thought.

"I know. Then it hits you that it's forever. And you wish you could tell fate a thing or two about how you want your life to go instead of just going along with whatever happens." Penelope shook her head, looking troubled.

"You could, you know," Megan said, feeling like a jerk for allowing Penelope to think they were talking about the same thing. "Fate hasn't told you anything hopeless, Pen. And even if it did, you just don't know. Sometimes our interpretations are wrong. I just know you're going to have children someday, and I know you'll be a *great* mother."

Penelope laughed again and waved the words away. "Oh sure, sure." She sighed and looked around the store. "I just wish it could happen right now. And here I thought I was the only one who took dreaming to this level of reality." She spread an arm out to encompass the wealth of mommy merchandise around them.

Megan laughed and pulled a white shirt from the rack, taking in its oversize cut around the middle. This kind of thing might work for her at the animal hospital, she thought. It looked like a normal shirt until you got to the center. She pictured herself wearing it to work, then remembered the damn pink uniform shirts she'd bought everyone. Did they make those in maternity sizes, she wondered. If they did she'd end up looking like a giant marshmallow Easter Peep.

"But Megan . . ." Penelope's voice interrupted her thoughts. "Even if you adopt you're never going to need *that* kind of thing."

Too late, Megan realized the kind of fantasizing Penelope was talking about didn't include the actual pregnancy. And for sure you didn't need big shirts to adopt a child.

She dropped the maternity shirt.

"Ma'am?" The saleswoman was back. "I've got you set up in fitting room number two."

Megan froze. "Uh, thanks."

Her eyes darted to Penelope.

"A fitting room?" Penelope said, looking confused.

The saleswoman floated inconspicuously away.

Finally Penelope's eyes widened. "Megan!" she nearly hissed, leaning toward her intently. "Are you—?"

Megan stopped breathing. She had to tell someone sometime. Was now the right time? And was Penelope the right person? She was becoming a dear friend, but she wanted a baby herself *so badly* . . .

Hesitantly, Megan nodded. Once.

Penelope straightened, looking at her in shock. "And it's . . . is it . . . ?" She leaned forward again and whispered, "Does Sutter *know*?"

Megan shook her head. She felt unreal. As if this were some kind of weird dream. Never had the pregnancy seemed so unbelievable as it did at that moment, transitioning from concept to reality as the news was absorbed by someone she knew.

She swallowed, feeling sick, and put her hands on her abdomen as if she could shield the baby from the world discovering its secret presence.

Penelope was clearly stupefied. "But . . . I thought . . ."

"I know," Megan said, low. "I did too. I thought it was impossible. But it's not. That's what I meant about interpreting fate. It's . . . real." She made a face between a smile and a grimace, so afraid the news must be *killing* Penelope. Penelope, who wanted children more than anything else in the world . . .

Penelope reached out and grabbed Megan's arm. "Come on," she said, then turned and nodded toward the white shirt Megan had dropped. "Bring that."

"Where are we going?" Megan asked.

Penelope gave her a look. "To fitting room two, of course!"

In the end Penelope had been excited for her. Megan had bought three shirts and a pair of jeans, and Penelope had purchased the little autumn-leaf overalls for the baby—just for fun.

Megan had never been so glad to have a friend as she was at that moment. Penelope had been up-beat and fun, and reassured Megan at every op-portunity that she would not want for help or company or solace whenever she needed it during her pregnancy and beyond. Megan had even cried at one point, so grateful for Pen's warmth and ac-ceptance she could hardly believe it was real.

Once or twice she thought she'd caught a wistful look on Penelope's face, but it disappeared quickly and was replaced by enthusiasm every time. The outing had ended up being tremendous fun.

On the way to the parking lot, Penelope brought up the issue that Megan had been holding at bay the entire day.

"So when are you going to tell Sutter?" Pene-lope asked.

Megan shifted her Mommy 'N Me shopping bag from her right hand to her left and fished around in her purse for her car keys.

"At least not for the next couple of weeks. He's out of town. After that . . . I'm not sure."

"I know you're nervous, honey, but you know,

he could really be excited," Penelope said, inject-
ing her earlier enthusiasm back into her voice.

Megan eyed her skeptically. "Come on, Pen.
We're talking about The Vault here. Even if he was
excited, chances are we'd never know it."

Penelope laughed. "I know, but The Vault has already surprised me a couple of times when it
comes to you. I don't think you have anything to
worry about."

That was taking optimism to new heights.

"I wouldn't be so sure about that," Megan said.
"You didn't see him that night at the concert,
when he reacted to me talking to that tabloid. He
was furious."

"But he apologized! Once you explained to him
what happened, everything was fine."

"Sure, but this is a little bigger than that,"
Megan said, touching her hand to her abdomen
again. "I'm just . . . I'm so afraid he's going to
think I did this on purpose."

Penelope gave her a reproachful look. "You
didn't do this alone, you know."

"I know. But he asked about contraception and I
told him I couldn't have children. What if he
thinks I lied? I'm so afraid he'll think I . . . I don't
know, trapped him or something."

"Trapped him! That's ridiculous. But even if he
did, you'd tell him the truth and he'd have to understand. In either case, ultimately I don't think
you'll have anything to worry about with Sutter."

She nodded her head and added, "He'll do the right thing."

Megan threw a glance at Penelope sideways as she opened the trunk of her car. "And the right thing would be . . . ?"

"He'll marry you, of course." Penelope looked at her as if there was no other answer.

Megan felt her insides drop. "Marry me!"

"Of course. Why? Don't you *want* to marry him?"

"No!" Megan vehemently slammed the trunk shut and turned back to her. "Absolutely not. I'm not going to marry someone just because I'm pregnant. Good lord, that's just begging for a miserable life."

"But Megan," Penelope protested. "It's his child too. Don't you owe it to the baby to be a family?"

Megan's heart raced as fast as if she were being chased down a dark alley.

"Plenty of kids grow up just fine in single-parent homes," she said firmly. "And it isn't as if we don't live close to each other. No, there's no way in the world I would marry Sutter Foley. Not unless he pops up and asks me tomorrow, before finding out."

Penelope eyed her shrewdly. "So you'd marry him tomorrow, huh? As long as he didn't know?"

Megan blushed. "I guess I walked into that one. No. I wouldn't even marry him tomorrow."

"Megan, if you're in love with the man, why

wouldn't you marry him when he finds out you're going to have his child? That just doesn't make any sense."

"Because I'd never get over the fact that we got married *because of* the child. I would feel . . ." She stopped, shaking her head. Damn hormones, she felt like she was going to cry again.

Penelope stepped closer and put a hand on Megan's arm. "Listen, if I know Sutter, he wouldn't do anything he didn't absolutely want to do anyway. And if he wanted to marry you because of the child, it would be because he wants both of you. Don't you see?"

"No," Megan choked out. "He'll love the child, I know that. But he won't love me."

It sounded so pathetic, she hated herself for it.

"Besides, we haven't even had a real relationship," Megan argued. "Would *you* marry someone you'd never even been on a date with?"

Penelope tilted her head. "Well, no, not if you put it that way . . . But don't just write him off because this has happened. There's still time for you to develop a relationship. You'll just have to give it some time, let your heart tell you what to do."

Despite herself, Megan smiled wryly. "You make it sound so simple."

"Maybe it is simple. Maybe his feelings will be clear once he finds out about the baby."

Megan eyed her warily. "Don't you *dare* go telling him, Penelope Porter." She wagged a finger at her friend. "I'm going to tell him when I'm ready and not before. He won't be able to fool me, either. If he proposes and I suspect it's because he already knows about it, I'm turning him down flat."

"Sure you will, honey," Penelope said, patting her arm.

"You don't think I will?" Megan demanded.

Penelope just smiled. "I think you're madly in love with the man and the two of you will eventually be very happy. And that's all I'm saying."

With that, she leaned over, gave Megan a kiss on the cheek and headed off for her car, leaving Megan to wonder how she would react if Sutter *did* actually propose.

"Nooooo!" Megan wailed, holding the tabloid Georgia had handed her in both hands.

The sound was so loud and heartfelt that for a second all the dogs in the dog park stopped to look at her. Two schnauzers, a boxer, a miniature poodle, a springer spaniel, four Labradors, three beagles and, of course, Peyton, Sage, and Wimbledon.

Peyton cantered over and rubbed her face on Megan's thigh, looking up at her expectantly.

"But this was just *last week!*" Penelope protested. "I didn't even *see* anyone. You'd think you'd notice someone taking pictures of you."

"There's one more inside," Georgia said, eyeing Megan.

"This is unbelievable," Megan muttered, folding the front with the picture of her holding her Mommy 'N Me shopping bag so that it was hidden and opening to the other shot, of her and Penelope actually in the store, Megan's hands on her abdomen. In the background of this second picture was the rack of tiny overalls.

"Oh God, oh no," she said, the words coming out as another pitiful moan. "This is so bad."

The headline of the article was "Sutter Foley: Expecting the Unexpected?" with the subhead, "Foley mistress adding peripheral to Sutter's system . . ."

"So you *were* there? They didn't just stick that lettering on the shopping bag?" Georgia asked.

"I've got to sit down," Megan said.

"Here. Over here." Penelope led her over to a large tree. "We can sit on the ground, it's plenty dry in all this heat."

"Now, c'mon y'all, I've got my good pants on," Georgia said, hands on her hips. "Only way I'm sittin' in the dirt is if Megan's really pregnant."

Megan and Penelope exchanged a glance.

"Then you better sit down," Megan said.

Georgia's mouth dropped open. "What? You mean this is *true?*"

Megan tapped a finger on the dirt. "Come on down."

Georgia sat gingerly. A moment later Sage,

catching sight of her on the ground—the universal dog-sign that the human is now fair game—loped over to check her out. He circled her once, then backed up so his behind came down squarely on her lap. He looked over his shoulder at her and panted happily.

"Sage, you big baby." With an *oof* she pushed him off. He lay down next to her.

Peyton and Wimbledon were apparently too hot to bother with their people.

"So tell me all," Georgia said, leaning forward, her elbow on her knee. "How long have you known?"

"A couple weeks. It's taken me this long just to believe it myself. But *this* . . ." Megan looked unhappily at the tabloid. "This screws up all my plans."

"You don't even look it. You're still skinny as a snake," Georgia said, frowning at Megan's figure. "It's Sutter's, I take it."

Megan looked at her. "Of course."

"Well, what did *he* say? Did he play the knight in shining armor and offer marriage, or did he run off like the fox who stole the chicken?" Georgia asked.

"He doesn't know," Megan said. "Or didn't. Oh God! What if he's already *seen* this? When did it come out?" Megan fumbled for the front page.

"It's the newest one, but it might not be on the

racks yet," Georgia said. "I subscribe so I usually get it a couple days early. There's a chance it hasn't hit the stands."

"You *subscribe* to the *National Tattler*?" Penelope asked. "What on earth for?"

"For obvious reasons, Miss High-and-Mighty," Georgia said. She gestured toward Megan. "Obviously, they sometimes get things right. And they get it before everyone else. Including, it seems, the father."

"I thought I had two weeks," Megan said. "Sutter's out of town until next Monday and I was going to tell him when he got back. Now . . ." She felt her palms breaking out in a sweat and she wrinkled the paper in her hands. "He'll know it all before I say anything." She looked up at them pleadingly. "You all know him. How do you think he'll react?"

"We don't know him like you do, honey," Georgia said. "Your guess is better than ours."

"I told you how I thought he'd react," Penelope said. "He'll offer marriage, of course. And I think she should accept, don't you, Georgia?"

Megan looked at Georgia.

"Hell, yes," Georgia said.

Penelope smiled and nodded her satisfaction.

Georgia snorted. "It's not every day a girl's got the means to land a friggin' billionaire."

"She's not *landing* him," Penelope objected.

"Besides, he owes you that much," Georgia continued. "He owes that baby a name, for one thing. And he owes you for bringin' it into this God-forsaken world. Even if you end up divorced you'll be sittin' on a pretty damn good nest egg."

"She's not going to *divorce* him," Penelope said, glancing at Megan. "She *loves* him. And I think he loves her. You should have seen him the night of the concert, Georgia. I never saw him anything but reserved when he was with Bitsy, but that night he was positively frantic to get to Megan."

"I told you, Penelope, and now I'm telling you, Georgia," Megan said, giving them each a stern look, "I am not going to *marry* him. At least not now." She looked back at the picture of herself in the parking lot once more. "But I do have to tell him the truth."

"And what's the truth, Megan?" Penelope said, looking as firm as Megan ever saw her. "That you're pregnant. That it's his. And that *you're in love with him*, for pity's sake. You can't tell him part of the truth without telling him the rest!"

"Why?" Georgia asked. "Why should she give him that kind of power over her?"

"It's not power," Penelope said.

"I've got to find him," Megan said, getting up. "I've got to call his office and find him. I've got to tell him before he reads *this*."

She called Peyton and headed for the gate.

Penelope sprang to her feet and Georgia pushed up slowly.

"Megan, wait!" Penelope called after her, fumbling for Wimbledon's leash. "Let me help you!"

But Megan was collecting Peyton and heading for the exit. "It's all right. I'll call you after I tell him," she called back with a wave. A second later she turned back again and said, "Don't worry!"

Penelope turned to face Georgia with a worried expression. "What do you think he'll do?"

Georgia shrugged, looking after Megan. "I have no idea."

They both watched Megan turn the corner.

"The good news is," Georgia said, brushing off her pants with both hands. "Doc got the DNA test results back and guess what. Sage is a daddy too!"

Eighteen

"I told you she'd come up with something." Montgomery marched across the hotel suite, her narrow silhouette and short-cropped hair making her look like a dart and Sutter was the target.

Twister jumped up from beside Sutter's chair the moment the door opened and trotted next to Montgomery, sensing excitement that might mitigate the lack of crumbs dropping from Sutter's breakfast plate.

Montgomery pushed the dog away, her face smug as she tossed the *National Tattler* onto the breakfast table in front of him.

Sutter put his knife and fork down on the side of his plate of eggs Benedict and picked up his coffee cup. He watched Montgomery sit down, antsy on the edge of her chair, took a sip of coffee, and put it back down.

"Good morning to you, too, Montgomery. There are some croissants on the piano, if you'd like one." He indicated the baby grand across the suite with a nod of his head.

"No thanks," she said brusquely and pointed to the tabloid. "You need to read that."

He did not look at the wretched tabloid, though he knew it must have more libelous conjecture about himself and Megan Rose for her to get wound up again. Montgomery had been getting a little too strident on the subject of Megan and he had no desire to invite more criticism.

"I could order something from room service," he said mildly.

"Uh, no, but thanks," she said, looking confused and slightly shamefaced at her own impertinence.

"Forgive me if I'm wrong about this," he said, picking up a piece of toast and buttering it, "but don't we have more pressing issues than what's made up for publication in the *National Tattler*?"

She sat straight in the chair. "I'm sure we do, sir, which is why I'd like to get you off of their pages once and for all."

"Montgomery, do me a favor. Have some coffee, maybe a danish, and relax, all right?"

She was silent a moment, watching his knife spread butter on the toast. Finally, she said, "I'd feel better if you'd just look at it."

He sighed, turned dispassionately to the paper and picked it up. On the cover was a picture of

Megan. His eyes lingered on her face, on the sweep of her dark hair blown away from her neck by a breeze. Her body was lithe and graceful, even in the still photo.

Grainy though the picture was, even this mere glimpse of her had him wishing she were close. He missed her laugh, her knowing eyes, her sharp wit and ultimate kindness. And he missed her touch. God, how he missed her touch.

She was standing in a parking lot with Penelope Porter and she carried a shopping bag. He read the caption, looked again at the picture, then read the heading. With a long exhale, he leaned back and opened up the paper to read the article.

Briana Ellis better pack her bags unless she intends to share Sutter Foley with more than just the other woman, it began. It then went on to say that Megan was seen in a maternity store and left with a large shopping bag. She and her friend were spotted picking out maternity wear and baby clothes from the local boutique and were heard conferring in hushed tones for several hours as they shopped. The friend, Penelope Porter, was not pregnant, according to sources close to both women.

Sutter finished, then tossed the paper across the table and picked up his fork again.

If that damn paper had gotten this right, there'd be no question he had to race home to be with her.

Fate, he would have to believe, had taken control. And wouldn't that make things simple and clear?

But he knew better than that. To believe the *National Tattler* one had to be out of one's head. Just as he'd been that night at the concert.

"I think you need to refine your reading tastes," he said to Montgomery, taking a bite of his eggs. He could master this longing, he thought. "If you like fiction, novels are better."

"But sir, don't you *see?*" Montgomery said, her voice urgent in the face of his indifference. "That Rose woman is going to claim she's pregnant! I *told* you she'd come up with something to get money out of you. And I've taken the liberty of doing a little investigating—her business is going down the tubes. She's down to almost no clients ever since her father was involved in that puppy theft. How much do you want to bet she asks for a huge settlement to get rid of this 'baby'?"

"Don't be daft," he said, dropping his hands to the table. "And don't *ever* 'take the liberty' of investigating someone I know again without telling me. Do you understand?"

She hesitated, momentarily thrown. "Of course. I'm sorry."

He held her gaze another moment, anger seething within him, and with an effort returned to his breakfast. "This is a nonissue. She's not pregnant."

Montgomery sat back in her chair, arms across

her chest. "Maybe, according to you. But Sutter, she's obviously got a different story and if I were you I'd ask for proof. It would be too easy for her to claim she'd gotten rid of a baby after you settled with her when there wasn't even one there to begin with."

"If I'd known you were so interested in fabricated gossip, I'd have bought you a subscription to that rag," he said. "The story's not true, Montgomery. Those pictures were doctored. She probably had a bag from Hecht's."

"How do you know it's not true?" she demanded.

He glared at her. "Trust me. I just know it."

What was she so upset about anyway? She was acting like his accountant at tax time, like he was being robbed in broad daylight.

She kneaded her hands in her lap. "I don't know how you can be so sure. You must know that contraceptives are not one-hundred percent—"

"Montgomery," he snapped. "I am not a teenager in need of a lesson on safe sex from you. Now tell me, why are *you* so upset about this? Even if this were true, it would be my problem. My *personal* problem. And nothing to do with you."

At that she looked as if she'd missed the bottom step. "Sir—your problems are my problems. This kind of thing affects your reputation, which affects our company. Don't you even want me to call the lawyers about it?"

"My reputation is not going to affect this company in the slightest. Not anymore. It's gotten too big and you know it. What's this really about?"

Mongomery rolled her eyes, but to Sutter she looked more than a trifle appalled. "Well, think of it, sir. You, a father. It would be disastrous! Your passion is your work. You can't be bothered with diapers and bottles and squawking all night long. Imagine if you couldn't sleep with all the mess and chaos a baby brings. No, *this* is our life, right here. Work, travel, meetings—changing the face of the business world! We can't be tied down by some drippy little baby."

Like dawn breaking, a small light grew in his mind, illuminating Montgomery's inappropriate, proprietary and misguided view of himself and the situation.

This is our life . . .

Montgomery, who worked all hours and showed up at his house on the weekends in a business suit. Montgomery, who cut off all her hair and wore mannish clothes as if to deny nature. Montgomery, who was desperate to dispute any place that Megan might have in Sutter's life. Montgomery thought that he and she were one and the same. They were both married to the company and therefore, perhaps in some way, married to each other.

To her, he *was* this company and nothing else.

And was he? he wondered suddenly. Was he as pitiable as he'd always considered Montgomery?

Had he really sold the very soul of his life to make this company what it was?

Montgomery clearly thought so.

Briana wouldn't have interfered with Montgomery's view of their life together, but Megan would. How had she known that Megan was different? How was it that despite her distorted point of view, she had seen almost immediately what it had taken Sutter months to see himself?

For it was obvious now, he told himself. He'd considered marrying a woman based on the same criteria he used in *hiring* one. Briana fit, she was appropriate, she had the diplomatic skills, hostessing abilities.

Megan, on the other hand, had brought laughter, passion, and freedom from a view of the world that was myopically corporate.

He hadn't wanted Briana, because he hadn't been able to let go of Megan. Somewhere inside, some small piece of humanity remained and *it knew* . . .

He couldn't love Briana. And he couldn't love her because—

Sutter stood up so abruptly his chair toppled over behind him.

"What is it?" Montgomery said, her eyes feverish. "Do you see what I mean? Should I call the lawyers?" She sat on the very edge of her seat, feet poised as if to begin the fifty-yard dash to the phone.

"No, damn it," he said, more fiercely than he'd intended. Twister scuttled from beside his chair to lie beneath the piano, watching him. "I've got to get out of here. Get hold of the pilot, tell him we're leaving in an hour."

"So you're going to confront her?" Montgomery asked, her voice high, her eyes bright with excitement.

"I'm going to save myself while there's still time," he muttered, striding to the desk and throwing papers into his briefcase.

"That's the spirit!" she said, picking up proposals and memos and handing them to him. "Just tell me what you want me to do, sir."

"Stay here and manage the meetings." He slammed the briefcase closed and strode toward the bedroom. "I've got to get to Megan before she gives up on me completely."

She was in the driveway, shoving an oversized suitcase in the trunk, when the black Jaguar pulled up behind her.

Peyton gave a friendly bark and trotted over to the vehicle as the driver shut it off, her tail fluttering in the soft evening air.

The sun had settled behind the trees but the sky was still bright. Honeysuckle along the river was just starting to waft its sweet scent into the late-summer breeze.

Megan straightened up, slammed the trunk, and turned. She froze when she recognized his car.

What could this mean? Visions of his angry face the night of the concert assailed her. He thought she'd done this on purpose. That's the only reason he would come here, to her. He wanted to confront her. Tell her this scheme wasn't going to work.

He probably thought that she'd not only gotten pregnant on purpose, but that she'd let the *National Tattler* in on it as a way of letting him know. He'd think it was all part of some unscrupulous plot.

He stepped out of the vehicle but faced briefly back inside. Megan could see Twister's tale waving as frantically as a conductor's baton at the end of Beethoven's ninth. Then he backed away from the door and let Twister jump out on the leash.

He turned and strolled slowly toward her.

Twister, by some miracle, did not drag him forward. Maybe because Peyton was sniffing her behind, or maybe because someone had been doing some training.

"Going somewhere?" he asked.

His voice washed over her, so missed in the last weeks, but his face was inscrutable. Or . . . maybe not. Maybe it was just that he didn't look the way she'd expected.

He wasn't angry.

Had he not seen the *Tattler*?

"Sutter . . . I . . ."

What should she say? If he hadn't seen the tabloid, there was time to tell him about the baby in another, more delicate, way. But her mind had been frantic for hours, as she'd packed and tracked down the directions to the New York Palace hotel. There was no way she could be calm about this right now.

"I was thinking about it," she said finally, leaning one hand against the back of her car.

"Most people decide and then pack," he said, stopping a few feet away from her. She had to be mistaken, but he appeared to be smiling a little bit.

Twister finished greeting Peyton and rushed over to her. She squatted and scratched the dog's ears. "Well, look at you!" she said to the dog, avoiding Sutter's gaze. Her mind worked furiously for a tack to take as she cooed over the dog. "You're getting so big!"

"Ah, listen, Megan," he said.

She scratched the dog one more time and looked up.

Sutter's gaze dropped to the ground.

Megan stood and Twister pawed at her leg.

She watched him, confused. Was Sutter . . . could he be . . . *nervous?*

"Well, first," he said, clearing his throat, "I want you to know that I saw the *Tattler* and—" He looked up. "Have you seen it?"

Megan's blood froze in her veins. She actually thought she might faint. She nodded jerkily. "Yes, I—"

"No." He held up a hand. "I want you to know that I know it's not true. I didn't believe it for a second. The way they doctor photographs these days is astonishing, but rest assured I am not here to bluster about in any sort of egocentric way, as apparently is my wont."

"I—" Her breath caught.

"I'm here because I realized," he took a step closer to her, "when I was away, and my VP, she's got this bee in her bonnet about you, but in talking to her I realized that I . . ."

"Sutter—"

"No, please, let me finish. Megan, I . . ." He looked heavenward, then glanced around the backyard. Peyton and Twister rolled next to each other in the gravel of the drive. "Jesus, I guess I could have picked a better location than this."

"Sutter, no—"

"Megan," he fixed her with his green gaze, "I've got to say this. I would give anything to be able to make up to you all I've done, all the mistakes I've made. I've given you short shrift, made you suffer through all that bloody tabloid business, and Briana—"

"Yes, what *about* Briana?" The words burst from her. Megan, in fact, was so paralyzed with shock and uncertainty that she was amazed even her lips would move.

"Briana and I have split. It was never serious, and it never could have been." He took a deep breath. "Not when I'm in love with you."

Megan's knees nearly buckled. "You—what?"

"I'm in love with you," he said warmly. "And I know this isn't a life that you wanted. This 'fish-bowl' existence, I believe you once called it. And who could blame you? Certainly not I. But I can't—that is, I don't want to live without you. You make my life—happy. You make me happy, Megan. And if you would let me try to make you happy—"

"Sutter, wait." Her voice emerged almost hoarsely. "We've got to talk about the *Tattler* article."

"No we don't. I told you. I don't usually make the same mistake twice, and I know that they're a lying pack of thieves. I promise you, I didn't give it a second thought—"

"It's true," she said, and felt as if she might be sick.

For a second, the expression on his face didn't change from the earnest one disclaiming any belief in the tabloid.

Then in a flash it switched, to one of incredulity. "I beg your pardon?"

She forced the words out in a toneless voice. "I said it's true. They got it right this time. I am pregnant."

The truth washed over him. His eyes searched her face. "But I thought—"

"I know what you thought," she said roughly. "Because I told you I couldn't have children. And now're probably thinking that I lied to you, that I'm trying to trap you. Well, I didn't and I'm not. It was a million to one shot and it happened. And I don't expect a thing from you, I just—"

"Marry me," he said then.

It was her turn to gape. "*What?*"

"Marry me," he repeated, taking a step closer. His eyes didn't leave her face.

She stared at him. Then breathed, "No." She shook her head, tried to say more, but tears clogged her throat and rose in her eyes. She swallowed.

"Megan, if you're going to have my child—"

"How do you even know it's yours?" she said impulsively, backing away. "We haven't even had a *relationship*, Sutter. We've slept together a couple of times. We barely even know each other! Why on earth would we marry?"

"How do I know it's mine?" he repeated.

She looked back obstinately. It was the only thing she could think of to stop his obligatory madness.

"Is that what you said?" he asked. "That it might not be mine?"

"I . . . My point is, you don't know anything about me. For all you know you aren't the only person I've been sleeping with."

After what seemed like an hour but was probably only a fraction of a minute, he gaped at her. Then he started to laugh.

"What . . . what are you doing?" she asked, utterly confused.

He brought his chuckles to a reluctant halt and said, slowly and with great conviction, "Megan, that child is mine, I don't doubt it for a moment. And there's nothing you can say to make me doubt it."

"That's—awfully confident." She frowned. "You're practically calling me a liar."

He smiled and gave a one-shouldered shrug. "If you are a liar, you're not a very good one."

She straightened, feeling as if she were not a part of whatever joke was making him smile. "Fine, I suppose it's no insult to be told I'm not a good liar. But, Sutter, don't you see? Marriage for the sake of this child would be a misguided sacrifice, one that I am not willing to make. I refuse to make all three of us miserable simply because of some outdated idea of respectability. Besides, neither one of us has a good track record when it comes to marriage."

He tilted his head and thought for a long moment. Then, with great patience he said, "Look, when I came here today it was to tell you that I love you. You, Megan Rose. I love *you*. And it's not because of a baby I did not even believe existed until this moment." His eyes held hers with an intensity she could not look away from. "But even if you don't believe that, surely you see that we owe that baby the effort to try to make this work."

Megan brought her hands to her lips, as if she might be able to hold back the tears by keeping her mouth shut.

"Make this work," she repeated finally. "Do you hear how that sounds? Like some horrible, endless homework assignment for both of us. That's no way to live. Not for me or you, or even for this child. We have a problem here but it's not the baby. It's us. I don't even know you, Sutter. I mean, my God, I tried to call you and I don't even know your home number! What kind of woman doesn't know the home phone number of the father of her baby?"

"That's not—"

"No, this is important!" Now that she'd uncorked the fears, she had to let them out, let him see what was so insurmountable. "I didn't know you'd split with Briana. I didn't know you were going away. I didn't even know you took Twister to work with you. You took her to New York! You've turned into someone I never even guessed was in there! Don't you see? I can't marry someone whom I don't even know!"

He laughed incredulously and she gave him a mutinous look.

"Megan, you know me better than I knew myself," he said. "Tell me the truth, now, you talked me into taking that dog because you thought she'd worm her way into my cold, lonely heart and I'd keep her, right? Well, that's exactly what happened. Nobody else I know would have guessed for a second I had that in me. But you did, didn't you?"

It wasn't quite a question and she didn't quite answer. But she felt herself weakening. She *had* thought that would happen. She'd seen it so clearly that first day she met him. He had so much soul in his eyes.

And now, here he was, telling her she was right. Not returning the dog. Not angry with her for the article. Not even running off at the thought of her presenting him with a baby.

In fact, he was looking at her with—was it? yes, *love!*—in his eyes.

"Megan," he said quietly, taking a step closer so that now he stood close enough to reach up and touch her cheek. "I understand what you're saying, but it's fear. Maybe I didn't choose the right words because for me it would be no work at all to be with you. But for you . . . ? I don't know. I see that it's up to me to convince you of my feelings, and perhaps coax yours out of you. So tell me the truth. Is there a chance that you could love me? I know we haven't had much time, and I promise you I'll do everything in my power to make up for my previous stupidity. Just tell me, have I got a chance to win your heart?"

Damn hormones! She was crying openly now.

She looked down at his shirt front, dying to put her hands to his chest and curl into his arms.

And the truth was wrenched out of her by a force greater than herself.

"I do love you, Sutter," she grumbled.

He tipped his head down, to catch her lowered eyes. "What was that?"

She glanced at him. He was smiling tentatively.

Reluctantly, she smiled back. "I said," she straightened and fought through her pride, "I do love you."

He reached a hand out, caught one of her teardrops on his fingertip. "Then what's the problem, love?" he asked gently. "We're in love. We're having a baby. What could be simpler?"

Megan took a deep breath. Joy, almost on a par with what she'd felt when she'd discovered she was pregnant, bubbled up inside of her.

He hadn't believed her for a second when she'd told him the baby might not be his, she thought. Not for a second. He did know her, she realized. What's more, he believed in her.

Was that enough? some stubborn part of her mind argued. She looked down.

"But I don't want to get married," she repeated petulantly. She was having a hard time not throwing herself into his arms. "Not . . . not right now. We haven't even dated."

He laughed and she pressed her lips together to keep from smiling with him.

"We'll date, then," he said, running a hand lightly up her arm and back down. "And I'll bring you flowers. I'll flirt with you, and woo you. Kiss you good night on your doorstep."

She let her fingers play with one of the buttons on his shirt. "For how long?" She looked up at him through her lashes.

"I'll kiss you all night on your doorstep if you want," he said, grinning. "Or anywhere else you want to be kissed."

She inched forward, putting her hands on his chest. After a moment, laughter bubbled up within her. "Lord, what'll the *National Tattler* make of this, do you think?"

He obviously repressed a smile. "Oh I don't think we'll have to worry about them anymore."

"What do you mean?" She gave him a quizzical look.

He let the smile emerge. "I bought the bloody thing," he laughed.

"You *what?*" She gazed at him incredulously.

"Hey, at least this way we'll be able to spin to our benefit what all the other gossip sheets have to say about us."

She laughed. And his eyes glowed as he watched her.

He lifted his other hand to her other arm and sobered.

"So after we've dated for a while . . . ?" he asked softly. "What then, Megan?"

"Then . . ." she said, looking up at him with a small smile, "then I guess I'll be as big as a house and I'll have to let my father get out his shotgun."

He laughed. "So *then* you'll marry me?"

"You'll just have to ask and find out." She put her arms around his neck.

He pulled her close. "I love you, Megan."

She regarded him long and hard. "I love you too, Sutter."

He bent his head and kissed her, a soft, sweet kiss.

"And . . ." He looked downward, between them, and put his warm hand on her belly. "I love you too. Whoever you are."